LOST SHADOWS

THE SHADOW PATRIOTS
BOOK SIX

WARREN RAY

This is a work of fiction. Names, characters, places and incidents either are products of the author's imagination or are used fictitiously. Any resemblance to actual events or locales or persons living or dead is entirely coincidental.

To my wonderful readers:
Sorry for all the cliff-hangers.
Well, no, not really. HAHAHAHA
But seriously, this is the last one.
Or is it???   BWAHAHA

CHAPTER 1

JACKSON MICHIGAN

Scar struggled to get up from his bed and had to push with his left arm to sit up. He began stretching his body, which ached from the failed mission to Canada. Not only did they not get any supplies but lost the funds to purchase them. After twisting his shoulders around and arching his back, he massaged his temples trying to relieve a headache that was pounding like a jackhammer.

Besides the stress he was under, the loud gunfire from last night's shootout didn't help any. He was also upset that he had lost his prized Kimber Model 1911 .45ACP to the cops in Canada. It had been a gift from his wife five years ago, and he had been carrying it with him since the beginning of the Shadow Patriots.

He stood up and arched his back again before jumping into the shower to wash off yesterday's failure. Coldwater had a way of forcing you to focus on the here and now, which is what he needed. Dwelling on the past tended to confuse your thinking on what needed to be done, and he had lots to do.

As he stepped out the shower and toweled off before putting on his clothes, he tried not to think about Sergeant Wilson's greed. Scar shook his head to get the man out of his thoughts. He wasn't worth the effort but hoped he would pay for his sins.

Thankfully, Hadley had spotted the cops sinking their canoe and decided to get back to Jackson for help. How different the night would have gone had the young Texan not done so. More than likely, the cops would have caught and tortured him for information before killing him as a traitor. They would have seen the Patriots coming back across the river, and that would have been the end of that.

Scar swallowed some Motrin for his headache before heading down to the cafeteria.

Since the food was still running low, he realized supplies continued to be his main priority, and they would have to get creative to either find more to eat or move the rest of these people out of Jackson.

He pushed the door open and was surprised to see Amber sitting there. She had on a clean pair of jeans and a dark purple cami top with a dark blue windbreaker. He was glad she was there because he had arrived in a different vehicle last night and hadn't had the chance to talk to her or Reese.

"Well, hey there."

Amber looked up. "Morning Scar."

"Didn't expect to see you here," said Scar picking up the decanter.

"It's a bit on the light side," said Amber commenting on the quality of the coffee.

"I see that, but it's better than nothing," said Scar as he poured a cup. He sat down across from her. "Sleep good?"

"Like a baby, but something out in the hall woke me up a bit ago."

"Well, that sucks."

Amber gave him a half shrug.

Scar took a sip of coffee. "So, was it miserable taking a cold shower last night."

"Believe it or not the shower actually felt pretty good. I guess I was still numb and besides, there was a lot of grime to wash off."

"Yeah, I'll bet," said Scar taking another sip of coffee. He set the cup down and looked at Amber. "You know, you and Reese, were amazing last night. I'm really proud of you guys."

Amber moved a hand to her heart. "Well, thank you, Scar. That's sweet of you to say so. We certainly weren't expecting to be in a firefight that's for sure. We thought we'd just be babysitting the garage. Reese even commented she shouldn't have been there, to begin with."

"I don't know about that. She definitely held her own."

Amber nodded approvingly. "So, what was it like over there? We were looking through the binoculars fantasizing about getting a beer, well I was, Reese just wanted pizza."

Scar couldn't contain his smile.

"What?"

"We had both."

Amber crossed her arms over her chest. "Ah, that's just not fair."

"I know, right, but then we were also in jail, so there's that."

"So, how did that beer taste?"

"The first one was pure ecstasy," boasted Scar.

"You had two?"

"Had to wash down the cheeseburger."

Amber feigned anger by giving him the evil eye.

Scar laughed. "Hey, we had just barely finished the second one before getting arrested."

"Ah, yes, always a price to pay now isn't there?"

Scar shook his head. "Always."

"Well, serves you right," said Amber sarcastically.

"I'll say this Amber. It was just nice having a normal night out with friends."

Amber gave him a thoughtful expression and nodded.

"Those Canadians have it pretty good despite everything that's going on here. The prices were higher than normal, but that's to be expected."

"Probably where the Jijis and cops are getting their supplies."

Scar put his cup down and stared at her.

"What?"

"Amber I think I could kiss ya."

"What?"

"Supplies. Mordulfah's got a lot of mouths to feed. He must have stockpiles of it somewhere close to feed his little army."

Amber started nodding recognizing what Scar was saying. "Sounds like we got a recon mission."

"Oh, hell yeah, we do."

Scar leaned back in his chair grateful he bumped into Amber. This could potentially solve their problem or at the very least put it off until they had a better solution. He liked the idea and was about to get up to go look for Bassett when he and Meeks walked into the cafeteria. He told them the idea, and both readily agreed to go out on a recon mission.

CHAPTER 2

GROSSE POINTE MICHIGAN

Surveying the progress of cleaning up the mansion, Mordulfah dug deep to control his emotions in front of his men. His father taught him at an early age to always maintain a blank facade. It was a source of power, and he would need it in spades because the rebels had embarrassed him again by attacking his home and taking his women.

Even after three days, the smell of burnt carpet and wood still permeated the air as he stepped around a charred window frame from the galley room that had fallen out. Broken glass crunched under his feet as he walked on the grass. He had just finished fixing this room from the last attack, and now it, along with the entire south side was completely ruined from the rebel's RPG. Thankfully, they were able to contain the fire and prevent the whole mansion from burning down.

Mordulfah turned toward the front of the house and saw some of the workers staring at him. There had been whispers among the men on how he was weak and not as powerful as they thought he was. He wouldn't be able to do anything about it because he could only behead so many people before they would desert him. He had already played that card after the battle on Robinson Road. Besides, he had lost close to a hundred men from this recent attack and couldn't afford to lose anymore.

What he needed were men who were real fighters, not these wannabes that filtered in from around the area. These men had the will to fight but just not the skills, and it showed. Over the past week, he had lost over half of these men to a smaller force. He hated Cole Winters but had to admire him for how he was able to accomplish so much with just a handful of men.

Mordulfah shook his head thinking about the RPG they had used. He could only guess where the rebels got their hands on such a weapon but figured it had to be the Canadians. They were quite interested in what was going on down here and thought they knew about his plans of conquering the upper Mid-West. Even though he purchased supplies and received electric power from them, they didn't want him as a neighbor and would do what they could to prevent such a thing. As soon as he had established control, he would deal with the Canadians and punish them for their insolence.

Mordulfah had seen enough and headed to the kitchen. He turned to his trusted aide, Wali. "I'm going to need to go and see Uncle Faisal."

Wali raised an eyebrow.

"I know, the price will be high, but we need his forces if we are to have our own country."

"I'll make the necessary arrangements."

"I need you to stay here this time and continue overseeing the repairs. I'll have Thomas accompany me."

Wali bowed. "As you wish."

A flicker of excitement shot through Mordulfah's veins knowing it would be worth the price to bargain with his uncle. He had a soft spot for him because of the unfair way the family had treated him. Mordulfah had many cousins to compete with, and his father was the youngest brother. He made his own path with the help of his Uncle's connections in the banking world.

He had made millions instead of spending millions like his spoiled cousins. This endeared him to Faisal, but at the same time cast him as an outlier because of his cousin's petty jealousies. Mordulfah never let it bother him and went about his business amassing a fortune and making connections that were now coming in handy. It was how he was able to meet and do business with the multibillionaire, Gerald Perozzi. Over the last few years, he allowed the old man to take advantage of him making him think he wasn't as sophisticated. It was how he manipulated the man to allow him to become part of the cabal in the takedown of America.

Perozzi only thought he was going to take him out after he did his part in taking over the upper Midwest. Little did the old man know that he had someone in his inner circle reporting to him and waited for orders to kill him. He would also take out that arrogant fat man, Lawrence Reed. He would personally pull the trigger on him and take his time doing it.

CHAPTER 3

JACKSON MICHIGAN

Scar and Amber stood in the parking lot and watched Bassett, Meeks, Burns, and Nordell take off to begin scouting out the Jiji's supply lines. If they were going to get the full outlay of the Jijis supply chain, then they would have to cross enemy lines. There were several hundred Jijis just up in this area alone, which was a lot of mouths to feed.

Did they have one or two trucks handling the delivers? If two, then where did they split up and were they out of Detroit? The trick was getting the supplies back across the border. This was a daytime operation, which was not the ideal environment when you're outnumbered. Their preference was to operate with night-vision optics where they owned the night.

Bassett drove north on Willis Road toward the interstate. Their destination was an abandoned manufacturing plant off Willis Road. Bassett had the multiple building grounds heavily guarded not wanting the Jijis to use the thirty-five acres as a base of operations. Besides patrolling this area, part of the security Basset put in place included, blocking off all exits from the interstate. He had tractor-trailers parked in strategic areas as well as keeping rotating guard units. There had been random encounters with Jijis looking for accommodations that were more comfortable in nearby houses, but for the most part, they stayed on the interstate.

Bassett drove into the plant and saw one of his men climbing up a ladder to the roof where they had a guard post.

"You boys up for a bird's eye view?" asked Bassett.

"Always up for that," said Meeks getting out of the SUV.

The four climbed up the ladder and were greeted by Craig and Rick Robertson who were cousins from Jackson.

"Hey guys," said Bassett extending his hand.

"What brings you guys here?" asked Craig.

"Wanting to get some info on the Jijis' food deliveries."

"That's easy," said Craig pointing across the field toward the rest area on the interstate. "Van makes deliveries twice a day. The Jijis come and go out of there all day."

Bassett lifted the binoculars up. "How big of a truck."

"More like a small moving van. Eighteen footer, I'd say," said Rick.

They chatted with the cousins for a few more minutes before leaving and heading east to the border. Bassett wanted to get in place before the next delivery in a few hours and threaded his way through the back roads. He had familiarized himself with the whole area because he was in charge of their borders and knew what roads were safe to travel.

This part of the state had a lot of open areas that were still being farmed up until the crash. While weeds started taking over the fields, there wasn't enough to keep you from being spotted. However, some of the roads had plenty of trees and foliage to keep you hidden.

Sylvan Road was one of these roads, and it was just west of Manchester Road or Michigan 52, which was the Jijis' border. It connected Interstate 94 where the Jijis were and US 12 where the cops kept watch. Bassett wanted to know if they used two vans or one van making delivers. If the deliveries came from Detroit, then this would be the logical place for them to go in separate directions.

All the windows on the SUV were down as Bassett drove on Sylvan Road. The guys stayed alert knowing they weren't too far from the Jijis. Bassett found the dirt road he was looking for and took a left. He drove around a small bend to hide their ride. Without formality, the guys exited the vehicle and jogged back to the road.

"This is Chrysler's Proving Grounds," said Nordell as he climbed over the chain-linked fence that surrounded the area. "You got around a hundred miles of road on 3800 acres."

"Sounds like a fun place to work," said Meeks.

"Can be if you like to test drive cars. They got all kinds of different road conditions out here."

"How far to 52?" asked Burns.

"A couple of miles," said Bassett looking at Nordell.

He nodded. "We'll have to split up though. We won't be able to monitor both roads at the same time."

Bassett partnered with Meeks and headed north towards the interstate while Burns and Nordell headed east. It took close to an hour to travel across the Proving Grounds' diverse terrain. They didn't dare walk on the road in case Jijis were driving around on them. Bassett had thought about just staying with the cousins up on the roof. It would have been easier, but he wanted to be sure if it was one or two vans and how long the deliveries took.

They came to the edge of the woods and were right next to the interstate. Bassett wished he could have gotten closer to the overpass, but this was why he sent Burns and Nordell the other way. He wanted eyes on both roads at the same time.

Bassett froze when he heard leaves crunching to his left. He shot up a hand to signal Meeks. Both hunched down and stared through the trees. Bassett squeezed the hilt of his tactical tomahawk when he saw a Jiji coming toward them.

The last thing Bassett wanted was to be in a firefight. They were exposed and out in the open with no backup. Their vehicle was a couple of miles away, which meant they'd be doing some running. He had no doubt Meeks could keep up and likely be able to outrun him, but it wasn't a great option if you got a couple of hundred pissed off Jijis chasing you. The better choice would be to take him out quietly and leave the area. The Jijis would find him, but they'd be long gone before.

The man stopped and unzipped his pants to relieve himself. Bassett turned to Meeks who shrugged his shoulders. It took a minute before he finished and turned back to the interstate.

Bassett rose back up and looked around realizing the Jijis had been using this area as a latrine. He motioned to Meeks who scrounged his face and started to move away when he spotted two more Jijis headed their way. his office.

CHAPTER 4

GROSSE POINTE MICHIGAN

Thomas boarded Mordulfah's jet and took a seat toward the front. He had never flown in a small jet before and was astonished on how luxurious it was. The G650 was considered the gold standard of business jets. The first-class-style seats, as well as the walls, were wrapped in white leather. The tables, cabinets, trim and door were all mahogany. The thick, deep blue carpet sported gold pin stripping on each side.

Thomas couldn't believe his luck when the prince asked him to come along. He knew he had moved up the food chain after the attack as some of Mordulfah' key men had been killed. It was why Wali had to stay. He didn't have anyone else he could trust to get the place cleaned up and reorganized.

Thomas leaned back in the leather seat and thought how promotion by death wasn't a bad way to move up the company ladder. He was excited because he knew he'd be able to give the Shadow Patriots valuable information from this trip. He hoped it would impress Reese whom he had a crush on. He was shocked when she came to see him back in Jackson. He thought he'd never see her again after she had escaped from the mansion with Winters and Sadie. She looked banged up, which made him wonder if she wasn't fighting with them. He had asked Mister Taylor about her, but he wasn't forthcoming with any information, which meant they were protective of her. Thomas had heard she had attacked a couple of the cops that were prisoners there and wondered why.

The G650 lifted off the runaway, and Thomas gripped the armrest tightly. He didn't particularly like flying and trusted smaller jets even less. He tried to push it out of his mind by thinking about, Cara.

He didn't know she was dead and had been wondering how she was doing now that she was back with her father.

It was a daring rescue and a crazy night. All the shooting and chaos had men running around not knowing what to do or where to go. Then the horror among the men when they found out Cara, and the twins had escaped. They were afraid that Mordulfah would exact revenge on them. The death of CC gave him satisfaction because he felt she deserved it after conspiring against, Cara.

During the attack, Thomas hid and didn't come out until the shooting stopped and then helped put the fire out by organizing the men. This endeared him further to Mordulfah because the man loved this mansion and what it represented, which is why he would rebuild it, regardless of the cost or time it took.

After the plane leveled off, Thomas fell asleep and didn't wake until it landed in Washington DC. The stewardess came up and escorted him and the pilots off the plane.

Two limousines were parked on the tarmac, and Thomas watched as a chauffeur opened the back door of one of the limos. A tall, middle-aged man with a receding hairline stepped out. He wore black-framed glasses and a red tie on a tailored dark blue suit. He jogged up the stairs and disappeared into the jet.

Thomas thought he recognized him and tried to remember where he'd seen him before. He turned to the pilot and asked him.

"No idea," shrugged the pilot.

"Yeah, you do," said the copilot. "He was with Perozzi that one time when we flew Mordulfah down to that private island in the Bahamas?"

"Oh yeah, that's right. That big get-together with all those mucky-mucks. That was a helluva a trip. Remember all the women?"

"Yeah, some were a bit too young though."

"Not for the prince," snickered the pilot.

The two pilots kept reminiscing while Thomas kept thinking he knew the guy from somewhere. He wondered what they were talking about and wished he was inside sitting in on this secret meeting.

After fifteen minutes, the mysterious man exited the jet and came down the stairs. His chauffeur must have said something funny to him because the man laughed in a high pitched tone. The odd laugh finally gave up the mysterious man. Thomas remembered where he had seen him before. He had given the commencement speech at his graduation at the University of Tennessee.

His name was Albert Sauer and was the son of German immigrants that came to America after the war. He had gone to all the right schools and worked on Wall Street as a stockbroker before climbing the corporate ladder to become a CEO of a major bank.

Thomas thought perhaps he was now working in the new government but wasn't sure. What was he doing here, talking with Mordulfah? There was an obvious banking connection, but why the secrecy of a meeting out on the tarmac?

Thomas put it out of his mind when the limo pulled away, and Mordulfah exited the jet. He joined the prince and climbed into the second limo. Mordulfah said nothing about the man and Thomas didn't dare ask him. He sat back and watched the passing scenery. He'd never been to Washington before and hoped they would pass by some of the sights.

CHAPTER 5

CHELSEA MICHIGAN

Meeks began moving away from the outdoor latrine when two more Jijis came their way. Bassett signaled him to stand still. If spotted, they'd have a lot of angry Jijis chasing them through the woods. There was no way to take these guys down quietly if they see them. All hopes of blending into the woods evaporated when one of the men stopped and stared at Bassett trying to figure out who it was.

Bassett let out a breath when the Jiji swung his rifle off his shoulder. Bassett had him beat and fired a single round taking him down. The sound of the Colt M4 echoed in the still air and alerted the rest of the enemy. Bassett aimed at the other Jiji and squeezed another round missing him. The Jiji had taken cover behind a tree and yelled for his friends. He then started firing wildly into the woods hoping to hit something.

"Let's get the hell out of here," said Bassett.

"And it was all going so well," said Meeks as he followed Bassett through the woods.

"Bassett," Nordell said over the radio, "give me a SITREP," which was short for Situation Report.

"We're busted here," said Bassett. "We're hauling ass back to the truck."

"Copy that, we'll meet you there."

He shoved the radio back in his vest and turned to see if they had anyone on their tail. Not seeing anyone, he yelled for Meeks to hold up. They needed a plan to get back the fastest way. When they crossed through the Proving Grounds before, it took nearly an hour. Granted they did it at a leisurely pace, but even at a jog, it would still take too long. It was eight miles to their nearest guard post, which was too far away to call for help on the handheld radio. He wasn't sure how motivated the Jijis were, but then he just killed one of them. The Jijis hadn't seen much action as of late so this would be the perfect opportunity for them to alleviate their boredom.

"Whaddya think?" asked Meeks.

"I think we just gave these guys their activity for the rest of the day."

Meeks let out a scoff. "Yeah, probably so."

"If these guys were smart, they'd start surrounding the area and cut off any chance of escape."

"But they're not, and they have no idea it's just two of us."

Leaves started rustling, and they turned to see six Jijis running through woods. Bassett and Meeks squatted down and watched them as they ran by them heading west. Meeks' eyes flickered up and down as he raised his rifle. Bassett whispered for him to wait. Sure enough, another group of four came bursting through the woods following the others. They were chattering in loud voices and had an air of excitement amongst them.

Bassett tapped Meeks on the shoulder and signaled him to get behind this group. He decided to take these guys out, which will make the others more cautious. These guys weren't professional and seemed a little too cock-sure and excited. They needed a reminder that if they continued, it was at their own risk.

Bassett raised his M4 to his shoulder and Meeks did the same thing as they rose up and got behind this group. They followed them as the Jijis came into a clearing exposing them. They were no more than thirty feet away as Bassett pulled the trigger first followed by Meeks. The nearest Jiji in the group took two rounds in the back sending him crashing into the man in front of him. Meeks also hit one in the back, and he dropped like a bag of rocks when both his lungs and heart were punctured. The third tried to veer away but caught multiple rounds exploding his head. The last one, who had been knocked down, rolled onto his stomach, raised his rifle and got one shot off that went wild before Bassett emptied his mag on him.

"Let's go this way," said Bassett pointing south.

They raced across a small clearing before entering another set of woods just as the first group of six Jijis came running back.

"That ought to slow 'em down for a bit," said Bassett.

"Hell yeah, it will."

They disappeared into the woods before turning around to watch what their enemy was going to do. To their surprise, the Jijis started following them and shooting into the trees.

"Well, that didn't work," said Meeks.

"C'mon."

They sprinted through the woods and soon came to a test road, which they had taken before to get in their original position. They crossed over, and Bassett grabbed Meeks' arm.

"We'll make a stand here."

It was the perfect place to wait for an advancing enemy. It was seventy feet of open ground from one side of the road to the other. They would need to wait until all six were in the open before they fired. Bassett was counting on the fact they weren't experienced enough to send one or two across at a time. He had hoped to leave a couple alive so they could tell their friends what happened. This would spread through their ranks and make them more cautious.

Bassett slammed in a fresh magazine, which left him with only seven. They needed to conserve their ammo if it was going to be an all-afternoon battle.

He turned to Meeks. "How many mags you got?"

Meeks patted his chest rig and counted six.

"Three-shot burst only," said Bassett.'

Meeks nodded.

They didn't have to wait too long before the Jijis came out of the woods to the road. They started to cross the road when one of them ordered them back to the safety of the woods. These guys or at least one of them was smart enough to pull back. Now it was a waiting game to see what they would do.

CHAPTER 6

WASHINGTON D.C.

The limo pulled into the entrance of the Saudi embassy and stopped at the gate. The guard then waved them through, which made Thomas' heart beat faster. He'd never been to Washington D.C. before, and here he was, by the side of an Ambassador's nephew.

It had been a short drive from the airport and besides seeing the Washington Memorial in the distance; he didn't get to see too much of the city. He was surprised to see so many cars on the road and wondered if it was like this anywhere else.

The limo came to a stop at the embassy, and he looked at the square building and wasn't impressed with how plain it was but figured the inside was much nicer.

Mordulfah looked up at him. "You are to stay by my side and to not say anything. You'll handle my briefcase and get me whatever I need. When we are meeting with my uncle, stand off to the side but within my view."

"Yes, your Highness."

They exited the limo and headed inside the massive building. The place was spacious and decorated ornately but not in a gaudy way. The blue carpet matched the gold curtains.

A representative came and ushered them into the Ambassador's office.

Thomas stepped to the side and watched as Prince Faisal warmly greeted his nephew. The prince was taller and heavier than Mordulfah and followed the trend of the monarch by dying their beards black. He appeared genuinely happy to see his nephew, which made Thomas wonder what kind of relationship they had. After catching up on family, Mordulfah got down to business telling his uncle his predicament.

"I have known about your troubles," said Faisal.

"Of course you do," said Mordulfah.

"I've been expecting you to ask for help. I'm actually quite surprised it has taken you this long to come."

"I thought I had the problem taken care of and didn't want to be a burden."

Faisal shook his head. "No, my dear nephew, you didn't want to divide up your deal with Perozzi."

"Yes, that too."

"Mordulfah, you are a businessman and a brilliant one at that. You have outshone your many cousins, most of whom don't do anything but spend money," said Faisal as he then changed the tone of his voice. "You've made your way in this world, but the one thing you are not is a military man."

Mordulfah ate up the compliment but seethed at the same time. Thomas had never seen him in a subservient position before and couldn't help but enjoy himself. Mordulfah wasn't so confident after all and was quite thin-skinned. The man sat stiffly in the chair knowing this meeting was going to be costly.

"I have what you need and have had them ready for some time," continued Faisal.

Mordulfah didn't seem too surprised by this information. "How many?"

"I have five-hundred highly trained and seasoned fighters ready to go."

"Where are they?" asked Mordulfah.

"They are nearby."

"When can I expect them?"

"You can have them today."

Mordulfah nodded in satisfaction.

"I'll have you meet their commander. He's a colonel and knows what he is doing, so do yourself a favor and listen to him."

Mordulfah stared at his uncle for a few moments before asking him the cost.

"Half the revenue from the North Dakota oilfields."

Mordulfah didn't move a muscle and continued to stare at his uncle.

"You think this is too steep a price?" asked Faisal uncomfortable with the silence.

Thomas forced himself to control his facial expression at this question. He had a degree in finance and knew a little about negotiations. You never question your own demand as it showed weakness. Thomas looked over at Mordulfah who still hadn't moved a muscle and began to appreciate his skillful handling of his uncle. He had been contrite during the whole meeting but was now a lion patiently waiting to wear down his prey.

Thomas could see Faisal grow nervous and figured he had realized the asking price was too high, to begin with. Half of the oilfield revenue would eventually be worth billions.

"Okay, I can see you think that is too much but I ask you, if you're not able to get your situation under control, you'll have nothing." Faisal fidgeted slightly and continued. "Since you are my favorite nephew, I'll go with twenty-five percent, and that is a gift."

Thomas shifted his eyes to Mordulfah wondering when he would move.

Mordulfah didn't flinch and took his time responding. "Is that really the best you can do?"

Faisal's eyes darted around the room, which surprised Thomas because he had the upper hand but gave it away too willingly. Perhaps, he had a soft spot for his nephew or was just a bad negotiator. He now appeared to be more of a pleaser or better yet, a diplomat.

"I'll go twenty percent."

"Ten percent sounds better," said Mordulfah finally making an offer.

"Fifteen."

Mordulfah then pounced. "Fifteen it is but for five years only, which will be worth billions and all for five hundred men."

Faisal nodded and extended his hand.

Thomas slightly shook his head in disappointment. He wanted to yell at the elder prince to ask for ten years and couldn't believe he hadn't. He watched as the two men stood up to shake hands and kiss each other to seal the agreement.

CHAPTER 7

CHELSEA MICHIGAN

Bassett and Meeks watched as the six Jijis who had been chasing them stopped at the edge of the woods. There was a lot of open ground between them and was an ideal kill zone.

"C'mon now," whispered Meeks, "no one's waiting for ya."

"That tall one there has some experience and seems to be in charge," said Bassett.

The tall Jiji waved his hands around and split the men into three groups. The two groups walked in opposite directions for fifty yards before crossing the road to start flanking their enemy.

Splitting the group was smart, but it would weaken their force if not done correctly. Not only was speed essential but also coming in without detection was crucial.

"I want that tall one," said Bassett.

"Shouldn't we be backing up and take out their flanks?"

"Normally yes, but that tall one is smart and needs to be taken out. The others won't know what to do without him."

"Gotcha."

"Few more seconds and he'll get his courage up."

They both continued to stand behind a tree when a bearded Jiji started coming forward leaving the tall one behind safely in the bush. He cautiously crept across the open ground darting his head from side to side.

"That tall one is smarter than we thought," smirked Meeks.

"Bit of a wuss if you ask me," whispered Bassett, as he pulled the rifle sling over his head. He laid the rifle on the ground before pulling his tactical tomahawk and blackened steel knife out.

"Poor bastard doesn't have a chance," said Meeks.

"Keep me covered."

The bearded man kept his AK-47 at his side on full auto, made it to the edge of the trees, and stopped. He stared into the woods looking for any movement. Not finding any, he entered the woods and crept toward an awaiting Bassett.

Bassett tightened the grip on his weapons and prepared to strike. He pushed against the tree upon hearing the man closing in. He took a deep breath and twisted around the tree swinging the tomahawk upwards into the pit of the arm. The move sliced through the joint and muscle, which disabled his trigger finger. Bassett then jammed the blade into the side of the neck. Blood sprayed in all directions as the bearded man collapsed to the ground dead.

Meeks pulled the corpse away before getting back into position. The tall Jiji still kept to the woods and didn't appear to be in any hurry to put himself in danger. Bassett and Meeks didn't have much time left before they would have the flanks closing in on them.

"C'mon, ya bastard," said Meeks who then turned to Bassett. "Oh, ah, nice work by the way."

Bassett gave him a firm nod.

"I think he's gone," said Meeks.

"Yeah, he was probably supposed to get an all-clear signal by now."

"Okay. So what now?"

"Let's head west. We should be able to avoid those flanks."

Bassett led the way disappointed the tall one decided not to engage. It would now be too dangerous to go after him. Too much time had passed not to have more Jijis headed their way. Bassett stayed close to the edge of the road to keep an eye on their flank. They ran another three hundred yards to where the road curved to the left. The road intersected with another road, which meant they were running out of cover. They would be forced to cross the road leaving them exposed for seventy feet or more.

"If I remember correctly, this road intersects with another just ahead," said Bassett.

"Roads everywhere in this damn place."

"No kidding."

They turned south and within a minute came to another road with plenty of exposed ground from one side to the other.

"Got no choice," said Bassett.

"Great."

Bassett raised his M4 to his shoulder and looked both ways before running across. Meeks followed paying attention to their six. Crossing safely, they let out a sigh of relief, but it didn't last long as voices penetrated the air. They both froze. Bassett turned toward the sounds and then pointed down the dirt road to their east. The four Jijis who separated to flank them were now walking towards them.

"Must have been frustrating not finding us," said Meeks.

"Don't see the tall one anywhere," responded Bassett.

"What ya think?"

"Hate to give away our position."

"Let them pass?" asked Meeks.

"We could then go south."

Meeks nodded and then squatted down behind some bushes.

The Jijis conversations were loud, and they were not happy with the tall one ordering them to flank the enemy while he stayed behind.

"Where the hell did he go off too anyway?" grumbled one of them.

"Right and where in the hell are these damn rebels?" asked another.

"I don't know, but I'm gonna love stringing those bastards up."

Meeks turned to Bassett and shook his head. Every word of this conversation was pure comedy gold. It was like listening to a bad sitcom with terrible actors. These guys had no idea what they were up against and acted accordingly. Their faux bravado would melt away if Meeks stood up. He yearned to do it but restrained himself because Bassett was right about not giving away their position.

The Jijis walked right on by and Meeks was about to stand up when more voices pierced the woods. They were coming in from behind them. Meeks turned his head and saw the tall Jiji leading a bigger group right towards them.

CHAPTER 8

WASHINGTON D.C.

Green spent all morning thinking about the message Reed left him wanting him to keep quiet about the shooting. Add to it the way Reed had the garage cleaned up spoke volumes about him. He was a calculating man, and an attempt on his life would only show a weakness. By pretending the shooting never happened, he could feign strength and demonstrate no one could lay a finger on him. That his men took out the shooters before it even began, like it was nothing; so don't bother trying again.

Deep down though, the man must be going out of his mind with rage and fear to know that his longtime ally had tired of him. He would have to start shoring up his forces and plan a counterattack on Perozzi.

Green had little doubt Perozzi was angry with Reed because of the recordings and the way he tried arresting Stormy. However, Green didn't think that was enough to get Perozzi too riled up. Something else needed to happen to get Perozzi to act decisively against Reed. Green wanted them both fighting each other not just one of them. He wanted all their forces involved and to get everyone out in the open. Green wanted it to be the talk of the town. It was the only way to show everyone in Washington D.C., that these two were vulnerable.

What would get at Perozzi? He was a proud man but was he thin skinned? He was old and liked having younger women hanging off him. He worked out and was in decent shape but still, he was old, and he knew it.

Green tapped a pencil on his desk trying to come up with something. It had to insult Perozzi but also have him think Reed had something to do with it. A knock on the door interrupted his thoughts. He looked up to see his secretary Grace.

"Sir, I'm going to lunch. You want me to pick you up something?"

Green remembered he had a lunch appointment with his friend Sam and waved her off. He headed outside and walked down the block to start his surveillance detection route, or SDR, he'd been using to shake off any tails that might still be following him.

Jacob Gibbs, the former FBI man, had instructed him on the tradecraft, and he had instituted it in his routine so often that it had become second nature to him.

After conducting his SDR, Green arrived at the small lunch counter where Sam was already waiting. The place was crowded, and they would have to keep their conversation to a minimal.

"Hey, sorry I'm late."

"No problem. I already ordered for ya."

"Thanks," said Green sitting down.

"So, how did it go?" asked Sam purposely talking in vague terms.

"Better than expected."

"Really?"

"Oh, yeah."

"Can't wait to hear all about it."

"Our new friend did well."

"Did she?"

Green couldn't help but break out into a smile.

Sam noticed. "You like her, don't cha?"

"Yeah, and once you see her you'll know why?"

Sam leaned back on the stool and patted John on the back. "My buddy finally has taken an interest in someone. Is this a two-way street?"

"I think so, but I can't say for sure. We haven't exactly been in normal situations together, so it's hard to say."

"What about her friend?" asked Sam referring to Kyle Gibbs.

"Just friends as far as I can tell."

Their food arrived, and they continued with small talk while they ate. Within twenty minutes, they finished their food and headed outside away from prying ears. As they walked through a park, Green caught Sam up on everything that transpired. He fist-pumped the air hearing about Reed's reaction but was most interested in Stormy's participation.

"She really took down one of them?"

"Yeah, she can handle herself."

"And she smart-mouthed Reed?"

Green nodded.

"Wow, John, I'm totally intrigued by this girl. I cannot wait to meet her."

Green raised an eyebrow, which Sam noticed.

"Oh don't worry I won't make any moves on her. I promise."

"Yeah, I'll believe it when I see it."

"John, that hurts. I wouldn't do that to my friend. Besides, I've got this other girl that I started dating."

"Which one is this?"

"Oh, someone new. You don't know her, but I think this is the one. We really have a connection."

Green shook his head at Sam who either didn't like being tied down or just hadn't found the right girl. "Can't wait to meet her."

"Hey, if you want to see if we can double date."

"Double date? I don't even know if Stormy likes me yet."

"All the more reason to get out on a double date. I'll tell ya if she likes ya. Just leave it up to me."

Green shook his head knowing Sam can be overzealous with women. He had no doubt he'd be asking Stormy to join him and his new girlfriend.

They exited the park and passed by a bus stop where Green noticed a small poster pasted on the side of the shelter. He walked over to it and saw it advertised a band.

Sam came up from behind him. "You into this kind of music, John?"

"No I'm not but look at this poster," said Green running his hand up and down on the poster.

"What about it?"

"It's really glued on there good."

"And?"

"We don't see a lot of graffiti in the district do we?"

"No, we don't.

"They don't dare with the way things are."

"Yeah, they'll get thrown in jail," said Sam noticing the smile growing on Green's face. "I know that look, John. Whaddya got in mind?"

"A way to insult Perozzi in front of the whole district."

Sam started to understand and nodded his head.

"Just got to find ourselves an artist," said Green.

"Someone who shares our view and we can trust."

"That shouldn't be too hard. I'm sure there's plenty of artists who hate what's going on."

"Some cash should help inspire them," said Sam.

"Let's bring it up at our meeting tonight."

Street art had a way of making a point and if done right can cause quite a sensation. With the right message, it has a unique way of getting attention. Graffiti is illegal, which makes it have an even bigger impact. Some people view it as art while others as vandalism. What he had in mind would no doubt be considered vandalism. Perozzi was his target, and he just found a way to embarrass him.

CHAPTER 9

The limo pulled out of the Saudi embassy and took a right on New Hampshire Avenue. Mordulfah had just made a deal with his uncle for experienced fighters and had done so with superb negotiating skills. Thomas wasn't sure if he should comment on the way Mordulfah dealt with his uncle. Thomas had a newfound respect for the way he handled the old man and wondered if he did all his negotiations like that. Thomas must have been staring at him too long because the prince took notice.

"What is it, Thomas?"

He turned red but took a breath and decided to ask him. "Your Highness, the way you handle that negotiation was quite brilliant and I am in awe."

Mordulfah looked pleased with the compliment.

"What I was wondering, is that the way you handle all negotiations?"

Mordulfah stared at him in silence the same way he stared at his uncle. The intensity of his stare was both impressive and eerie. Thomas found himself starting to fidget.

"Uncomfortable isn't it?"

Thomas nodded at the revelation.

"People don't like silence, and if you can control yourself while staring someone down, you'll achieve the upper hand."

"Wow! I don't remember learning something so valuable in all of my four years of college."

"Nor do I and I went to Oxford. It is something you learn in life. I learned some of it from the man, we're going to go see next."

"May I ask who?"

"Gerald Perozzi. He's America's puppet-master and controls all the strings of power. He's the one I deal with, and while we're in town, I need to pay my respects. He'll want an update, but I know he's well aware of our current situation. He has ears everywhere."

Thomas looked out the window to admire as much of Washington as he could. He knew they'd be no sightseeing, but he no longer cared because he had learned about Mordulfah's plans and couldn't wait to tell Captain Winters. They needed to know he was sending experienced fighters to fight them. He hoped they were going to meet this colonel before they left so he could learn even more.

The limo pulled into what looked like a mansion but was a converted office building. The chauffeur parked and opened the door. Mordulfah didn't say anything to him as he exited the car and figured he had the same instructions as before. Be available and don't say anything. Thomas laughed to himself thinking it was like being a fly on the wall.

The receptionist greeted Mordulfah in friendly terms as if they knew each other, so Thomas figured she'd worked here for some time. She escorted them to a side room with a large open entrance where you could still see the reception area. The room had hardwood floors with an area rug centered in the middle of the room. The wallpapered walls had heavy wooden oak trim, which gave the place a sturdy appearance. She offered Mordulfah a drink, which he declined. Thomas stood off to the side and figured he was not to sit down. He never saw Wali ever sit down when he was around him.

After a few minutes, Thomas heard some laughter and turned his head to see an older man walking with Albert Sauer, the man who met with Mordulfah on the tarmac. Why was he here? Thomas looked out his peripheral vision to witness Mordulfah pretend not to know the man. He figured the old man must be Perozzi and watched as he acknowledged Mordulfah's presence. Albert Sauer didn't, and it finally dawned on

Thomas why. He was Mordulfah's inside man, which is why he met him in secret out on the tarmac. Thomas again had to control his emotions as he realized just how cunning Mordulfah was. He didn't take any chances on not knowing what was going on and wanted to have the upper hand.

Perozzi said goodbye to Sauer and then came inside where Mordulfah patiently waited. He looked at Thomas and then Mordulfah expecting to be told who he was.

"This is Thomas, he is filling in for Wali who I have doing other things."

Thomas wasn't sure if he should extend his hand out but decided to wait to see if Perozzi was forthcoming. He tried to act like Wali and gave him a slight bow. The old man then turned away and invited them into his office.

Thomas began to follow them, but Mordulfah turned around and told him to wait here. His heart sunk as he hoped to learn more about his business. Thomas turned around to go back to the side room. He was about to sit down when the receptionist asked if he like something to drink.

"Don't worry you'll have time, I've seen their meetings take over an hour and never less than thirty minutes."

"Well, thank you. I'm Thomas, by the way."

"Hello, Thomas, I'm Alicia. This your first time?"

"It is. It's actually my first time in Washington."

"Oh, how exciting for you. Where are you from?"

"Nashville."

She gave him a curious look. "You don't speak with much of a southern accent."

Thomas laughed. "My parents are from Pakistan and heavily influenced my language. They didn't mean too, but they did."

"Well, there you go. Now, what will it be?"

"Excuse me?"

"Drink?"

"Oh, yes, do you have Coke?"

"Coming right up."

Thomas watched the receptionist scoot down the hall. He liked her bubbly personality and thought it matched her small size, which he figured was about five-foot-two without the heels she wore. The pixie hairstyle went well with her round face and kept her looking young, even though she was probably in her late thirties.

She came back and handed him a glass full of ice and cola.

"If you don't mind me asking," asked Alicia "but how did you get to Michigan from Nashville?"

"I graduated college with a degree in finance and was offered a job. There weren't many other prospects at the time, so I took a chance."

"How bad are things there?"

Thomas thought her line of questioning was strange. Didn't she know what her boss was doing to the country? He looked at her and realized she was just a receptionist and wasn't on the inside of things so to speak.

"Most people have left the state, but there are still many in the area."

"I'm always so inquisitive because we're so insulated here in the district. Heck, if you didn't know any better, you'd never even know we're even in a war."

"I've noticed that. I was surprised to see so many cars on the road with actually traffic jams. Do you have any food shortages here?"

Alicia slowly shook her head. "No, not really. I mean sometimes, yeah, but for the most part, you can get what you want. It's way more expensive, that's for sure."

Thomas took a sip of his drink. "I'm fortunate I work for who I do because I don't know how everyone is doing it."

"Gardens I suppose," said Alicia not really giving it much thought.

Thomas could see she didn't lack for anything. Her hair was perfect and looked like she just had her nails manicured. He figured Perozzi paid her well but wondered if the rest of Washington was like this. He turned his thoughts to his parents and was glad they lived in the south. He hadn't talked to them in about six months, but during his last call, they told him they had stocked up on plenty of food. They lived in an upscale-gated neighborhood, which kept them safer than most people. Now that he'd seen Washington, he knew this was the ultimate place to be. All the influential people worked and lived here, which almost guaranteed you could get anything you needed, even during times of war.

CHAPTER 10

JACKSON MICHIGAN

Reese slid out of bed mid-afternoon still tired from last night's operation in Port Huron. She had put too much pressure on her leg and was feeling the pains today. She managed to swing her feet onto the linoleum floor and decided to take another shower to wash off any remaining filth from the river. The cold water would also help numb the aches and pains that were coursing through her body.

She gritted her teeth and hopped into the cold water, which caused goose bumps to explode across her skin. "At least the water is clean," she said to herself. After a couple of minutes, she got used to the cold water and washed around her wounds before rewashing her hair.

She got out of the shower and stood in front of the mirror looking at her wounds. The leg had an entry and exit wound and didn't look nearly as bad as her arm, which was missing a chunk of flesh. A yellowish blue bruise surrounded the stitches and even though she had full mobility, the whole area was still delicate to the touch, even more so having rolled around on it last night.

She remembered the slow-motion realization that she'd been shot. The first thought that goes through your head is at any moment you could actually die. An odd thought when you are in the middle of a gunfight but being struck with a bullet gives it more credence. Then the pain hits you, and you know you've never felt such pain. Never even imagined it could be so bad, which is quite a statement for someone who had been brutalized over the course of ten days. Besides the sexual abuse, she had to endure, some of the cops were downright cruel to her. A few would beat her with a variety of instruments from wooden paddles to leather belts sometimes to the point of drawing blood.

She shook her head at the memory and turned to the side to look at the bruising from the blow she'd received from the cop she killed during the hospital attack. He had punched her ribcage after slamming her down on the conference table. The size of the blue and red bruise had shrunk considerably, and it didn't bother her as much as it had. She tilted her head from side to side realizing she had been lucky none of her injuries had been life-threatening. She debated on whether she should have Doctor Lunsford examine them. She didn't want her wounds to get infected from who knows what was in the river and was glad she'd been taking her antibiotics.

Deciding to speak with him, she dressed in a yellow cami and a pair of jean shorts, grabbed her red crutch and headed downstairs. Thankfully, she had only one flight of stairs to hobble down, as she was still sore from last night.

The cold river had been helpful in keeping the pain at bay, but it had caught up to her on the way home. She and Amber drove back to Jackson by themselves with the heater blowing at full blast.

She laughed at how no one wanted to drive back with them with the heater going. The air did get stuffy enough that they had to crack open the windows for fresh air. It took nearly an hour before the heater had any real effect on their wet clothes. It was then that the pain started coming back as it got warm. The leg hurt the most as she had been walking on it without using her crutch. Between the adrenaline, the numbness and her resolve, she managed to ignore the pain while fighting.

"Reese," greeted Sandy, the nurse, who had been looking after her. She was the one who had an emotional break down after the hospital attack while trying to care for Reese.

Reese closed in for a hug. "Hey, Sandy,"

"You okay? I heard what happened last night."

"In some pain and my dressings are off," said Reese twisting around to show her bare legs.

"Ah yes, well let's take a look. You've been taking your antibiotics?"

Reese nodded just as Doctor Lunsford walked in. He'd served as an Army surgeon in the Middle East and had seen his share of gunshot wounds.

"Good afternoon Reese, how's it going?

"I'm good."

"Heard what you did last night and was hoping you'd come by."

"You were?"

Lunsford smiled at her. "You went for a swim, yes?"

"Yeah, you could say that."

"Well, who knows how polluted that river is," said Lunsford examining her arm and leg. He had Sandy weigh her and check her blood pressure before examining her eyes and ears and listening to her heart. "You in any pain?"

Reese nodded. "I was walking without my crutch."

"How did that go?"

"Between the adrenaline and the cold river, great at first."

Lunsford laughed. "Afterwards, not so much eh?"

"You could say that."

"Sandy, go ahead and re-bandage those wounds," said Lunsford. He then turned back to Reese and said, "The wounds are healing up nicely. I don't see any infection from last night. Just a couple more days for the bandages should do it. Keep taking the antibiotics until you finish the bottle. Do you still have those painkillers?"

Reese let out a scoff. "Oh, yeah."

"Have you taken any of them?"

"A couple, but they make me loopy, and I don't want to get hooked on them."

He gave her a knowing nod. "I understand. Why don't you bring those back here and we'll put you on some 800 mg Ibuprofen. I don't see any reason why you shouldn't be able to get rid of your crutch over the next few days.

Reese nodded glad she came to see him. She wanted to be reassured she wouldn't get sick from last night. It was bad enough she had stomped her feet to go on the mission, but it would have been worse if she had become a bigger liability to the team. She should never have put Meeks in the position to give in to her. She couldn't help, but blurt out that she wanted to go, and knew she had an issue of self-control.

Since Cole left, she'd been battling a bout of depression by keeping herself busy and was afraid if she stopped it would come back and swallow her as it had done to Cole.

Reese walked out into the hallway and saw Scar and Amber walking in from outside. They were headed to the cafeteria, and she decided to join them.

CHAPTER 11

Nate pushed the door open and entered the cafeteria. He hadn't been down here since the attack on the hospital last week. His nurse, Sandy, had been waiting on him hand and foot since then. He was in the mood for a fresh cup of coffee and didn't want to bother anyone. He picked up the decanter and saw what was left of the weak coffee. He looked around for more coffee but didn't find any, so he walked into the storage room. He checked all the cabinets before finding a box hidden way in the back. He tore it open and found it full of coffee packets. He drummed his fingers on the cabinet and yelled out in excitement.

He opened a fresh packet and brought it up to his nose inhaling the rich aroma deeply into his lungs. He eagerly poured it into a filter before sitting down to wait for it to finishing brewing.

He was in a much better mood now that Elliott was doing better. Despite what Elliott had been saying, the last few days he didn't look so good. However, Doctor Lunsford had given everyone an update this morning assuring he was going to make a full recovery.

The water finished pouring into the glass decanter, and Nate got up and filled his cup to the top. He breathed in the aroma before taking a sip. He sat down with his hands wrapped around the warm mug. It was one of the few things around here warm.

Between the generator and the solar panes, the hospital used the power they produced in a limited way. The kitchen, cafeteria, operating and examination rooms were the only areas with full power. Not all the hallways had working lights or any of the hot water heaters, which explained why most people showered every three or four days. It took a lot of motivation to jump into the cold water. Nate let out a scoff thinking how motivated Amber and Reese must have been to get in that cold river.

Nate took another sip of coffee and looked up when he heard the door open. Scar and the girls walked in.

"I was just thinking of you guys," said Nate toasting them with his cup.

"Is that fresh coffee I smell?" asked Reese.

"Damn right it is."

"Where'd you get it?" asked Amber. "I looked everywhere."

"Apparently, you didn't look in the very back of the storeroom. Got a whole box of it here."

"Oh, Nate, you're my new hero," said Amber.

"Haven't I always been?" asked Nate with a smirk.

Amber leaned down behind him and wrapped her arms around his chest. "But of course."

"How's my favorite cripple?" Nate asked Reese with a wink.

"She's feeling it today," said Reese plopping down next to him and leaning her head on his shoulder. "Pain is my companion today."

"I heard what you guys did. My hats off to ya."

"They were something alright," said Scar as he poured a cup of coffee. He then poured two more for the girls. "Helluva night, that's for sure." Scar handed the girls their coffee and sat down next to Amber.

"I suppose Canada's no longer a friendly place," said Nate.

"We still have Winnipeg," countered Amber.

Scar took a sip of coffee and agreed.

Nate shrugged. "Bit far from here."

"Hopefully, Bassett will come back with good news."

"Where is he?" asked Reese.

Scar briefed her on the reconnaissance mission. "Amber's idea."

Reese held out her hand for a fist-bump across the table to Amber.

"Speaking of supplies, I need to go see Mayor Simpson and give him an update."

Reese's eyes lit up. "I just love that man. He's always so sweet to me."

"Come with me then," suggested Scar.

"I couldn't possibly climb those stairs today," she said in a disappointing tone.

"It is a lot of stairs," said Amber.

"The last time I was there, Badger had to carry me down."

"He did?" Nate asked in a doubtful tone.

Reese nodded.

"How?"

"On his back."

"Bill Taylor? Our lovable curmudgeon? Badger?" Nate asked again still not believing what he just heard.

"Yes," Reese responded annoyed with his disbelief.

Nate scoffed, "I'm surprised he can even get up those stairs himself."

Scar laughed and then turned to Reese. "I'd be more than happy to carry you up."

"Careful there Scar, you think you can handle…what are ya, Reese, about a buck five?"

"I'm a one-fifteen, thank you. Sandy just weighed me."

Scar laughed again. "I think I can handle that. Amber, you can join us if you like."

"You gonna carry her up too?" asked Nate in a deadpan manner.

"If she wants me too."

"Hmm, that is tempting," joked Amber."

"Say yes, Amber, please say yes," pleaded Nate.

Reese bumped Nate's shoulder. "You are a trouble-maker today."

"Yeah, well, I haven't been out in a while. I'm getting a little antsy."

"I can see that. You should go out for a drive. I do it all the time, and it works wonders."

"Just might have to do that."

"I'll take ya out later if you'd like," offered Reese.

"Careful Nate, her driving is a bit reckless," said Scar.

Reese shot him a squinted glare.

"Right up my alley, then," said Nate who since being wounded, had only left the hospital once to go watch the executions. Since then, he'd been keeping his childhood friend, Elliott, company. This wasn't ideal for a man who always liked to be on the move. He desperately missed being in the heat of battle and needed something to do.

CHAPTER 12

CHELSEA MICHIGAN

Before heading west back to their SUV, Nordell and Burns decided to hold their position for a few minutes to see what kind of action the Jijis had in mind. They kept watching across the overgrown field to Manchester Road. It didn't take too long before four cars came speeding down from the interstate. The cars all turned into the Proving Grounds entrance, which meant they were going to cruise the maze of roads to look for Bassett and Meeks.

"Let's see if we got a clean exit south," said Nordell.

Burns nodded and then pointed to more cars coming down Manchester Road. Another four cars turned into the same entrance and disappeared behind the trees blocking their view.

"Looks more like a contest to see who gets them first," quipped Burns.

"Probably so."

Nordell followed Burns through the thin strip of woods, which would end as soon as they came to the shutdown buildings. He had been here many times over the years as a guest. A friend of his was an engineer at Chrysler and worked at this location for most of his career. On more than one occasion, he had invited Nordell to come out and test drive cars. It was one of his favorite things to do whenever he came back home from the Marines.

It was a big place with lots of different types of roads and terrain, which made it an ideal place to keep hidden. It would take a lot of men to go through the whole area, let alone surround it. If the Jijis were smart, it's just what they would do, but there was no telling how motivated they were. If it took too long, they might get bored and call off the search figuring they had escaped.

After zigzagging around the property for an hour, they finally came to the southern end of the Proving Grounds. By the time they reach it, their mouths were dry, and their bodies were covered in perspiration, with their legs were on fire. Nordell grabbed the canteen and took several gulps of water. They sat down to rest for a few minutes, and Burns pulled out some granola bars handing one to Nordell. They eagerly at the food having burned through a lot of calories.

Across the field was Lehman Road, which was a dirt road that connected Manchester Road with Sylvan Road where they left their ride.

"Got a patrol down there," said Burns handing the binoculars to Nordell.

"Looks like they're trying to surround the place."

Ten men stood guard paying attention to the southern edge of the property.

"Let's check out the other end," said Nordell.

They started heading west keeping to the cover the trees. A straightway racetrack was to their right, and they had to stop when two cars came racing down the road. One of the cars jammed on the brakes coming to a full stop. Four Jijis got out and started patrolling the woods where Nordell and Burns had just come from.

Nordell shook his head. "Damn it."

"Where's Bassett when you need him," said Burns.

"Yeah, I'm too old for those kind of moves."

"That's what these are for," said Burns, as he raised his rifle.

"Was really hoping to keep out position quiet."

"Suppressors sure would come in handy."

"Yes. They're on my wish list if we ever get back to your friends in Winnipeg."

Nordell pushed forward to keep ahead of the Jijis who were coming in behind them. Voices broke through the air as the Jijis spoke to one another. Nordell shook his head at the rank amateurs but was happy they were gabbing because it made it much easier to keep track of them.

Burns put his finger to his ear and then pointed west. New voices were coming from that direction. The other car had stopped, which meant four more Jijis were ahead of them.

Nordell turned to the left and started heading south. Burns followed keeping his eyes peeled to their six. The crunching leaves were making them paranoid, but the Jijis' chatter helped drown out any loud sounds.

"Damn it," said Nordell, as he raised his rifle and pulled the trigger.

A pair of Jijis unexpectedly appeared in front of Nordell, and he had little choice but to engage. A single shot to the head dropped the first before he even raised his weapon. The second one was quicker and got a shot off before Nordell planted one in his chest. The impact threw him back off feet as his trigger finger kept firing the AK-47 until he hit the ground. The errant rounds snapped and whistled through the canopy of trees dropping leaves and launching a branch through the air.

"So much for keeping hidden," said Burns.

"Let's get around these two and wait for their buddies."

"Don't want to hide anymore," quipped Burns.

"Screw that. Let's take these bastards out."

They dashed through the trees to an ideal ambush spot. Nordell crouched down behind a tree, as sweat formed on his forehead. He looked over at Burns who was also crouching down behind a tree just to his right. Burns gave him a firm nod and then turned toward the corpses about fifteen yards away. It didn't take long before two more Jijis came to investigate.

"Those four must be from the same car," whispered Burns.

Nordell nodded. "Let's wait for the others."

The Jijis had their AK's shouldered and jerked around at the slightest movement. One yelled out for help. A minute later, the other four Jijis showed up, and all started freaking out.

"Now," said Nordell, as he aimed and pulled the trigger on full auto. Shell casings flew out of the Colt M4 as rounds thundered through the air.

A bloodied Jiji spun around and dropped to the ground dead. Another pulled on his friend while taking a couple of rounds to the chest. The friend was pulled down but not before taking a round to his head.

The rest of the Jijis took cover behind trees or falling to the ground. They were scared and unsure where the enemy was. They yelled at each other to do something. Finally, one came around the tree and started randomly spraying bullets at anything.

Burns pulled the trigger and sent a tight grouping of three rounds into his chest. Another Jiji who was lying on the ground lifted his head to find a target. He pulled the trigger in haste not aiming at anything. Burns ignored the rounds flying by and squeezed a single shot and a second later, another dead Jiji.

"That's five by my count," said Nordell.

"I'll flank 'em."

"I'll cover ya," said Nordell as he threw in a fresh magazine. He switched to a three-shot and nodded to Burns. He aimed at the Jijis who were in a prone position. He squeezed the trigger and hit the ground in front of them throwing dirt and pine needles in the air.

Burns swung around and headed south for a few yards before turning toward the enemy. He could see them up ahead with their heads buried in the dirt. Once in position, he emptied his magazine and took out the remaining three Jijis.

"All clear," yelled Burns.

Nordell came jogging in and surveyed the area. "Let's grab an AK and ammo. No telling how long we'll be in here."

Burns began rifling through their jackets and found a set of car keys. "Look what I got."

Nordell nodded. "Might as well have a getaway car in here."

They took all the ammo they could carry and hightailed it to the car the Jijis left on the track. Nordell got in the driver's seat and said he knew just the place to hide.

CHAPTER 13

JACKSON MICHIGAN

Leaving Nate and Amber back at the cafeteria, Reese insisted on driving Scar to city hall in the beat-up Chevy pickup she'd been using all week. She liked the way it handled the tight turns, in other words, she loved the way the wheels squealed whenever she over-steered the backend.

Scar smiled as she revved the engine before throwing it in drive. He grabbed the door handle when she tore out of the parking lot.

"Don't worry, I won't kill ya."

"Ya damn well better not. What will my wife think if she hears I died with a hot looking chick?"

"She'll think you're a stud," laughed Reese.

"She already knows that."

Reese laughed again while shaking her head.

She pulled in front of city hall and parked the truck. She turned to Scar and gave him a look that said, I told ya I wouldn't kill ya."

Scar chuckled and headed for the front door.

"You wanna jump on my back or would you prefer I carry you in my arms?"

"Oh, my! That's a hard choice," said Reese as she put a finger to her chin. "I think I'd like to be carried."

Reese put a hand around Scar's neck as he lifted her up while she held onto the crutch in the other.

"My knight in shining armor."

Reaching the top, he set her down and said, "My lady."

Scar turned to corner and saw Mayor Simpson in his office. "Good morning, Mayor."

"Mister Scarborough, come in, come in, oh and I see you brought Miss Reese with you," said Simpson as he got up and moved around his desk to greet them. He shook Scar's hand and then took ahold of Reese's hand. "How's our brave young lady doing this morning?"

"I'm good, sir," responded Reese breaking into a big smile while shaking his frail hand.

"I heard about your harrowing experience in that cold river. Oh, but look at you now, you couldn't look any more beautiful."

Reese blushed at his compliment. "Thank you, sir."

"Did you climb all those stairs just to come see me?"

"Actually, Scar was my knight in shining armor and carried me up."

"Well, how nice of you."

Simpson pulled Reese's hand and guided her over to a chair. "Come, sit down here."

"Mayor, I brought you a gift," said Scar handing him several packets of coffee.

"Oh my, Mister Scarborough, thank you."

"You're very welcome."

"Would everyone like a cup?" asked Simpson moving over to the coffee pot he had hooked up to a car battery with an inverter. He emptied the contents and poured the water before moving back around his desk.

Scar sat down next to Reese amused at how excited the mayor was with his gift of coffee. It was sad yet fun at the same time. Sad they were running out of what was now a rare commodity but fun to see the excitement and appreciation at the same time. The smell of coffee began to saturate the office and Simpson got back up and poured a cup for everyone.

Simpson inhaled the aroma before taking a sip. "It's the little things in life that give us the most pleasure."

"Indeed it is, sir," said Scar thankful he thought to bring the coffee. Despite the mayor's overall optimism, the poor man looked to be on edge and needed a boost.

After a few sips of coffee, Scar briefed him on their trip to Canada and apologized for the failure.

"Please, don't apologize. You have nothing to apologize for. We're all just grateful for your help."

"Well, we might have a solution albeit a temporary one," said Scar.

Simpson's bushy eyebrows rose high on this face.

"We're gonna see about raiding the Jijis' supplies."

"Oh, that sounds like a grand idea," said Simpson.

"I already have a squad scouting it out as we speak."

Simpson toasted Scar with his cup before taking another sip.

After they finished their coffee, Simpson offered them a refill, but Scar declined the offer because he had other things to do.

"Yes, of course, you do," said Simpson rising up and thanking them again for their help as he walked them out to the hallway. He grabbed Reese's hand and said with a glint in his eye, "I look forward to seeing you race your truck around town some more."

Blood rushed to Reese's cheeks, and she said in an apologetic tone, "I'll be careful, I promise."

"I know you will, dear," he responded with a wink.

Scar waited until Simpson walked back into his office before turning to Reese. "Getting a little reputation, I see."

"Oh, my gosh. I'm so embarrassed."

"You probably scared the wits out of some little old lady," said Scar.

"I know, right."

"I wouldn't worry about it."

They got to the staircase, and Reese opted to get on Scar's back this time. She handed him the crutch before wrapping her arms around him. Reaching the first floor, Scar opened the door, and they walked outside.

"Thanks for helping me up there. I just love visiting him. He reminds me so much of my Grandpa," said Reese.

"Does he now."

"Yeah. They're so much alike and both so sweet."

"He's a very kind man. I just hope he can hang on. Every time I see him, he looks older than before."

"He's stronger than you think."

They hopped back in the pickup.

"How long has it been since you've seen your G'pa?"

"Oh, he's been dead, like, eight or nine years I guess. I was, like thirteen or fourteen, I think. He died not long after my G'ma died."

"They lived nearby you?"

"Yep. Just down the street. I used to ride my bike there all the time."

"Well, that's nice."

"Yeah, it was. I really relied on them a lot when my dad left us."

Scar hadn't known her dad left her. "I'm sorry to hear that."

"It's okay. You get used to things and then move on."

Scar sat in the passenger seat admiring Reese's inner strength. She was beaten to hell but still carried on trying to help in any way she could. Winters departure had initially affected her attitude negatively, but it had changed to a more positive one over the last couple of days. He was glad he carried her up to see Simpson. He could see that it helped her out as well as the mayor, who was obviously excited to see her. The mayor had been right; it is the little things that give the most pleasure.

CHAPTER 14

CHELSEA MICHIGAN

The sound of voices got louder as a group of ten Jijis came right towards Bassett and Meeks. They had just let another group of four go by in hopes of staying hidden. They were still a mile from their ride and hoped to get there without having to engage an overwhelming force. They were in a precarious position not knowing where the Jijis were waiting for them. Also, they had four more roads to cross, which meant a lot of open ground.

Bassett raised his head and saw the tall Jiji he had been hunting earlier leading another group. It was too late to try to sneak off, as they were too close to them. They had no choice but to engage.

"I'll take the tall one," whispered Bassett. "Hit the left side."

Meeks nodded.

"We'll have to head south right after."

Bassett lined up his first shot. The tall Jiji was in charge of these men and needed to be taken out first. Bassett let out a breath and squeezed the trigger. A three-shot burst hit the man center mass throwing him on his back. Panic ensued as the others stared at him for a split second before trying to take cover.

Meeks switched his rifle to full auto and emptied the magazine sweeping it back and forth. With such a large pack to aim at, he justified wasting the precious ammo by hitting three Jijis. He ejected the empty mag and shoved in another one as he looked for more targets. The rest of them were taking cover, and not a single one dared to return fire. Meeks wanted to flank them and take out a couple more, but Bassett tapped him on the shoulder to move out.

In situations like this, Meeks always showed deference to the more experience Bassett and was glad he was on their team. He followed him out on the dirt road just as he let loose a burst on the group of four they allowed to pass by earlier. Blood-curdling screams came from the group as they all took bullets to the chest. Bodies spun around before collapsing to the ground in a bloody heap.

Bassett jumped into the woods in a full gallop wanting to put as much space between them as possible. He wanted to get to the next road before they had too many of them on their tail. Taking out the tall one and the others bought them a few extra minutes, and besides, some of those guys were more than likely wounded, which always slowed down a team.

Gunfire in the distance got their attention, and they stopped to listen. They recognized the different sounds of the M4 and AK-47 as the gun battle continued. The final sounds were from the Colt M4.

"Sound like they took care of business," said Meeks.

"Yes, it does. Let's start heading west," said Bassett.

Bassett was hoping Nordell and Burns would be able to keep hidden and be able to get to the truck first. That way they could at the very least, get in radio range and call for help. As things stood, it was reminding him too much of the Battle on Robinson Road. It was similar because the enemy had the opportunity to surround them in a small area. Granted the Proving Grounds was much bigger than the woods behind Robinson Road, but still, it was very reminiscent. The enemy certainly had the manpower to do so if they desired.

Bassett looked at his watch, which read sixteen hundred hours. They had five hours of daylight left with no night-vision optics and not enough ammo. Thankfully, both carried a canteen of water and several snack bars.

They reached the first of four roads they needed to get over. They stopped at the edge of the woods. It was a hundred feet of open ground with too many places for the enemy to be lying in wait.

"What ya think?" asked Meeks.

"Don't like our options but we got no choice."

"One at a time?"

"No. It'll give them a heads up for the next guy."

"Alright. On three," stated Meeks.

Meeks counted down, and they bolted across the road each looking the opposite way for any signs of Jijis. Four seconds later, they reached the safety of woods with neither of them seeing anyone on the road. They continued running and quickly came to the next road, which was narrower than the last one. They were about to cross when a loud popping pierced the air. It was a pickup with a bad muffler approaching.

Bassett crouched down next to Meeks and watched a truck with armed men in the back zip by them.

Meeks shook his head in disbelief. "Thanks for the warning."

The car stopped several hundred yards south of them, and everyone disembarked. A few walked into the woods, but the rest stayed with the truck.

Bassett lifted his binoculars and focused on the group. There was ten, and none of them were paying attention in their direction. It was now or never.

"Follow my lead," ordered Bassett as he started to do a low crawl across the road.

Meeks usually beat Bassett or anyone else when they were running because of his athletic ability. However, this didn't include crawling, which wasn't as easy as running especially at his age. The much younger Bassett had him beat by a few seconds and had time to look through the binoculars again. No one took notice of them, and they dashed through the woods to the third road. They made it to the other side when their radio came alive.

CHAPTER 15

WASHINGTON D.C.

Thomas walked behind Mordulfah after he exited the limousine in a warehouse district on the outskirts of Baltimore. The whole area was rundown but still had plenty of activity with tractor-trailers backing up and pulling away from shipping docks. They were here to meet with Colonial Khan. He was the man Mordulfah's uncle put in charge of getting rid of the Shadow Patriots.

They approached the door that had a camera above pointing down at the entrance. Thomas pushed the intercom button and expected someone to speak but instead, the door buzzed. He pulled the door open and waited for Mordulfah to enter first.

The two-story open interior was close to ten thousand square feet and had dorm rooms sectioned off on each level. Gym equipment sat in the back, with some men working out. There was another area for daily prayers and an open kitchen.

Thomas was stunned when he realized this was where Colonel Khan had his men living. The conditions weren't the best, but then they were probably used to much worse. The battle-hardened men stopped what they were doing and turned to watch Mordulfah.

An older man approached them. He wore a beard, which he dyed black. He was physically fit, stood five-foot-eight, and had an air of confidence about him.

"Prince Mordulfah," said Colonel Khan as he bent down slightly to show him deference. "I am Colonel Khan."

"Colonel," said Mordulfah not bothering to introduce Thomas to him.

"I understand I'm to help you with your situation in Detroit."

"Yes."

Mordulfah was putting his practice of silence to good use on the colonel who was being forced to fill in the gaps of silence. Thomas noticed Khan already had a slight change in his mannerisms.

"Perhaps I can show you the men."

Mordulfah nodded.

Khan looked over to his assistant and gave him an order in Arabic, which Thomas didn't speak. The assistant then yelled out in Arabic, but Thomas didn't need to understand the order to know what it meant. Khan's men began pouring out of the dorms to line up. It was impressive to see how quickly and organized five hundred men lined up for inspection.

Thomas followed behind Mordulfah as he walked from one end to the other inspecting the men. These were unlike the fighters he had with him in Detroit, who mostly drifted in from the area looking for work and a chance to kill. These men standing at attention were experienced and had serious looks in their eyes.

"These men seem up to the task," said Mordulfah.

"They're all battle-tested and are my best men."

"You'll be up against a formidable enemy."

"My men have all fought the American military. They do not frighten us."

Mordulfah turned and stared at the colonel for a moment. "They are not American military, but ordinary men, fighting for their homeland. They fight with a passion and have been quite successful. Do not underestimate them."

"I can assure you, we are up to the task."

"We shall see. Can you be ready today?" asked Mordulfah.

"Yes."

"Then I'll arrange transportation, and you can fly in tonight."

"Perhaps you could give me an overview of your situation?" asked Khan.

Mordulfah turned to Thomas and motioned for his briefcase. Thomas held it open while Mordulfah grabbed a map of Michigan. It already had areas marked off as to where the Shadow Patriots were stationed and where his men were as well as the National Police. He gave him an overview of the skirmishes and how many men he had lost. Khan listened until Mordulfah was finished.

He studied the map and asked how many men he had as well as the amount currently guarding the town. He then laid out a solid battle plan to force the rebels into a corner.

Thomas had to fight to maintain a straight face because what he was hearing was disheartening and he realized the Shadow Patriots were in for an intense fight. This Colonel knew what he was doing and would show no mercy to the people of Jackson.

Mordulfah nodded and headed back to the limo with Thomas in tow. Once inside the car, Thomas didn't say anything but wanted to know if the prince liked what he heard. Mordulfah was difficult to read and seemed indifferent to Khan.

"What did you think?" asked Mordulfah.

"Sir?" asked a surprised Thomas.

"Don't play coy with me, I know you want to know what I think, but first I want to hear your thoughts."

"Well, sir, I'm not a military man, but I'd have to say those were some scary looking men."

Mordulfah nodded.

"They're different from what we currently have," said Thomas. "His battle plan seems good as well."

"Indeed. These men are exactly what we need to break those rebels."

Thomas continued to watch Mordulfah for the rest of the trip back to Detroit and noticed the man's spirits seemed lifted. Thomas began to formulate an excuse to leave Grosse Pointe on an errand so he could warn the Shadow Patriots. They needed to know an attack was imminent and they would be fighting an experienced army. Unfortunately, he couldn't come up with any ideas and thought perhaps it was time to run off permanently.

CHAPTER 16

JACKSON MICHIGAN

Reese was in her element as she tore down the street showing off her driving skills to Nate, who was the expert on cars. He never bothered to put his seatbelt on, mostly because the strap would have caused his shoulder too much pain. Regardless, he was enjoying the company and the wind blowing across his face to worry about safety. He hadn't been too active since the hospital attack where he fought a cop hand to hand. During the struggle, his stitches tore open and set his healing back by a few more days.

Thankfully, the girl sitting next to him pulled his butt out of that jam. Had it not been for her, he wouldn't be here enjoying the drive. He glanced over at her and admired her tenacity. She went full on beast-mode by jumping on that cop and slicing his throat. Even after he slammed her on the table and punched her ribcage, she was still able to gather her wits and kill him.

The separation between houses grew as they were now out in the country. Nate hadn't been in this area before and didn't recognize where they were. Not that it mattered much because that's why they had maps.

Reese wasn't doing many turns because it put too much strain on his shoulder. He'd rather see her push the limits of the truck as it was something he did in his youth. Burning rubber was a lot of fun and quite exhilarating. He let out a sigh because it was another thing to add to the list of things he couldn't do.

He wasn't living up to the Attila the Hun moniker Bassett had given him. It was frustrating being a drag on the group, but mostly he hated missing all the action. This is what gnawed on him the most. So much had happened and he wasn't able to get in on any of it.

Lost in thought, Nate leaned his head back when he heard a noise in the distance. He sat back up and stuck his head out the window.

"What?" asked Reese.

"Did you hear that?"

"Hear what?"

"I thought I hear a gunshot."

Another round of popping got their attention. Reese slowed the truck down and then came to a full stop. Neither said anything but stared at each other while straining their ears. More gunfire erupted, and Reese let off the brake and continued heading east toward the shooting.

"Isn't Bassett and Meeks out this way?" asked Reese.

"Yes, they are."

A shiver shot through Reese as she stepped on the gas. They were on Old US Hwy 12, which emptied out on the interstate.

"How far do you want to go?" asked Reese.

"In radio range," answered Nate, as he grabbed the radio off the dash. He tried to raise Bassett to no avail. The range on the small handheld radio varied on line-of-sight, but typically, they were only good for a couple of miles at best.

Reese reached into her backpack and took out a Colt .357 Python. The nickel-plated four-inch barrel was compact and easy to carry as a spare. Badger had loaned her the revolver to use while driving alone because it would never jam.

She checked the cylinder before shoving it between her legs and then pulled a map out throwing it to Nate. "We're on Old Hwy 12 and just passed Francisco Road."

Nate unfolded the map and quickly found their location. "We're about four miles from the interstate."

Nate then put his Colt M4 on his lap and racked the lever back. Ever since the hospital attack, he never went anywhere without his weapon. It had been a painful yet valuable lesson, one he'd never forget.

The red needle on the speedometer topped ninety as Reese kept the pedal to the floor. The old Chevy's engine screamed as they flew down the road. Nate took another look at the map and told her to slow down and take the next right. She eased up on the gas pedal, and the engine quieted down as the truck began to coast. She saw the turn and braked before taking the turn onto Braeburn Circle. She stopped at the entrance of what was a small neighborhood with only four houses.

Nate keyed up the radio. "Bassett come in."

After a couple of more tries, Bassett responded.

"Who is this?"

"It's Nate and Reese out for a drive."

Bassett gave a quick heads up on their situation.

"Copy that. We'll go for help."

Reese began backing up the truck when two cars were approaching from the left. They were full of Jijis. The hair on the back of her neck bristled with a combination of excitement and fear. Her job had just gone from easy to complicated and dangerous.

She grabbed the Python and pulled the hammer back. She fired two shots hitting the windshield with one round striking the passenger.

"Hang on," she yelled, as she shoved the gearshift into drive. She rocketed through the small neighborhood but ran out of road. She swung the truck onto a grassy field hitting the turn so hard, it threw Nate into the door.

Both cars fell in behind them in hot pursuit.

Reese let out a breath of relief seeing an open field. It was almost guaranteed you could get anywhere you needed to go, but as she passed by a small pond, it reminded her to not get cocky.

"Swing to the left and then make a wide right turn," said Nate, as he lifted the M4 to the window. "I want to take some pop shots at these guys."

Reese gave him a lopsided smile knowing what he wanted her to do. The field was big enough to draw these two in, and she knew just what to do to get these guys to follow her. She slowed down before swinging to the right. The second car started to turn away to try and cut her off. She gunned the engine, and the truck went into a full controlled spin. Had the situation not been so serious, she'd be laughing in hysterics as the tires kicked dirt and grass high in the air.

The second car came into Nate's sight. He had to brace himself with his leg against the floorboard while holding onto the M4 with his one good hand. He lined up a shot and pulled the trigger. Rounds penetrated the windshield before the driver swerved to the left to protect himself leaving his passengers exposed. Nate took advantage and fired directly into the passenger side. Multiple rounds hit the windows killing both passengers as blood splattered throughout the interior.

The first car broke off the chase while Reese continued spinning the truck around. Nate emptied the magazine but this time on the driver's side.

"They're done," yelled Nate.

Reese let go of the steering wheel, and the truck jerked the other way before she grabbed the steering wheel again. Just up ahead was a road and she tore off towards it.

"Take it easy hitting the asphalt," warned Nate.

Reese nodded and slowed down before making a right onto Sylvan Road to head south. The first car followed but stayed far back.

"That was friggin awesome," screamed Reese. "Hell, those poor bastards didn't stand a chance."

"Nice driving kiddo," said Nate.

"Nice shooting."

Reese's heart raced as she took in a couple of hurried breaths. She white-knuckled the steering wheel as she the punched the accelerator. She had no idea where this road would take her and ordered Nate to find them on the map.

He reached for it and found what he was looking for. "Take a right on Heim Road."

"Where is it?"

"Coming up."

Sweat beaded on her forehead when she saw cars sitting up the road blocking their turn onto Heim Road. Now she understood why the car behind her didn't bother following too close. They were boxing them in.

CHAPTER 17

WINNIPEG

Winters had arrived with the injured Findley along with her family early in the morning. After arriving he had taken Laney and Collette to the big cafeteria to get something to eat where Sadie came charging in.

It had been a joyous reunion, and Sadie had taken it upon herself to give the two girls the grand tour. This had given Winters the chance to get some sleep before his meeting with General Standish later in the afternoon.

Winters had just finished debriefing General Standish and Colonel Brocket on the Shadow Patriots activities, and as always, the two military men were impressed with what they heard. They admired the Shadow Patriots enough to continue supporting them with supplies.

Brocket then informed Winters of some Americans who wanted to volunteer. They had been waiting for the last week in hopes of finding out where they could go. It was excellent timing because he needed drivers to bring supplies back to Jackson. He had considered asking the girls but didn't want to put their lives at further risk. They had done enough last night, and there was no sense in pushing his luck.

Brocket led Winters to the sleeping quarters where the men had been staying. He explained to him they were from Minnesota and knew Bill Taylor.

He gave the door a short knock, and a man who was in his early forties answered the door. Jack Butler stood at five-foot-nine and kept what remained of his hair short almost to the point he could shave it rather than cut it.

"Mister Butler, this is Captain Winters of the Shadow Patriots."

"Captain, my friends and I have been waiting to meet you."

Winters noticed the roughness of his hand as he shook it and figured he had been in construction or something of that nature. Definitely, someone who wasn't afraid to get his hands dirty, which was the sort of person he liked having around. The harder the man, the better fighter he typically was, at least it was with what he had observed over the last few months.

"I understand you want to join us," said Winters.

"We do. Me and my two buddies that is, you know. We, all ah, grew up and went to school together and been itching to do something."

"How did you know to come to Winnipeg?"

"Well, you know, we're from Minneapolis, and I know Bill Taylor, so, you know, I heard through the grapevine that, ah, you know, that this was the place to come."

"You know, Bill?"

Butler nodded.

"Well, any friend of Bill's is a friend of mine. Glad to have you aboard."

"When will we be heading out and where?"

"Tomorrow night and we'll be heading to Michigan. You guys can help me drive some trucks there."

"With supplies and such."

"Yeah, food, medicine, some weapons."

"That sounds great."

"Are your friends around?"

"Oh, they're off somewhere, I'm not too sure. I can go find 'em if you want."

"No, that's alright, I'll catch up with them later."

"It's ah, a real honor to meetcha."

Winters shook his hand and was pleased to see he had three new guys who were in their early forties, which was a good thing because they typically had a lot more energy than a lot of his guys. The younger guys they had on their team, the better.

Winters headed to the infirmary to visit with Finley. He hadn't had the chance to see her yet and wanted to find out what she and her mother's plans were. Did they want to stay in Canada or head back home? He also needed to get with Laney and Collette to find out the same thing.

Winters found Finley's room and gave a gentle knock as he pushed the door open.

"I was wondering when you were going to come visit me," said Finley.

"Just saving the best for last is all," smiled Winters as he bent down to give her a light hug. "How ya doing?"

"Still hurts some, but, like, my fever and headache are gone."

"Glad to hear it."

"Thanks for bringing me here."

"Please. You deserve it after what you did. I couldn't have done it without you guys."

Finley's face lit up hearing the compliment.

"I'm sorry for not thinking they'd be waiting for you at your place."

"It's alright. They would have, like, taken my mom and sister anyway, so I'm glad I was there with them."

"Well, it all worked out, and now you'll have a couple of badass scars to remember it all with."

"Right. Now I'm gonna have some street-cred."

Winters sat on the edge of the bed.

"I met Sadie."

Winters smiled.

"She is just the sweetest. I absolutely love her. She came right in, and like, took my sister under her wing and cheered her up."

"She's very good at that."

"She told me you and her, and another girl were, like, taken hostage, and she was supposed to marry some prince."

Winters nodded his head.

"And that you were rescued, but then you had to, like, fight your way out."

"That pretty much sums it up."

"Wow! It sounds like a good plotline for a book."

"It does, doesn't it!" said Winters with a curious look.

Tears started to run down her face. "I'm so glad you came home."

"What's wrong?" asked Winters, as he grabbed her hand.

"Laney told me why you, like, came back home. I'm so sorry, Cole."

More tears streamed down her face, and Cole gave her a comforting hug telling her it was okay.

"But if it hadn't been for your daughter, then we'd be, like, still having to…" cried Finley not wanting to finish her sentence.

The whole ordeal was finally hitting her and the realization that her good fortune came at the cost of another's. It was a hard truth. How do you celebrate with something like that in mind? The only thing you can do is not forget the sacrifice someone else made.

Winters began to wish he hadn't told anyone because it would be easier for the girls to be grateful for their rescue. They had already paid a big enough price as it was. They would have to accept what they did for food and be okay with it. This wouldn't be an easy thing to do, and it would be something they'd think about it for the rest of their lives. Now they had an additional string attached to it. Perhaps down the road, it would give it more meaning in a spiritual sense.

Winters continued to hug her for a few more moments. "Hey, hey, don't think that way, okay. It was an honor to help you girls, and it gives Cara's death meaning to me. It helps me deal with my sorrow."

"But."

Winters leaned away. "No. No, buts."

Finley nodded and used her hands to wipe away her tears. "Okay, but still, it just sucks for you."

"Hey, everything happens for a reason, alright?"

"I guess."

Winters wanted to change the subject and asked if she knew if her mother wanted to stay in Canada.

"I think so. She was, like, hoping to talk to someone about that."

"I'll mention it to the right people. Where is everybody?"

"Oh, they went to get something to eat so I could get some sleep."

"Then I'll leave you to it. I'll come back by in the morning."

Winters gave her another hug and then headed to the smaller cafeteria. He found Finley's mom and sister sitting with Laney, Collette and Sadie. Everyone turned their heads when he walked in.

"Cole," said Sadie scooting over to make room for him.

Winters sat down between Sadie and Laney, greeted everyone, and told them he just came from seeing Finley.

"She's on the mend thanks to you," said Finley's mom, Debbie.

"Just glad we had somewhere to take her."

"Sadie has been regaling us with some of your adventures," said Debbie.

Winters turned to Sadie. "Has she now?"

"Of course I have," said Sadie, "how can I not brag about you? You've saved so many lives, like, Amber and Reese."

"Reese?" asked Laney. "Your girlfriend, Reese?"

Sadie's mouth dropped open and turned back to Winters. "Reese is your girlfriend?"

Winters nodded unsure how she'd feel about that.

Sadie grabbed his arm. "Oh. My. Gosh. That is so sweet. My big sister deserves someone nice like you."

Winters let out a sigh of relief.

"I'm going to have to write her a letter."

"That's a lot of cards you need to get done. You'd better hurry."

"Why? When are you leaving?"

"Tomorrow night. It's one of the things I wanted to discuss with you guys," said Winters as he turned to Debbie.

"Can we stay here?" she asked.

"Absolutely. If that's what you want. I can get with General Standish, and he'll have someone work out the details with you."

Debbie turned to her daughter Kayley. "You think you'd like to stay here for awhile?"

Kayley was about the same age as Sadie and nodded her head excessively. "Yes. Yes. As long as Sadie is here."

"Heck yeah, I'll be here. Ahh, I'm so excited I've got a new friend."

"Tired of all the grownups, eh?" asked Winters in humorous tone.

"No. It's just that I need a girlfriend."

Winters turned to Collette. "What about your mom?"

"She wants to stay here too," grumbled Collette.

"What's wrong?"

"I can't stay here with her. I'd rather go back home than stay here."

Winters nodded having witnessed the friction between them. She had been looking forward to going to college and getting away. Winters turned to Laney assuming she wanted to get back home to her mom and sister but asked anyway.

"Yes. Of course."

"Alright then, we'll be leaving tomorrow night. I have some new volunteers who will help drive the trucks back to Jackson. We can drop you guys off on the way."

"Cool," said Collette.

"Tomorrow if you guys want, I can have some instructors give you a crash course in weapons training. This way in case you need to defend yourselves again, you'll be ready."

"Oh yes, I love it," said a wide-eyed Laney. "Will you give us some guns to keep?"

"Remember what I said? We go everywhere armed."

Both Laney and Collette shook their closed fits in front of them.

Winters liked the idea of arming these girls in case there was any more trouble back home. No need to have all his work go to waste by having a power vacuum filled with more criminals.

Satisfied with the plans, Winters excused himself and headed to back General Standish's office to use his phone. He needed to contact Major Green tonight and give him an update.

CHAPTER 18

CHELSEA MICHIGAN

After taking out one of the cars that were pursuing them, Reese swung the car out of a field and onto Sylvan Road. There was still a car behind her, and she was headed toward a roadblock. The Jijis were about to box her in, and she had few options.

One of the things Reese learned over the past few months was never panic. There was always a few seconds to figure out what to do and when there's adrenaline pumping through you, a few seconds was all you needed.

She let off the gas while looking in the mirror to see their tail was about hundred feet back. Small hills bordered both sides of the road so swinging back into a field wasn't an option. They could try and ram the blockade while shooting their way through, but she had no idea how many cars would be there. Coming up on the left was a house with a dirt road in front of it. Taking a left was appealing, but they were too close to Manchester Road, which was the Jiji border. She was running out of options when suddenly the hill to her right leveled out. It was what she was hoping for, another option.

"Hang on," she said as she swerved to the right through a small opening of trees, which broke out onto another field.

The engine raced as the front-end rose up off the ground before diving back down. The pickup bounced violently rocking them on the bench seat. Reese fought to control the steering wheel and was able to wrestle the truck to avoid hitting an evergreen tree. They crossed through over-grown lawns and two driveways before reaching Heim Road. She took a quick look to her left and was surprised to see at least six cars at the intersection.

"You see 'em all?" asked Reese.

"Looks like they got a party going on," grunted Nate.

"You all right?" asked Reese noticing Nate's painful expression.

"Yeah, I'm good. Again, nice driving."

Reese broke out a smile at the compliment. She always ate up accolades from Nate because he so rarely gave them. He wasn't an emotional guy and had little patience for stupidity.

Nate took another look at the map and told her to take a right when the road ended. The last Jiji broke off the chase the closer they got back to Jackson. Nate kept calling on the radio and wasn't able to reach anyone. He threw it up on the dash having grown frustrated with its limited range.

It took fifteen minutes before Reese pulled into the emergency room entrance.

She opened the door and looked in the back surprised her crutch was still there. She reached for it and rushed inside with Nate. It took a few minutes before they found Scar down in the cafeteria with Taylor and Amber.

"Are they together?" asked Scar after getting their report.

"No. Nordell and Burns are on the south end," answered Nate pointing on the map. "We came out here on Sylvan Road. They had a blockade of five or six cars down here."

"Cops?" asked Taylor. "Any cops?"

"Can't say for sure," said Nate.

"They might not be invited to the party yet," said Taylor.

Scar studied the map and thought about their options, which were few. The north end of the Proving Grounds was the interstate, and the east side was Manchester Road, which was the Jiji border, so neither side was an option. It was either come in from the south or the west, with the latter looking more appealing. It was a much larger area and had more places to enter unnoticed. Scar glanced at his watch, which read five o'clock. They had four more hours of daylight. Using their night-vision advantage would be preferable, but if their friends couldn't hold on, then they'd have no choice but to come in guns blazing.

"Badger, alert all the guard post to be ready for an attack. Get Eddie down here with some of his men. Oh, and get Nordell's friend Hollis with us. We might need a sniper." Scar turned to Reese and Nate with an apologetic look because neither of them would be coming.

Reese recognized the look. "It's okay. I've had my fill of action."

"I'm pretty banged up from her driving anyway," smirked Nate.

"I thought you liked it rough," said Reese with a twinkle in her eye.

Nate scoffed. "Touché."

"Oookay," said Scar, "I'm leaving on that one. Amber you joining us?"

"Wouldn't miss it," she replied.

"Then let's go," said Scar.

Scar didn't have any particular plan in mind and wouldn't until he got a lay of the land. He needed to know where the Jijis were posted and if the cops were involved. More importantly was to get an update from Bassett and Nordell, which meant they needed to get in close enough for the radios. If their positions were secure, then they'd wait until it got dark before attempting any rescue. It was always the best option because they owned the night and it was still their main advantage over the enemy's superior numbers.

CHAPTER 19

Talking with some of the locals about the area by the Proving Grounds, Scar had an idea on where they could set up to get in radio range with Bassett. He sent Eddie and his men to the south to scope out the Jiji force, while he would lead a squad of ten to the west side. He kept another fifty men a couple of miles away with orders to stand ready and the rest of their men back in Jackson to leave at a moments notice.

Scar didn't necessarily want to engage the Jijis if he didn't have too. Mostly because he still wanted to raid their supply lines. If there was a battle, then he might have to put it on hold. Getting supplies was his top priority because without them the town would soon starve.

Taylor stopped the SUV when he came to Hoppe Road. Hollis had given them directions to a trail, which would take them through the fields to keep hidden while they got in radio range. The SUV rocked from side to side as Taylor drove through the tall grass and small bushes that had started to grow in the fields.

Scar grabbed the radio and tried to raise Bassett. It took a few tries before he finally reached them.

"What's your status?"

"So far we've been able to avoid any contact for the last hour."

"What about you Nordell?"

"Same here," responded Nordell over the radio. "We're hanging out in a car that we hijacked."

"Can everyone hang on till it gets dark?"

"Roger that," said Bassett.

"Same here," confirmed Nordell. "Once it gets dark, we'll take the car and head towards Bassett's position."

Scar turned to Taylor with a dubious look before replying to Nordell. "You sure?"

"There's tint on these windows. They'll never recognize us."

Scar considered Nordell's suggestion but told him to hold off until he scoped out Sylvan Road. If they could get across without being seen, then they could bring Bassett and Meeks out while Nordell and Burns just drove out. If anything, they could always create a diversion if needed.

"Let's recon Sylvan Road," said Scar as he turned to Amber in the back. "You up for a hike?"

She nodded, and they exited the SUV. Scar walked to the truck behind him that Hadley was driving and told him to hang back while they did a recon. Scar then took off through the trees with Taylor and Amber behind him. The trip to Sylvan road was a short one, and they were about to break out of the woods behind three houses when Scar noticed movement in one of the windows. He lifted his binoculars and saw men through the windows.

"Got Jijis in that house."

"What the hell are they doing?" asked Taylor.

"I think they're looting the place."

Taylor shook his head.

"They probably haven't been down here before," said Amber.

"Probably not," said Scar.

They moved away to look for another entrance to the road but weren't able to find one that wasn't open ground. So they hustled back to the safety of the woods to wait for the thieves to leave. It took nearly an hour for what looked like ten of them to go through all three houses before heading down road. Each carried a sack full of booty, and all were laughing as they left.

"Glad to see they're enjoying themselves," grunted Taylor.

"C'mon," said Scar as he got up and started across the back lawn. They crept to the side of the house and discovered the Jijis looked to be having a party on the road. They were at least a hundred armed men milling around the streets, but they seemed more interested in chatting with each other than standing guard.

"Them boys aren't paying too much attention," whispered Taylor.

Scar nodded.

"Yeah but there sure are a lot of them," said Amber.

Scar nodded. If these guys were still here when it got dark, then they would not be able to cross the road. He'd have no choice but to create a diversion to draw these men away. While he didn't want to engage them, push come to shove, he wouldn't hesitate.

Scar studied the map and figured the best place for a diversion was on the corner of Sylvan and Lehman Roads. It would draw the enemy down the road giving them access to the Proving Grounds. That would keep the Jijis busy while allowing Scar enough time to get his guys out of there.

CHAPTER 20

WASHINGTON D.C.

Green put the phone back in its cradle after receiving a coded message he had a call coming in tonight from Cole Winters. He was anxious to talk to him and get an update. He would wait to see if he mentioned his daughter Cara before deciding what to say to him about what she tried doing to him.

More importantly, he needed to give him an update on what they were doing here in the district. It couldn't be easy for Winters and his men not knowing if this "war" was ever going to end. They needed some reassurances things were happening in the Capital and that they were not fighting a lost cause.

Grace knocked on the door and to say goodnight. Green hadn't realized it was time to head home and prepare for his meeting tonight in

Manassas. He was excited to tell everyone about his idea for some street art around the district. Dwelling on it during the afternoon, he had become even more convinced this would be a great way to show the people that not everyone was afraid of Perozzi or Reed. No doubt, it would become the talk of the town and piss them off.

Green grabbed his jacket and headed down the garage. He contained his glee smelling the fresh paint while passing through the area where the shootout occurred. He hadn't heard from Reed today, but the car Green drove back was gone.

Green pulled into his driveway later than usual because of a traffic jam. He walked inside just as the phone rang.

He picked it up just as his mother was reaching for it. "Hello."

"Major?"

"Yes, it is."

"It's Cole. How are you doing?"

Sarah motioned him to put it on speaker so she could listen.

"I'm good, Sir. How about you?"

The question opened their conversation, and it started with them entering Jackson and ending with burying his daughter back home. After hearing about her death, Green decided not to tell him everything she had done while in Washington. There was no sense in it, and it wasn't necessary. Regardless of what she had done, he still lost his daughter. The conversation took nearly thirty minutes for each of them to give each other an update on what they had been doing.

Green said goodbye and stared at his mother.

"That poor man," said Sarah.

"I can't imagine going through that."

"And then to come home and find out what's going on there," said Sarah shaking her head in disgust.

"It's almost unbelievable."

Sarah directed her son to the kitchen for dinner. "Tell me what happened with Reed this morning?"

"Like it never happened," said Green.

She gave him a confused look, so Green filled her in on how Reed had the garage cleaned up and painted.

Sarah tilted her head to the side and nodded. "Or that it did happen but was a complete failure."

Green gave that some thought and nodded in agreement.

"What do you suppose he's going to do?"

Green shook his head. "Can't say for sure, but I'm sure he's shoring up his forces."

"What about Perozzi? What can we do to get him more riled up beside him not seeing Stormy again?"

Green told his mom about his idea for some street art aimed at Perozzi around the district.

A small smile grew bigger the more she considered the impact it could have. "He'd start blaming Reed for not getting it under control."

"Exactly."

"All we got to do is find an artist."

"Yeah, easier said than done."

"We should go," said Sarah getting up and clearing the dishes off the table.

The drive there was uneventful, and they arrived just as Sam was getting out his car.

"Sam cannot wait to meet Stormy," said Green as he parked the car.

"I'll bet. If you wait too long, he'll put the moves on her," grinned Sarah.

"Mom."

"I know you like her and I'm sure it's mutual."

"Well, I'm not so sure."

"I'll watch her and let you know."

"Now, you're starting to sound like Sam. He made the same offer."

"Glad to see he's got your back," smiled Sarah.

Green shook his head and stepped out of the car. They greeted Sam before heading inside where the rest of their team anxiously waited for them.

Sam's eyes lit up when he saw Stormy getting up off the couch. "You must be Stormy," he beamed as he approached her with an outstretched hand. "I've heard so much about you."

Stormy shook his hand. "Hello, and you're Sam?"

"I am. I was told how beautiful you were, but the description wasn't nearly enough."

"Well, thank you."

"And I also heard you're a bit of a badass too."

A flush swept across her face. "I don't know about that."

"No need to be modest," said Sam. "What you did was awesome."

Green rolled his eyes and approached them to rescue Stormy from his friend's flirtatious ways.

Sam backed away while grinning at his friend knowing what he was doing. He then observed the way Stormy leaned in and kissed Green on the cheek. To him, this was evidence this girl had the hots for him.

CHAPTER 21

WINNIPEG

Winters sat alone in Standish's office having just got off the phone with Major Green. He was pleasantly surprised to hear how much progress Green had made in taking down Perozzi and Reed. It was comforting to know he wasn't alone in this fight and perhaps there was an end in sight.

Winters couldn't wait to tell the Shadow Patriots what was happening in Washington. The news would help morale knowing others were fighting and its participants were important people who could make a big difference. The people Green had enlisted were an impressive group. Some State Department people, a former Assistant Director of the FBI, even a former Senator. These people will have the right contacts to help put an end to Perozzi's diabolical plan to take over the country.

Winters leaned back in the chair thinking about Green's fake assassination attempt on Lawrence Reed. That was a gutsy move and had surely put the fear of God into him. And sending those recordings to Perozzi and Reed was a stroke of genius. This had to have them freaking out, which would help force them into making mistakes.

Winters had struggled to report about the death of his daughter but could hear it in Green's voice that he knew who she was. He had no doubt his daughter was involved with something nefarious in Washington before coming to Michigan. He didn't press him on it mostly because he didn't want to know. It no longer mattered anyway. She paid for her sins, and that was the end of it.

Speaking of daughters, he needed to visit with Sadie, that is if he could pull her away from her new friend. Now that she had someone her age, he didn't think she'd be so easy to compete with. Which was perfectly fine with him, it couldn't be easy to be around a bunch of grownups all the time.

Winters left Standish's office to find Sadie. After getting no answer at her door, he found her a few doors down in Debbie's room with her daughter Kayley.

"Come on in," said Debbie who answered the door.

"Cole!" said Sadie getting up from the floor to hug him.

"Hey, whatcha guys doing?"

"I'm making my Get Well cards for everyone."

Winters debated on whether or not he should pull her away. She was having fun with her new friend, but he hadn't had the chance to tell her about Cara yet and didn't want her to hear it from anyone else.

"Is something wrong?" said Sadie.

"No. I just needed to chat with ya."

"Why don't you guys go for a walk," suggested Debbie.

Sadie grabbed Winters' hand. "Okay."

Winters turned to Debbie and mouthed, "Thank you."

They walked into the hallway and headed outside to an area, which had a couple of picnic tables and benches.

"I'm so happy I've got a new friend."

"I can see that."

"But I will still miss you when you leave again," said Sadie as she sat down on the bench.

"I will too," said Winters. He paused for a moment trying to get his thoughts together. He didn't want her to walk away sad and would try and candy coat it as best he could. "How much do you know about what happened to the girls?"

"Kayley told me that every day they had to be with a different boy.

That if they wanted food, then they had to do it with them."

Winters looked at her unsure if she knew exactly what that was.

Sadie tilted her head. "I know about sex. I know what Reese had to go through and remember, I was almost married off to Mordulfah."

Winters let out a sigh. "You know Sadie, sometimes I forget how old you really are. You're still a little girl, but you've been forced to grow up."

"I'm almost twelve."

"Yeah, twelve going on thirty."

"But, I still like to sleep with a stuffed animal."

"Good. I'm glad to hear that. Listen, I need to tell you the reason why I was able to help the girls. Why I was back home."

Winters inhaled a deep breath in an attempt not to sound too emotional when he told her. That effort didn't go so well earlier when he told Standish and Brocket. He chocked on the words and could feel the same lump forming in his throat again.

"Are you alright, Cole?" asked Sadie who took ahold of his hand.

Winters bit his lip.

She scooted closer to him.

"Honey, I was back home to bury my daughter, Cara." Winters blurted the words out as fast as he could and then fought back the tears.

Sadie looked confused for a second. "Wait, you found her?"

Winters nodded.

"And she died?" asked Sadie as tears started running down her cheeks. "Cole, I'm so sorry."

"It's okay, really."

"But how? What happened?"

Winters told her a sanitized version of events but left in the important parts, especially since it concerned Mordulfah, the man who tried to marry her.

Sadie wiped her tears and looked up at Winters. "So, it was like she led you back home, so you could help all those poor girls."

Winters patted her shoulders. "It's exactly why I'm okay with it, really. And I don't want you to be sad about it. Okay? Everything happens for a reason."

Sadie nodded. "I know. It's kinda like why I have you in my life. You know because my mom and dad are dead, so, like, now you're my new daddy."

Winters' heart began to melt hearing those words. Although he knew it to be true, hearing her say the words meant so much more. He leaned in and squeezed her hard.

"I couldn't be prouder to be your daddy."

"And I love that you're my daddy."

They embraced for a few more moments then Sadie backed away. "I'm glad you told me the truth."

"With everything you've been through, you deserve the truth."

"Will this ever end?"

Winters nodded. "At some point, it will. It can't go on forever."

"When it's over, we can all go back to your hometown to live. I'll have my new friends there. You can marry Reese, and she can be, like, my new mom."

"That sounds like a great plan," praised Winters.

Winters escorted Sadie back to her friend with a lightness in his step. The smile he wore didn't wear off as he laid down on his bed. She had once again helped to fill a void he didn't think would be possible to fill a few days ago. It had been devastating to lose his daughter but life goes on, and he had other people counting on him. He needed to get back to his men and get back to work. The people in Jackson were counting on him, and he would deliver the needed supplies to them.

CHAPTER 22

CHESLEA MICHIGAN

Nightfall finally came, and Scar was ready to rescue Bassett and Meeks. He packed two extra pairs of night-vision goggles and plenty of spare magazines. Scar led the way as they hiked back to Sylvan Road. Like before, Taylor and Amber were accompanying him. He liked having Amber there because of her youth, which gave her better hearing than him or Taylor.

They reached the road and hid behind bushes to get ready to race across. There were still about a fifty Jijis scattered up and down the street in a few groups. It was doable without the need for a diversion from Eddie's team, so he called him and told him to hold off.

The Jijis were enjoying their time away from guarding the interstate for the past week. A few Jijis were walking by their position chatting loud enough that Scar could understand what they were saying.

After they walked by Scar looked both ways and saw the coast was clear. Without having to give an order, Amber and Taylor fell in behind Scar as he flew across the road and jumped over the chain-linked fence that bordered the Proving Grounds.

Safely hidden in the woods, they began moving toward the first of two roads they needed to cross. Scar slowed the pace when he spotted headlights through the trees as they approached the first road. It was cluttered with large groups of Jijis standing around.

Amber tapped Scar on the shoulder and pointed north.

Scar nodded.

She then took point, followed by Scar and Taylor bringing up the rear. The three of them darted their heads around looking for anything out of place. There was just enough light from the moon for the goggles to enhance their view as they stalked through the woods. After about five hundred feet, Amber started stopping every few yards. She turned her head to listen before taking a few more steps, then froze. Someone was closeby.

She moved her head to the right to peek around a tree and finally saw what she had been hearing. Up ahead were two Jijis talking in low tones. She turned to Scar and pointed at them.

Scar let out a shallow breath when he saw them. He still couldn't hear them but was glad Amber was leading them. Any noise they made would have alerted them. They still wouldn't be able to see them in the dark, but if there was enough noise, then they might have started firing their guns blindly.

Nobody moved for a couple of minutes as they waited to see if they would leave. Taylor gritted his teeth as he was losing his patience. He pulled his knife out before handing his rifle to Amber. She took it and threw the sling over her head while Scar withdrew his knife as well. They weren't nearly as fast as Bassett and would have to take these two down at the same time.

They padded toward them like a cheetah stalking its prey. Slow and silent. Scar could hear them talking now, but their chatter wouldn't be loud enough to hide the snapping of a twig.

"Just a couple more feet," thought Scar as he angled the blade of his knife. As if they done it a thousand times before, Scar and Taylor pounced in unison. They grabbed them around their heads covering their mouths and stabbing in their throats. They let go of the bodies and then acknowledged each other. Amber came in and handed Taylor his rifle before they continued north.

They traveled a thousand feet north along the road to find it wasn't as congested up this way. A few cars had headlights on, which forced them to move a little further north to avoid them. It was a hundred and fifty feet across the open road, and it would take the slower Taylor at least seven seconds.

Amber whispered to Scar that she would guard their six. He tapped Taylor's shoulder and told him to go when he was ready. They were between two groups, and it took a few minutes before Taylor got up and bolted across the road. Amber followed Scar as they made it to the safety of the trees.

Taylor was breathing rapidly and grabbed Amber's jacket to stop her.

"Give an old man a second," he whispered.

"You did alright," she replied.

"Yeah, right."

"Badger, I'm serious."

Scar took advantage of the break and called out to Bassett telling them they were across the first road.

"Copy. We'll look for your signal."

Scar gave Taylor another minute before he motioned them to continue. Once again, Amber led the way, and she expertly led them around another group of Jijis who were using flashlights to aid in their search.

The road Bassett and Meeks were waiting by was five hundred yards away, and it took nearly thirty minutes to get to it. They finally made it to the next road, and they could see why Bassett decided to stay put. Jijis roamed around, and a couple of cars were racing up and down the road.

"You'd think they were celebrating something," snorted Taylor.

"They don't get out much," said Amber.

Scar keyed the radio. "Bassett we're here. We're just north of the two dragsters."

"Roger that. Not too far south."

"You want me to get them?" suggested Amber.

Scar thought it was a good idea and gave her the okay. He handed her the bag with extra ammo and the night-vision goggles.

Amber kept looking both ways while waiting for the right moment.

She was excited to operate on her own. A couple of Jijis peeled away from a larger group and were approaching their position. As she waited for them to pass by, she judged the distance across figuring it was about the same as running to first base. She'd been a speedster back in college when she played softball. She could run to first base in two and a half seconds, but she wasn't as fast as she used to be.

The two Jijis strolled by carrying weapons on their backs. A bearded one was laughing at something his friend said. He then split off from his friend to head to another group on the other side of the road.

Scar turned back the other way just to make sure that side was clear before giving her the all clear. He tapped her on the arm and whispered to go. She got up and started pushing her arms back and forth and pumping her legs as fast as she could. She reached other side of the road in full stride but couldn't slow down when she saw the bearded Jiji in her way.

CHAPTER 23

MANASSAS VIRGINIA

Having just rescued Stormy from the clutches of his friend's flirtatious ways, Green sat down next to her on the couch. He then began to give everyone an update on what happened with Reed.

"That sly old fox," said Gibbs. "He's playing the long game for sure."

"But he believed the assassination attempt?" asked Kyle, the younger Gibbs.

Green nodded. "Yeah, I mean it was convincing. You guys did it perfectly. I almost believed it myself after it was all done with. The placement of the bodies was spot on, and you had the right amount of shots fired."

"I'll tell ya, it was touch and go for a few seconds. His bodyguards were better than I thought they would be," said Kyle.

"Oh?"

"Yeah, I mean, as soon as we started shooting, they yanked Reed back behind that car. We hit them both, too, didn't we, Dad."

"They were both wounded but kept fighting," said Gibbs. "But as soon as they tried to return fire, you could tell they were just off their game."

"Good," said Green, "Probably sold Reed on it even more."

"So, what's next?" asked Stormy.

Green turned to her and said, "Before we discuss that, I need to tell you about a phone call I received from Cole Winters."

"He called?" asked Gibbs. "He's not in Jackson?"

"No, he's not, and he has a good reason for it."

All eyes were on Green as he told them about the death of Cara Winters. He didn't find it easy telling them even though she had tried to expose him to Reed. It was still a horrible thing regardless of her actions.

"My goodness! Such a terrible thing," said Senator Seeley. "I can't even begin to imagine losing my own daughter this way."

"I was listening to the conversation," said Sarah Green. "You can tell the man is in pain."

"But then he goes and saves his hometown from a bunch of rapists?" asked Stormy.

Green nodded.

"This guy sounds like the real badass," said Stormy turning to Sam.

"Well, you'd never know it by looking at him," said Green.

"Oh?"

"Yeah, he's very unassuming and doesn't look like much of a warrior. Which probably works in his favor because you underestimate him, at least I did."

"How so?"

"Before we were on the same side, I was tasked to capture him and let's just say he put one over on me."

Stormy gave him a surprised expression. "Really?"

"Yes. I'm not embarrassed to admit it, but he was able to capture us after we stormed their camp and took his men as prisoners. And he did it with just seven men. It was actually a brilliant plan and well executed."

"How many of you were there?" asked Stormy.

"I guess there was about thirty of us," said Green hoping he wasn't disappointing the girl he liked.

"Did he kill any of your guys?"

"No. He did it without firing a shot. It turns out he's a skilled strategist. It's how he's been able to do so much with so few men."

"I get that," said Kyle. "Kinda like us, right now."

"He also saved us from an ambush my former commander set me up for in Detroit Lakes, Minnesota."

"What?" asked Stormy.

"Colonel Nunn, my former CO was working for Reed and didn't like that I was questioning him on what we were doing, so he set my men up."

Stormy's eyes grew wide.

"Had the Shadow Patriots not happened upon us, then I would not even be here."

"What happened to this Colonel Nunn?"

Green hesitated as he searched for an answer. He hadn't told anyone this but his mother. His men never ask him about it even though they knew he had done it. They were just happy they were no longer part of it. He looked around the room as everyone waited for an answer. A month ago, he wouldn't have brought up the subject but seeing how they just murdered two of Perozzi's men, the people in this room deserved the truth.

He turned to Stormy. "I tried to arrest him but he resisted, and we came to fisticuffs, which resulted in me killing him in his office.

Stormy placed a hand on Green's arm.

"Our family friend, David Crick," interrupted Sarah Green, "was killed in that ambush. He was John's Lieutenant and grew up with him. Nunn got what he deserved."

Green turned to his mother and gave her a firm nod. She was just as devastated at the news of Crick's death as she was practically his second mom.

There was a palatable silence in the room, and Sam spoke up. "John, why don't you tell them about that idea you had today."

Green glanced over at Sam thankful he had changed the subject. "So, I had this idea that I think will help drive Perozzi nuts or at the very least show him, he can't control everything. It's just something we can do until we can make another big move."

"What?" asked Stormy as she placed her hand on his arm.

"Street art. Graffiti or whatever you want to call it. You know, political cartoons pasted on buildings targeting Perozzi and Reed."

"Oh, that is good," said Gibbs. "That's a big no-no in the district, and it would get people talking."

"Yeah, kinda what I was thinking."

"I love it," said Stormy. "Street art in New York is fantastic, and some of it really makes a statement."

"Only problem is finding someone to do it?" asked Kyle.

"I know someone," said Stormy.

"In New York?" asked Kyle.

"No, at work. One of the busboys is an artist and quite good. He was showing me some of his work, and he could easily do this."

"Will he do it though?" asked Sam.

"I'm sure he will if I asked him. Maybe give him some money."

"Can we trust him?" asked Green.

Stormy let out a scoff. "Oh yeah. He hates the government and everything about it."

"That works in our favor," said Green. "But we'll have to tell him that if he does this, he can't tell anyone because I can assure you Reed will have the cops all over this. They'll interrogate every artist in town for any morsel of information."

"Or maybe just make it about Perozzi," said Sam. "If you just make it about him, Reed won't be so motivated to find out who it is."

"I like your thinking," said Gibbs. "He'll secretly enjoy it."

"Exactly."

"Sounds good to me," said Green.

"I'll call him when I get home?"

"You have his number?" asked Green.

Stormy shrugged her shoulders. "Yeah, a lot of guys give me their number."

Green let out a silent sigh. Of course, tons of guys give her their number. It's almost comical to think these guys actually think she'll call them like she is desperate for a date. She almost seemed embarrassed by it, but she can't help how others act around her, and it doesn't seem like she encourages it by any means.

"Well, in this case, it works in our favor," said Green.

"Okay, then it's settled. I'll call ya and let you know."

"If he's up for it, let's see about meeting him tomorrow night," said Green as he gave Stormy his business card with his home phone on the back. He laughed to himself thinking here he was, another guy giving her his number.

CHAPTER 24

CHELSEA MICHIGAN

Skulking through the proving grounds to extract Bassett and Meeks, Amber ran across the last road to where they were. She was the fastest and could cross the road without being seen by the numerous Jijis that were patrolling the area.

She tore across the road in a full sprint and wasn't able to stop before crashing right into a Jiji. She tumbled over him before landing on her back. The impact ripped the goggles off her head, and she lay there unable to think. Her head pounded like a gavel, and she tried to rub the stars out of her vision. A warm liquid adhered to her fingers as blood oozed from her forehead. She tried to get up, but before she knew it, he was on top of her pressing a blade against her throat.

He leaned down to her ear and whispered, "Scream, and you're dead."

Amber was disoriented but felt the blade biting into her skin and nodded instinctively.

The bearded man had one thing on his mind, and that was to have Amber all to himself. His free hand moved to her breast, and he started to fondle them while keeping the knife to her throat.

The man's touch repulsed Amber, causing adrenaline to explode through her, which brought back her senses. She had to do something, if she didn't, it would be all over.

She moved her arms around the ground to feel for her weapon but found nothing.

"C'mon Amber, remain calm and keep your wits." She inhaled a deep breath to calm down. She didn't dare yell out, not because he told her not to, but if she did, then there would be a lot more Jijis to deal with.

She still had options, and her next move was to get the knife in her right boot. Thankfully, she took up the habit after witnessing how it saved Reese on several different occasions. She just had to remain calm and give this guy false hope.

She couldn't bend her knees or even move her legs with him on top of her. She stretched her hand as far down as she could but wasn't even close enough. She needed a better position.

His hand moved down to the button on her jeans to undo them. His breathing increased with excitement as he pulled down the zipper but then became aggravated when he couldn't pull her pants down.

Amber formed a slight smirk because her jeans were so tight fitting that she struggled to get them off.

"Take your pants off," he ordered.

She pretended to push them down a little bit. "I can't if you're on top of me. Scoot down some."

The bearded man let out a frustrated scoff as he shuffled backward while keeping the knife pressed on her exposed belly button.

Amber still couldn't bend her knees. She just needed to get him a little further back so she could grab her knife.

She could sense his growing irritation and didn't want him to change strategies. The excitement and nervousness were clouding his judgment. If he were smart, he would smack her around and use that knife to tear the pants off her.

She needed to give in a little and give him false hope. She slid the jeans off her waist and was thankful she wore white underwear. The contrasting color in the dark blazed like a beacon in the night. The bearded man's face lit up in anticipation of a pleasurable conquest.

"Lift up some so I can bend my knees."

Staring at her white underwear seemed to put the man in a trance, and he did as she asked without thinking. The bearded man lifted up from her legs giving her the room she needed.

She lifted her butt off the ground and pushed her pants down past her thighs. His breathing now came in short rapid breaths as she sat up to just inches from his face. The stench of his breath was overwhelming and forced a gag reflex. It was all she could do not to turn away, but she needed to keep him distracted while she reached down into her boot.

Gripping the knife handle brought much-needed comfort. The coolness of the metal hilt never felt so good as she pulled the blackened steel blade out.

The bearded man leaned in and tried to kiss her. His bristled beard scratched her cheeks as she turned away while thrusting the blade into the back of his neck with all her strength.

The razor-sharp tip of the blade burrowed deep through muscle tissue and bone with a crunching sound. Blood splattered out and ran down the knife.

He let out a short gasp and coughed blood on her purple cami top. The whites of his eyes glowed in the dark, as they turned glassy while staring dumbfounded at her. He then fell forward resting his head on her shoulder.

Disgusted, Amber pushed the dead corpse to the side.

She lay down to pull her jeans back on and to recompose herself. She took a couple of deep breaths before holding a third one for a moment. Killing this guy reminded her when she wrestled with her first kill. A cop had come out of the bathroom surprising both of them. It was up close and personal like this one was and had the same desperate feeling. Kill or be killed.

A car burning rubber interrupted her thoughts, and she sprang back up. She struggled to see in the dark and had to get on her hands and knees to find the goggles. It took what seemed like an eternity, but she finally brushed up against them. She threw them back on and found the bag and her weapon. She then continued through the woods and found Bassett and Meeks.

"Hey," whispered Meeks.

Amber didn't say anything and wrapped her arms around him.

"You alright? You're shaking. What took so long?"

"Yeah, sorry. I'm alright. Had to take care of something first," said Amber not really wanting his pity. She just needed a comforting hug to help calm down. She was still high from the adrenaline rush but began breathing in short gasps.

Bassett reached into her bag and found the night vision goggles. He threw them on and looked at Amber. "You're bleeding!"

"Am I?"

Bassett pulled out a bandage from his pack. He blotted the blood from her forehead before putting the bandage on. "Let's give her a minute."

"No. Really, I'm alright."

"Drink this," said Meeks as he handed her a canteen.

Amber gulped down the rest of the canteen. The cool water helped clear her mind, which made her realize she was not operating at full capacity.

They gave her a few minutes before heading back towards Scar. Bassett led the way, and they soon came upon the dead bearded man lying face down. Bassett bent down and pulled the knife out from his neck. He cleaned the blade off and handed it to Amber.

"Lose this?" asked Bassett.

Amber took the knife and put it back in her boot.

"He gave you that?" asked Meeks pointing to her forehead.

"Yeah, I kinda ran into him and then he tried to rape me."

Meeks shook his head. "Dumbass."

Bassett gave her a firm nod and said, "good job."

Amber returned the nod and was glad they didn't coddle her but treated her like one of the guys. Granted they still looked after her and Reese, but both had proven themselves enough to earn their respect. Just being out there with them had given them a certain amount, but their performance was what made them one of the guys.

CHAPTER 25

Nordell and Burns decided to stay until they heard from Scar that they'd gotten Bassett and Meeks back to safety. Push come to shove; they could drive up to where he was and assist them if it had been needed. They were still sitting in the car they had hijacked earlier in the day. Since Nordell was familiar with the track having test-driven cars on it over the years, he had known of a good place to hide until it got dark.

They had been going stir-crazy waiting for the sun to set and Nordell cursed himself for not bringing night-vision goggles with him. Never again would he go anywhere without them. Of course, this was supposed to be a quick mission. However, like any operation, something can and does go wrong. Running into an area, the bad guys used as a latrine was a new one for him. Add to the fact the Jijis had been inactive over the past week and bored, so this was some welcome excitement for them.

Had Reese and Nate not stumbled onto them and brought help, Nordell had thought about driving their new ride during the daylight. It had tinted windows and would have given them decent cover, but nighttime was the better move. He fantasized about driving over some of the Jijis and shooting them in a drive-by fashion. They would have no idea the approaching car was the enemy. He let out a chuckle thinking about it.

Burns turned to him. "Care to share?"

"Oh, just thinking about killing some of these guys is all. You know, do a little gangster drive-by. Maybe run over a couple of them."

Burns let out his laugh. "I'd be up for that."

"Would you now?"

"Gunny, we've been sitting in this hot car all damn day. I could use a little reward."

Nordell slapped the steering wheel. "That's what I wanted to hear."

Both needed to vent and shooting the enemy would loosen that valve.

Back in Vietnam, Nordell liked to go out on patrol and engage with the Vietcong. He liked it so much he volunteered for a second tour. He'd learn a lot about himself and was surprised at how good of a fighter he was. He'd even earned a bronze star on his second tour.

He continued musing about his career in the Marines and how difficult it was to transition back to civilian life. He'd taken up woodworking to help pass the time and give him something to do. His wife insisted he start doing something physical to keep him out of her hair. He never thought he'd have another chance to fight for his country. But, here he was fighting for his fellow countryman, which still seemed surreal. It was almost unbelievable to be fighting his fellow Americans in order to defend innocent Americans. They were in a bloody civil war very few people even knew existed.

Thinking about it always made his blood boil. Damn bastards were setting this whole thing up so they could over the country. What kind of maniacal person would do something like that? And what kind of people were these National cops or the Jijis that would turn on their fellow Americans? Nordell let out a sigh because he knew the answer.

They had been fed a bunch of anti-American propaganda from the time they entered grade school until they graduated college, so it was easy to turn them. Add in a little greed here and there, and you got your answer. Little did they know how much worse it was going to be for them once their task-masters were in charge. They would have to do what they were told to do or suffer the consequences of death.

Nordell almost felt sorry for them to be under such disillusionment. Almost was the keyword. Better to just kill the whole lot of them. They would be a lost generation, but in the bigger picture, it would be worth the price to save their country.

The radio came to life interrupting Nordell's thoughts.

"We are out. I say again, we are out," said Scar. "Gunny, you and Burns head out and we'll cover you."

Nordell started the car up and put the car into drive while Burns racked the slide back on his M4. He took a right knowing the exit was just under a mile. They passed a couple of cars and Nordell tapped the horn at them.

"Look at 'em, just standing around," said Nordell.

"Where do ya want to hit them?" asked Burns.

"I know just the place," said Nordell. "As soon as we get out of here, we'll take a right on Manchester Road. The first road south of the Grounds is Lehman, and they'll have a bunch of people there."

"Cool."

Nordell approached the exit and tooted the horn a couple more times at the Jijis who thought he was one of them. Once on Manchester Road, he picked up some speed and passed by more parked cars. The men just stared at them as he drove by.

"These guys are idiots. If they had any sense, they would have stopped us," said Nordell.

The mile and half drive to Lehman road took a couple of minutes, but finally, their targets were up ahead. Fifteen guys were leaning on cars or standing in small groups on Lehman road.

"You got nothing up ahead," said Burns.

"Perfect. We'll go through, stop the car and get out to take 'em down. We'll take a right on the next road, which is just up ahead."

"You're the boss."

Nordell slowed the car down and passed through the intersection. He again tapped the horn and waved at them through the dark tint. A group of four had to move out of the way to let them through.

"Thank you, boys," grinned Nordell. "You ready?"

"Good to go, Gunny."

Nordell came to a stop and threw the car in park. He grabbed his M4 and switched it to full auto. They would have only a couple of seconds before they realized what was happening and scatter.

Nordell was the first to get out of the car and waited for Burns to get to the back before pulling the trigger. Some of the Jijis turned around to see what was going on as Nordell squeezed off the first shots.

The intersection erupted in strobes of muzzle flashes as Burns and Nordell emptied their magazines. The hail of gunfire took down the group of four who had moved out of their way. Death curling screams were heard between the deafening sounds of rifle fire.

Nordell yanked out an empty mag before slamming in another one. They agreed on just one reload before they hightailed it out of there. He aimed at three Jijis who tried fleeing in the field. Unfortunately, for them, a car headlight pointed in their direction exposing them. He squeezed the trigger and took them down with one sweep of the rifle.

Burns crouched down after reloading and aimed under the cars. He fired and took out two as he flattened the back tires. He got back up and angled around the car to finish them off.

The intersection went quiet but for a few groans of dying men.

"Let's go," ordered Nordell.

Nordell spun the tires and sped down the road to Grass Lake Road. There was no one to stop them or get in their way.

"Boy that felt good," yelled Burns.

"Damn right it did. Damn bastards."

It was just what Nordell needed to work out his frustrations and not have this be a wasted day. Any day his enemy died was a good day for him, and he looked forward to engaging them again.

CHAPTER 26

JACKSON MICHIGAN

Amber struggled to get out of bed because her head was still hurting from running into the bearded Jiji last night. She looked in the mirror and removed the bandage. The blood had clotted, but there was a sizable bruise around it. She needed some painkillers and left to go to Reese's room to get some. She knocked on her door a few times before Reese answered.

"Amber," said Reese as she rubbed her eyes. "What time is it?"

"I don't know. Early I think."

"Come in. Sorry, I fell asleep before you guys came back."

"That's alright. It was late when we got back anyway."

"How did it go?" asked Reese reaching for a water bottle.

"Good. We got 'em out. No one got killed…so a good night."

Reese took a gulp and invited Amber to sit with her on the bed. She then looked at her closely. "You look like hell," she said with a disarming smile. "What happened last night?"

Amber started fidgeting

"You have a cut?" asked Reese motioning to the bandage on her forehead.

Amber nodded and then cleared her throat before blurting out, "I was almost raped last night."

Reese's left highbrow hiked at the news. She grabbed Amber's hand and squeezed it. Her friend had come to the right person to get this off her chest. She would let her tell the story at her own pace.

"We were deep in the Proving Grounds, not too far from Bassett. I offered to go to them because I'm faster than they are. So, I was running across the road like I was stealing home plate but ran headfirst into the catcher. I didn't see him until, like, the last second and bang. I mean I hit him so hard that I flipped over him. I landed on my back, and all I saw were stars. Lots of stars. I didn't know what was what and then he jumped on top of me. Friggin bastard put a knife to my throat and ordered me not to scream."

Reese continued to hold her hand and not interrupt her. She remembered how she liked to get things off her chest with Cole because he never interrupted her. He was a good listener and didn't always offer advice, which was good because she mostly just needed to vent.

"And of course, the first thing he does is start grabbing my boobs."

Reese formed an uneven smile and nodded.

"About turned my stomach, but that's when I started to regain my senses. Then he tried taking my jeans off and thank God they're on the tight-side."

Reese let out a small laugh. "Gotta love tight jeans."

"The idiot actually asked me to take them off."

"Seriously?"

"Yep. And let me tell ya. Once he saw my white undies that's when I knew I had him. He was so excited and distracted that I was able to get the knife out of my boot. And bam! Right into the back of his neck. Bastard coughed blood on my shirt though."

"Gross."

'Oh, it was disgusting."

"Wow though! I mean, just wow, girl," said Reese as she wrapped her arms around Amber and squeezed hard. "You're so awesome. You did good."

"Thanks," said Amber as she let her go.

"Your head still hurts?"

"Yeah, you got anything?"

"Of course, I do," said Reese as she got up and grabbed the 800mg Motrin. "This should do it. Take one and see how it does before you take another." She got her a glass of water and handed her the pills. "You should have Doctor Lunsford take a look at that."

"Yeah, you're probably right," said Amber after she took a pill.

Reese sat back down next to her recognizing she had more to get off her chest. Amber was a tough girl and had gotten tougher over the past few weeks. Reese admired her calm nature and the fact that she was intelligent. She was always coming up with good ideas for the group. However, she didn't have the experience of being repeatedly raped. Not that she wished that upon her or anyone else.

It was too horrific of an experience for anyone, but it toughened Reese up like nothing else could. While she knew she'd never get over it completely, she had come to terms with it. She was starting to recognize the anxiety symptoms, like shortness of breath or suddenly becoming claustrophobic in a room. Violent thoughts like it were normal.

It was why she liked lots of action and not sitting around. It was also, why she liked to burn rubber on crazy drives. The distraction helped her deal with the symptoms or avoid them outright. The look on Amber's face told her she had some of those symptoms.

Amber's eyes began to water and a lump formed in her throat. "I wasn't sure at first, you know."

Reese grabbed her hand again.

"When he had that knife on my throat and told me not to scream. I was so scared, you know, because I thought, well, okay, he's gonna rape me, but if I can just stay alive, maybe Meeks or Bassett will find me."

Reese continued to stay silent as more tears fell down Amber's cheeks. She reached over to grab a tissue and handed it to her.

Amber blew her nose. "But then when he undid my pants that's when I knew I needed to calm down and think. But, that first minute, I just wasn't sure, you know."

Reese nodded.

"And he tried to kiss me…oh, his breath was disgusting."

Reese scrounged her face. "Eeeww."

Amber slumped her shoulders. "I'm sorry. I know, I'm whining about something that doesn't even compare to what you went through."

Reese remembered the advice Scar had given her when she was complaining to him about feeling guilty in regards to Winters' loss and his disappearance. He told her it wasn't a competition and that his loss was his own. It was good advice, and it had helped her.

"Amber, this isn't a contest. What you went through was traumatic. It was real. It was real to you, and that's what matters. Okay?"

Amber nodded. "Thanks. I just don't how you do it."

"None of that matters right now. Okay? This is about you."

Amber threw her arms around Reese. "Thank you. I don't know what I'd do without you. I love you so much."

"I love you too, girl. You're my big sister now, and we need to look out for each other."

Amber held onto her sister, grateful she had her in her life. Her admiration for Reese grew tenfold because of the way she had just taken care of her. She was so unselfish when she had every right not to be. Amber's experience paled in comparison to hers, but it didn't matter to Reese. She put aside her own damaged self in a genuine way to help her deal with a traumatizing experience. It was just what she had needed and after a good crying session began to feel better. The last thing she wanted to do was break down in front of the guys. That would change the way they saw her, and they might start treating her differently. She had worked too hard for their respect to let something like last night change things.

CHAPTER 27

WINNIPEG

Winters opened his eyes and realized he had slept through the night without any bad dreams or racing thoughts. His mind was at ease as he lay there but then the day's agenda started to get in the way of his peaceful moment. He needed to get Laney and Collette set-up with some weapons training before he got with the supply sergeant to figure out a shopping list. Besides food, medicine was a top priority, so he decided to get some advice from a doctor. He also needed to go visit with Murphy who had been wounded in the Sandpit Battle. He was in physical therapy but would still be out of commission for at least another month.

After a quick shower, he headed to the big cafeteria and grabbed a tray. The place was crawling with military personnel coming and going. He waved at a few and shook hands with some others. After piling his tray full of food, he looked around and found the man he came to see. He was in charge of the training department and had been instrumental in putting together a program for the Shadow Patriots.

"Captain, good seeing you again," said Sergeant Hicks. He was a bulky man who specialized in training snipers, who were among the best in the world. He was also one of several who had been giving Sadie some lessons.

"Sergeant, just the man I wanted to see," said Winters shaking his hand before sitting down.

"Let me guess? Those two girls you came in with?"

Winters took a sip of coffee before answering. "Yes, sir. They're in need of some training. Think you can you fit them in today?"

Hicks nodded his head. "We can do that. What's their story?"

The sergeant shook his head in disappointment hearing about what happened to them. Winters also gave him an update on what was going on in Jackson. Hicks took an interest because he had trained most of the men fighting in the Shadow Patriots.

Hicks scratched his chin and said, "Captain, it seems every time I see you, you tell me something even worse than before. I keep thinking, that's the worst, but nope, it's not. And the thing with those girls, I don't know why that shocks me especially since I know about the party house you broke up. How is Reese doing by the way?"

Winters let out a small chuckle and put his cup down. "Oh, she's good. Although she took a couple of bullets."

"Whoa. Has she now?"

"Oh Yeah. But boy, you should have seen her. She stayed in the fight."

"That girl's got something to prove."

"Well, it's more complicated than that. Let's just say she's got her demons," said Winters not wanting to go into detail.

Hicks didn't push the subject and took a bite of his toast. "So, when are these two girls going home?"

"Tonight. I'm dropping them off back in Iowa before heading back to Jackson."

"Do I have them for the whole day?"

"Absolutely."

"Bring 'em on by then. We'll get 'em fixed up."

Winters thanked him and then left the cafeteria to make sure the girls were up and ready to go. A full day with Sergeant Hicks and his team would be enough to prepare them to defend themselves. He would not only show them how to properly handle weapons, but he'd put them through the Urban Warfare Course as well. This would be valuable for them since they lived in small town.

It was seven am when he knocked on their door. He wasn't holding out too much hope they would be awake but was pleasantly surprised when Laney answered the door ready to go.

"Morning, Cole," said Laney.

"You girls up and about?"

"We've, like, already showered and eaten," said Laney.

Collette sat at the end of the bed and got up when Winters entered. "Surprised, aren't ya."

"Just a little," affirmed Winters.

"We've already seen Finley and have been sitting here waiting for you."

"Glad to hear it. I've already gotten the okay from Sergeant Hicks. He's in charge of the training program, and he's waiting for ya."

"Well, then let's go. Chop, chop," said Laney.

They left the room and headed down the hallway to the training center.

"Is he a nice man?" asked Laney.

"Oh yes. He's even been training Sadie. Not quite sure why, but he has been."

"That's so awesome," said Laney.

Winters stopped walking. "Now look, girls, I hope you don't mind, but he asked about your background."

Collette looked at Laney who shrugged her shoulders.

"Okay, good. I just wasn't sure if that was something that would upset you."

"We're not ashamed of it," said Collette. "We survived it, and that's all there is to it."

"Good. That's a good attitude," said Winters.

"Now, Hicks and his men trained all of us including Amber and Reese. So, he's very patient with rookies. Don't hesitate to ask him anything you don't understand. By the end of the day, you'll know more about guns than most people."

The girls couldn't contain their glee as they entered the training facility. Weapons hung from the walls, and glass cabinets were loaded with all types of pistols.

Winters introduced the girls to Sergeant Hicks and then decided to hit the range himself.

Winters spent an hour with an instructor and brushed up on his own shooting skills. Even though he'd become proficient with weapons, he always learned something new whenever he spent time with the real experts.

He thanked the instructor and then walked to a window to watch the girls firing pistols for a few minutes. They seemed enthused as the instructors were talking to them. Winters was about to leave when a man came up and introduced himself.

"Excuse me, but you're Captain Winters?"

Tom Fowler was a lanky man in his forties and sported a goatee and mustache. He had a bad habit of invading your personal space when he talked to you.

Winters backed up a step before speaking. "Yes, and you are?"

"Tom. Tom Fowler. I'm one of your drivers tonight."

"Oh, yes, I'm sorry. It's nice to meet you," said Winters extending his hand.

"So, glad to finally meet you, sir. We've been here for the past week and have heard all about you. We're very excited to be joining you guys."

"Your timing couldn't be better. So, I'm the one who's excited to have you guys."

Fowler looked through the window. "Who are those girls?"

"The girl with the spiky black hair is, Collette, and the other one is Laney."

"Are they volunteers too?"

"No. No. They're just getting some weapons training. We'll be bringing them back to Iowa before we head to Michigan."

"Why are they here?"

Winters didn't want to go into full detail on the girls, so he gave him a rough sketch.

"Alright, cool," said Fowler. "I need to get going so if I don't see you again, what time did you want to leave?"

"Let's say 9pm. You can meet us down at the motor pool."

"Okay. Hey, again, so glad to meet you," said Fowler as he shook Winters' hand.

Winters watched him leave thinking he was a bit of an odd duck. Not that it mattered much. The Shadow Patriots were filled with all sorts of personalities and characters.

Fowler hurried back to his room excited having just met Cole Winters. He opened the door and found his friend Butler sitting in an easy chair watching television.

"You're not going to believe who I just met?"

Butler grabbed the remote with his rough hands. He turned the TV off and waited for Fowler to continue.

"Just ran into Cole Winters."

"So? We're going to be leaving tonight with him."

"Yeah, but did you know that we've got a couple of passengers?"

This got Butler's attention, and he sat up straighter. "Who?"

"A couple of teenage girls."

Butler let out a sigh. "Oh, jeez. I thought it was more men. That'd be the last thing we need."

Fowler grew frustrated by his friend's disappointing response. He sat on the bed next to Butler. "Dude, these girls are friggin hot, and I want them."

"We're hijacking the trucks. Is that not enough?"

"Hell no! Not when there's also a couple of hot girls. And once we're done with them, we can sell 'em. Trust me these girls are worth good money."

Butler leaned forward. "They're that good looking, huh?"

"Oh, yes. And from what I gather, they were some kind of

prostitutes."

"Prostitutes huh? Now they don't sound so hot."

"Trust me, you'd never know it by looking at them. And they're young. I mean, they're like sixteen or seventeen."

Butler leaned back in his chair and gave it some thought. They came to Winnipeg when they heard the Shadow Patriots came here to get supplies. They thought they'd be able to take advantage. So they came pretending to want to join them. However, they were growing tired of waiting and were actually getting ready to leave when Cole Winters arrived last night. Butler couldn't believe his good fortune when he learned they'd be driving trucks filled with supplies worth tens of thousands of dollars. Now their luck had improved even more with the addition of two attractive girls. Fowler was right when he stated they were worth money. There was a growing sex trade happening, and they could sell them after having their own fun.

"Alright, we'll take them on one condition," said Butler.

"What's that?"

"Only if it's easy. The trucks come first, then the girls. I don't want to get into a gunfight with this guy. I've heard he's pretty damn lucky."

"Fine. All I want is a chance," said Fowler as he rubbed his hands together.

CHAPTER 28

WASHINGTON D.C.

Stormy Robinson reached for the coffee decanter and remembered she was out. The former model with the long raven black hair cursed aloud. She needed coffee first thing in the morning to get herself going. She didn't have the mindset to go to the grocery store, so she decided to go to the coffee shop. She threw on a pair of baggy gray sweatpants, to go along with the white t-shirt she slept in. She took a quick look in the mirror and ran her fingers to comb out her messy hair. Satisfied, she grabbed her keys and hopped in her white BMW.

With all the excitement over the last couple of days, she'd forgotten to go grocery shopping and more importantly, buy coffee. Never did she imagine her life would change so drastically when she decided to leave New York to come help her friend Kyle Gibbs. The idea of assisting in the capacity she had been doing was both surreal and exciting. Never before had she experienced such a high than when she took down Perozzi's man in the parking lot. It wasn't some competition where you can tap out to a referee. No, this was the real thing with real consequences.

She'd done some crazy things in her life but nothing like this. Growing up in Minnesota, she was a tomboy and liked to ride dirt bikes and skateboards. She was always trying to keep up with her cousins who kept daring her to do dangerous things. They lived near an abandoned rock quarry and would often go swimming there. One day, she jumped from a fifty-foot cliff, which was higher than even the boys dared go. This alone put her in the coolness category with the boys.

She pulled into the parking lot of the coffee shop and was glad it wasn't too busy. She decided to spoil herself and ordered a Mocha. She usually didn't get sugary drinks as she kept to a strict diet to maintain her athletic figure.

She looked around the place disappointed not to see anyone on a laptop. The days of hanging out at a coffee shop to use the free Internet were gone as was the Internet. Strange thing to get rid of but if you want to control the population, then you didn't want any free flow of information.

Stormy set the troubling thought aside and remembered what Green told them last night about him killing his commanding officer in hand-to-hand combat. Talk about a life or death situation. You either win or die. Now that was the ultimate in fighting, one she briefly experienced the other day. Of course, she knew in the back of her mind that help wasn't too far away. Still, it was dangerous and thrilling.

She broke into a smile thinking how different John was from the men she had dated in New York. They had expensive toys and pretended to do dangerous things to impress the ladies, but in reality, they were nothing but posers. John, on the other hand, was the real deal. Brave, loyal, selfless and kind. An appealing combination that added to his good looks.

"Mocha," yelled the barista.

She snapped out of her thoughts and grabbed her drink. She then exited the shop and got back in her car. She took the lid off and her mouth watered as the mocha vapors rose to her nose. Every delicious sip warmed her mouth as she drank the creamy liquid.

After leaving the parking lot, she started heading home and wasn't paying attention to the speed limit. It was an easy thing to do in this car, as it was a smooth and quiet car. She had purchased it in New York before moving down here and hadn't driven a car for some time. She always used the subway and taxies in the city. A loud siren sent a charge up her spine, and she looked in the mirror to see a cop behind her.

"Oh, fudge," she said aloud.

She pulled into a quiet residential street. She set her coffee down and grabbed her license and insurance card. She then looked in the mirror to run her hand through her long black hair and combed out a few loose strands.

The cop got out of the car. Stormy figured he was about five-foot-seven and weighed a buck sixty. She learned to size people up while taking martial arts. Her instructor told her to always make a habit of it in case she ever needed to take someone out in a hurry.

She lowered the window and gave him a big smile. "Good morning officer."

The officer's eyes grew when saw how attractive she was. "Morning, Miss. Uh, the reason I pulled you over, was because you were doing forty-five in a thirty mile per hour speed zone."

"I was? I'm so sorry. The car's new and quite frankly, I'm not used to even driving."

"You have New York tags. Are you visiting?"

"I just moved here," said Stormy as she noticed him looking at her chest. She then remembered she had forgotten to throw on a bra.

"You need to get new tags."

"It is on my list. I just haven't had the time yet."

He knelt down to her level, which was an unusual move for a cop. "You look familiar. Have we met before?"

Usually, Stormy would think this was a pickup line, but he genuinely looked puzzled. "Well, I have done modeling work, so maybe something like that."

"It'll come to me. Can I see your license and insurance card?"

"Oh, sure, got it right here."

The cop stood back up. "Stormy Robinson? That's an unusual name."

She was used to the response as she'd gotten the same comment all her life. "I was born at home during a blizzard."

The cop laughed. "Your parents must be pretty cool."

"Yeah, they are," she said as she watched the cop call her name into the radio mic attached to his shoulder. He didn't walk back to his car as was typical but stayed there so he could keep talking to her. He obviously liked her, and she thought she might get out of the ticket.

The cop snapped his fingers. "Were you on the cover of Muscle and Fitness?"

Stormy's mouth dropped. "I was."

"I knew it. I knew I knew you from somewhere. That was a great cover. You looked amazing. If memory serves me, you were wearing a yellow bikini."

Stormy had to think back to which cover he was referring to, as she had done covers for various magazines. Not that it mattered, because she had made such an impression on him that he remembered a cover that was at least a year old. "Say goodbye to this speeding ticket," she said laughing to herself.

"I was wearing a yellow bikini. You've got a helluva a memory."

"Hey, I never forget a pretty face."

"Well, thank you."

"Listen, I won't write you up, but please pay attention and get those new tags," said the officer as he handed back her license and insurance card.

"I will. Thank you, so much."

The officer started walking back to his cruiser and Stormy was just getting ready to hit the window button when she heard his radio come alive. The cop stopped in mid-stride and paused for a moment before turning around. He came back to the window and said, "Stormy Robinson, I'm sorry, but there's a warrant out for your arrest."

CHAPTER 29

JACKSON MICHIGAN

Scar headed to the cafeteria bothered by the empty results of the last two operations to bring more food into Jackson. It seemed like a simple task, but they had failed both times. It wasn't like he ordered inexperience guys to do the job. Hell, if Bassett and Nordell couldn't get it done, then it was just a streak of bad luck. Bad luck or not, he would try for a third time tonight. This time he'd send just Bassett and Burns to cross the border before sunrise and let them scout out the supply line.

The one good thing that had happened over the last few days was that they had gathered more fuel. Bill Taylor kept the men busy by siphoning gas out of the Jijis' vehicles that sat on the interstate. They had plenty of fuel to take a large number of citizens across tonight. If the western border was penetrable, then that's what they would do. It would certainly lighten the food demand and stretch those rations out.

After grabbing a cup of coffee, Scar headed outside to get some air. The sun was out, and it was starting to warm-up. He walked outside to the back parking lot and sat down on a bench. He looked at Winters' truck that Reese had been driving.

The twenty-year-old white Chevy Silverado hadn't been washed in close to a year. The windshield had a crack that ran along the bottom from one end to the other. Both sides shared numerous scrapes and dents with rust spots on the wheel wells. Surprisingly, the gray interior was clean despite the dashboard fading from the onslaught of the sun. It was covered in mud from yesterday's escape from the Jijis who were chasing Reese and Nate.

Scar let out a laugh at how her wild driving skills came in handy. Poor Nate didn't look too good after that ride. His bruised body appeared worn out after being bounced around.

Scar took a sip of coffee and let out a sigh. It had been four days since Winters drove that truck and his return needed to happen soon. The streak of bad luck started the night when they stormed Mordulfah's compound. They needed a win. Otherwise, morale would deteriorate if things didn't start changing.

He wouldn't blame the men if they lost faith as it was challenging to keep while in constant danger. If he needed to step aside to change things, he'd be more than happy to do it. Not that he thought it would come to that because he had no doubt Winters would return.

Scar coughed on his coffee thinking if not for the mission, then certainly for Reese. She was too good of a catch not to come back for. He told her that, and he meant it. It wasn't every day a hot twenty-year-old falls in love with an older man with no money.

Scar took another sip of his coffee when he heard the door open. He turned his head to see Reese coming outside. Her Colt M4 hung from the sling on her back as she walked over on her crutch.

"Hey, Scar," said Reese sitting down.

"I was just thinking of you."

"You were?"

"Yep. Just thinking about Cole and when he'll come back…for you," said Scar as he motioned his hand to her.

"Glad to see you have faith in me."

"C'mon, I told ya, you're a catch."

She flashed him a smile. "I'm going crazy waiting though, which is why I was going for another drive. I thought I try to find, like, a hose and wash her as well. You wanna come with?"

"As tempting as that is, I got other things to do."

"Can't they wait?"

Scar thought about it for a moment. He thought it prudent to check the borders to see if anything changed after yesterday's event in the Proving Grounds.

"Tell ya what, as long as we can visit the border guards, I'm in."

"We can do that."

"You got a radio."

"In the truck. Batteries all charged."

"Let's go."

Scar followed Reese to the muddy truck and heard her crutch land in the back before getting in.

"How much longer on the crutch?" asked Scar after he shut his door.

"Doc thinks next few days."

"How does it feel? You look like you're walking better now."

"I am but kinda screwed it up the other night."

"In Port Huron?"

Reese let out a scoff while she started the truck and revved the engine. "Yeah. I never should have asked Meeks to go."

"He never could say no to a pretty girl."

She flashed him another smile. "I knew there was a reason I wanted you to come along."

"Hey, who doesn't like compliments?"

"Right? Now hang on," said Reese as she stomped the gas pedal and peeled out of the parking lot. "Where to first?"

"Head over to Nordell's place. He's got a hose we can use."

"Cool."

Reese tore through the quiet streets and had them at Nordell's in no time at all. She pulled into his driveway and spied the hose off to the side of the garage.

"Let me see if he's home," said Scar as he opened the door.

After a few knocks, Nordell came outside.

"Hey, Gunny. Reese wants to wash this beast and needed a hose."

"She does? That thing?"

"Just go with it," whispered Scar.

"Alright," said Nordell as he waved to Reese. "I got a bucket and sponge you can use in the garage."

"Awesome," cheered Reese as she approached the garage.

Scar watched as Nordell got Reese set up and wondered just how silly it was to be doing this. He then remembered what Nordell said the other night while they were in jail about how eating in that restaurant made you think everything was normal.

Now, here they were, out in the driveway on a beautiful day with a truck in need of a bath. It was an ordinary thing to do, and it did make you forget, if just for a moment.

"What's on your mind?" asked Nordell. "You didn't come over here just to wash that piece of junk."

Scar laughed. "Don't let her hear you say that."

"I won't," said Nordell as he watched Reese spray the mud off the side of the truck.

"We've got enough fuel to take some people across tonight."

Nordell nodded. "Good. Lighten the load on the food supply seeing how we're struggling in that department."

"Don't remind me."

"Not all missions go as planned, Scar."

Scar nodded.

"How many you thinking?"

"We can easily do ten vehicles depending on the size."

"I've still got some short church buses still laying around, and they run on gas."

"What are those, like, fifteen passengers?"

"Around that depending on who we put in there. I'll get with Badger and see how much fuel he's got and have it all ready by nightfall."

Scar liked what he was hearing and knew he could count on Nordell to have everything ready. He knew the people and knew the order in which they needed to go. He'd been in charge of them from the get-go and had assigned "Block Captains" to expedite things.

CHAPTER 30

WASHINGTON D.C.

An arrest warrant was the furthest thing from Stormy's mind when the cop pulled her over for speeding. Her heart began racing after hearing those words. Apparently, Lawrence Reed still wanted her and Perozzi's influence stopped at the water's edge or the restaurant's edge. Reed's reach and determination in finding her were more than she had considered. Since Perozzi prevented her arrest the other night, she figured that was where it would end. She began cursing at her naiveté. She should have known better, and she should not have been driving anywhere.

No way could she let herself be arrested. No doubt, they would question her, maybe even torture her to get what they wanted. She'd never see the light of day again.

Options? She couldn't outrun him with her car, so she had only one option, and it had to be physical.

She took a deep breath to calm down and then formed the biggest smile she could muster. "A warrant? That's so weird. Are you sure?"

"I'm sure it's a mistake, but I still need to take you in. If I don't, they'll literally have my hide."

"Okay. Well, I don't want to get you in trouble. Should I lock my car?"

"We'll wait for a tow truck, so you won't have to worry about that."

Whenever Stormy modeled, she always played a character and right now, she was playing a meek and cooperative weak-kneed girl. She was already planning the moves she would make on him.

She'd never been arrested before but thought for sure he'd want to frisk her. Any excuse to put his hands on her. Guys were all the same when it came to wanting to put their paws on her, especially out at the bar scene.

She opened the door and climbed out.

"I need to search you. Do you have any weapons or anything sharp that I need to know about."

She continued smiling. "I do not."

"Okay, so put your palms on the hood."

She leaned against the fender and put her hands on her car. His hands then touch her shoulders and then down her back. Then came the icing on the cake for him as he slid his hands under her boobs. She regretted not putting on a bra. He then moved down her waist and groin area. *Pig!* She could almost hear his heart pounding in his chest from the excitement. If she were a betting girl, she would guess he was aroused. *Perfect distraction.*

She heard the rattle of handcuffs as he went for her left hand. Just as the cop grabbed her left wrist, Stormy uncoiled. She transferred her weight on her left foot as her hips rotated. Her clenched right fist landed on his temple with her knuckles digging in. The surprise blow snapped his head a quarter turn to the left.

The hit only needed to stun him for a split-second to set up her next move. His eyes went blank, and it hadn't registered yet in his mind as Stormy leaned back and used her forehead to strike his nose.

It was enough to break it and splatter blood in different directions. The lightning-fast strike didn't give the cop a chance to react as he swayed back and forth before she finished him off with a knee to the groin. He let out a yelp as he collapsed to the ground.

By far, her favorite move on guys, especially with ones who had just groped her.

"Sorry, sweetie but I can't let you take me in," she said as she looked around to see no one had taken notice of them.

She picked the cuffs off the ground and pushed him over on his stomach to cuff him.

"You were sweet to remember me, but it was also a little creepy, but not as creepy as you feeling me up. Is it proper procedure to grab my boobs?"

He didn't answer but only moaned in pain.

Wanting to give herself more time, she yanked the radio off him and smashed it on the ground. "Don't want you to call this in too quickly."

She walked to his still running cruiser, opened the door, pushed the lock button and slammed it shut.

After getting back in her car, she looked at him through the open window. "Don't be too embarrassed, though I'm sure you'll come up with a good story."

She hit the gas and took off speeding down the street. She didn't get her rapid heart rate under control until she reached her house. She wouldn't take any chances of being caught and grabbed a suitcase. She was pulled over too close to home for them not to start looking in the area for her. She had to leave and take the BMW, which stuck out like a sore thumb and ditch it. She wasn't sure how long she'd be gone for or if she'd ever come back here.

She gathered some clothes and toiletries and threw them into the suitcase. She was good at this, as she had lived out of one for many years while traveling to modeling gigs. She took one last look and headed back to her car. She figured the cop hadn't escaped yet, which gave her some breathing room.

"What to do? Where to go?" she said aloud as she pulled out of her driveway. She scratched her head and decided she needed help.

After ten minutes, she spotted a payphone and pulled over. She grabbed the change out of her purse and dialed Kyle's number. "C'mon, pick up, pick up."

Fifteen rings later, she hung up.

The quarters came jingling back down. She tapped her fingers on the phone. "Oh, I do have it."

She began digging in her purse and grabbed a business card. "Major John Green."

Green saw the light blinking on the phone. His secretary had transferred a call back to him. He wondered if it might be Reed checking in on him. He had prepared a script in his mind on what to say to him if he did.

He hit the button and said, "This is Major Green."

"Hi John, it's me, Cheryl. I was wondering if you'd like to get some lunch today?"

Green's mind began to race around because he recognized Stormy's voice but she used a different name. She was in trouble and knew enough not to raise any suspicion on the phone. He had told her he thought the lines were tapped and never to call him there. She had to be desperate if she was calling.

"I would love to get some lunch. What did you have in mind?"

"Well, I'm over at Ballston Mall in Arlington. You think we can get something around here?"

Green had to think for a second where that was. It was about seven miles away. "That'd be great. What time?"

"You know I haven't even had breakfast yet, so right now, if you could. We can beat the lunch rush."

"Give me thirty.

"Meet me up front."

"You got it."

Green put the phone back in its cradle and took a deep breath. He kept his calm as he walked out of the office. "Grace, I'm gonna get an early lunch."

"She sounded pretty," she smiled.

"She is."

"Glad to hear it. You have fun. You've got nothing on your schedule so take your time."

"I will, thanks.

Grace had been trying to set him up with some of her friends, but none of them was his type, so he just avoided the subject whenever she brought it up to him. This *date* was going to be a most interesting date. No telling what has happened. He gave his M9 a reassuring pat as he got on the elevator.

CHAPTER 31

JACKSON MICHIGAN

Scar held the water hose as Reese finished washing the mud off the last wheel. Overall, it didn't look too bad, despite it being a beat up truck. He understood the attraction to older vehicles. They had character and often held special memories. He had owned one similar to this one and had used it in his construction business. He put a lot of miles on it before trading it in for a new one. While the new one was nicer, he couldn't help but pine for the older one. It was comfortable and fit like a glove.

"Whaddya think?" asked Reese getting up.

Scar sprayed the wheel. "She looks pretty good. You did a bang-up job."

"Thanks," said Reese as she grabbed the hose to give it another rinse. "You know, I've never owned a car before."

"You haven't?"

"We could never afford a second one. Weren't any jobs around, so, I'd always drive my mom to work if I needed to go somewhere."

"Yeah, the years before the crash were hard. I had to lay off a bunch of guys. I didn't want to, but I had no choice."

"I couldn't find a job if my life depended on it."

"You know, Reese, you could literally choose any car around here to drive."

"I know, but I had my first kiss with Cole in this one," she said as she dropped the nozzle in the bucket.

Scar gave her a knowing nod.

"And besides, it burns rubber really easy," smiled Reese. She began rinsing the soap out of the sponge and bucket.

Scar returned the smile while looking at the lack of tread on the tires. "You're going to need new tires."

"I know. Badger has a new set for me," said Reese as she turned the water off and began looping the hose around the holder.

"Oh?"

"Yep. Said he'd put them on this afternoon."

"Perfect. Why don't we check out the borders and we'll head over there."

"You done out here?" asked Nordell as he came back outside.

"Yepper," said Reese. She handed him the bucket. "Thanks so much."

"No problem. You know, it looks better than I thought it would."

"Doesn't it though?"

"You guys out of here?" asked Nordell.

"We are, Gunny. Gonna check the borders and then go get her some tires."

Nordell leaned his head over to look at the tires. "Good idea."

"You wanna come with us?" asked Reese.

Nordell scrounged his face. "I've risked my life enough this past week."

Reese's mouth dropped open as she put her hands on her hips. "I won't kill ya."

"I'm good, really, but thank you."

"Okay," said Reese as she hugged Nordell.

"I'll see you later this afternoon then," said Scar.

"You got it. Remember, to buckle up," joked Nordell.

Reese feigned insult before getting into the truck. She started it up and revved the engine a few times. She looked over at Scar who pretended to buckle up before cracking a smile. Reese cocked her head at him as she backed it up and throwing it in drive while stomping on the gas. The tires squealed before they caught and rocketed them down the street. "I didn't want to disappoint, Gunny."

"No, of course not," said Scar. "One must always uphold their reputation."

"Riiight."

Scar was glad he came along with her and was enjoying the day. He could see why Winters was attracted to her. Besides her beauty, she was resilient and tough while keeping a sweet side to her. She had a way of putting you at ease and always included you in whatever she was doing. This wasn't something everyone could do, but her outgoing personality naturally allowed her to do it without effort.

If you didn't know her, you'd think she was this delicate, innocent girl, which was her true self, but circumstances made her into something else. He had heard the stories of her taking pleasure in gutting a cop. He had witnessed her satisfaction when Nordell executed the cops the other day. She was dealing with inner demons he could only imagine.

How could she not?

Ten days of torture would do damage to anyone, especially the kind she had endured. However, when allowed to do something ordinary like washing your car, her true self came out shining, and it was good and sweet.

They made it up to Lansing Road in quick fashion and found Eddie Perlee standing in front of the house they'd been using as sleeping quarters. The tall grass on the lawn was matted down with vehicles coming and going.

Reese threw the truck in park, and they climbed out. Eddie gave a casual salute and noticed the pickup had just been washed.

"Did you wash this ole heap?"

Scar motioned to Reese.

"It doesn't look half bad," said Eddie.

"She was in dire need of a bath," beamed Reese.

"So what's up?" asked Eddie.

"Just wanting to inspect the borders," said Scar. "Anything change?"

Eddie shook his head. "No, not really."

Scar detected a hesitation. "No, or not really?"

"Well, my guys did report on a meeting the Jiji commander had this morning, which isn't all that unusual, but it took longer than usual."

This got Scar's attention. "Oh?"

"I didn't think anything of it and figured it had something to do with the firefight yesterday."

"But?"

"One of my guys mentioned that he thought the commander had a map laid out on the pavement. He couldn't really get a good look at it, so he wasn't too sure.

Scar gave it some thought. "Maybe they're moving their guys around after yesterday."

"Which is what I was thinking."

"Or they're getting ready to attack," interjected Reese. "These bastards aren't gonna wait forever."

She was right of course, and it had been worrying Scar, which is why he wanted to check out the borders. It had been too many days since they attacked Mordulfah's compound for him not to want to strike back. Yesterday's firefight certainly had to affect that timetable. He wished Thomas would get back with them to report on Mordulfah's activities. Perhaps his absence said more about what was about to happen. Thomas had promised he would come back and tell them about Mordulfah's plans. It was inevitable at some point they would attack Jackson again.

The only question was when?

The best thing he could do was get his men ready, so for the next couple of hours, Reese drove him to all of their guard posts to keep the men motivated.

CHAPTER 32

The traffic was light as it was mid-morning and the lunch crowd hadn't hit the streets yet. Stormy hadn't given him specific instructions but figured she'd be on the lookout for his vehicle. He had thought about switching the cars out, but it would have taken too long, and she sounded desperate.

He was coming down Glebe Road and saw the mall up on the left. It was a big mall with a multi-level parking garage. An Iceplex was connected to it where they used to play professional hockey when there was still a league.

He wasn't sure where to go but figured out front meant the parking garage. He slowed down and took a left just as the light was turning red. The entrance to the mall swerved to the right, and as he came around the bend, he saw a girl with baggy sweatpants and a white t-shirt. He did a double take as the girl approached the car and opened the door.

"Thank God, you're here," she said leaning over to kiss his cheek.

"What's going on? What happened?"

Green parked the car as she filled him in.

"So, I didn't know what else to do," she finished.

"You did good, Lady Storm,"

Stormy smiled hearing the nickname.

"You played it smart by coming here. A lot of nice cars in this garage."

"Kinda what I was thinking."

"We're going to have to get rid of your car. We can take it to one of my storage units."

Stormy let out a sigh of relief. "I feel so much better now that you're here."

"This is my fault for not thinking about this. I should have known better."

"No. The fault is mine for mouthing off to Reed in the first place."

"Well, regardless, we need to stash you somewhere."

"I grabbed a suitcase before I left."

"Okay. Good. Where's your car?"

"One level up."

Green backed the car up and drove up another level.

"Towards the back…and there it is."

Green parked next to it, and she hopped out to retrieve her suitcase. She threw it in the backseat and jumped back in.

"Did you get a chance to call your artist friend?"

"I did, and he's totally up for it. Said he can meet us tonight."

"Okay."

Stormy put her hand on his arm. "Thanks for this."

Green's pulse quickened making him wonder again if she liked him. Their eyes met, and he didn't have to wait long as she leaned in to kiss him. Her lips were warm and soft making Green melt in his seat. He hadn't kissed a girl in quite awhile and hoped he wasn't disappointing her.

She pulled back with a grin. "Sorry, for being so forward."

"That's a bad thing?" asked Green with a lopsided smile.

"It's not?" she asked.

"Does take out all the guesswork."

"You've been guessing?"

Green's cheeks blushed. "I have."

"I thought so. I was wondering if you were going to make a move."

"It's not that I didn't want to, but with all the craziness I wasn't sure."

Stormy leaned back in her seat. "Well, now you know."

"Yes," said Green as he put the car in reverse. "And now my mother is going to go absolutely crazy."

"I love your mom. She's so sweet."

"That's good because that's where we're headed," said Green as he pulled out of the garage. He could still taste her lips and couldn't wipe the smile off his face. The casualness of their encounter was pleasing because he didn't like a lot of awkwardness. With their experience the other day, it was probably the main reason for the ease. He was still smiling as he glanced at her to see the same expression on her face. A bit of relief came over him, as he didn't want to be the only one giddy about this.

She met his gaze and reached over to grab his hand. "This isn't so awkward, is it?"

"I was just thinking the same thing."

"Really?"

"Yeah."

"It's nice."

Green had to force himself to concentrate on the road. She was an enjoyable distraction, and he feared he'd lose focus because of her over the coming days. Business and pleasure were often a bad mix. He had a lot to think about, and a relationship could get in the way. Then again, he deserved to be happy, and it had been a long time since he had a relationship.

He pulled into the driveway and saw her mom tending her flowers. She turned and then stood up.

"Oh, this is going to be so much fun," giggled Stormy.

Green bowed his head and shook it.

"C'mon, your mom is going be so excited."

"You have no idea."

"Oh, I think I do," said Stormy as she opened the door.

Green got out as his mom approached the car.

"Stormy, what a pleasant surprise," said Sarah. "What are y'all doing here?"

"Oh, your son is being my knight in shining armor," said Stormy as she grabbed ahold of his arm and leaned on him.

Sarah's eyes grew. "Is this what I think it is?"

"It is," exclaimed Stormy."

"John?"

"Mom! Try to control yourself," said Green.

"Oh, John, don't worry. I'm not going to embarrass you…too much," she said with a wink.

Green looked at Stormy and said. "I told ya."

"Oh, she's adorable."

"C'mon inside. I'll make us some lunch."

While she made lunch, Stormy told her about what happened with the cop. With everything Sarah and her son had been through, she took the news in stride. They had all faced some dangerous situations and knew they'd face even more in the coming weeks. Sarah served them lunch and suggested that Stormy change her appearance. They could go to Manassas and let Alison O'Connor change her hairstyle as she had worked in the business.

CHAPTER 33

WINNIPEG

Winters rounded the corner to find Murphy finishing his physical therapy session. It had been a few months since he'd been shot in the sandpit after they rescued the girls from the party house. He was with his friend Burns when they took up a position behind their truck to help Nate protect the rescued girls. Four cops outflanked them by climbing up a sand dune and firing down at them. The cops killed nineteen girls and injured many more including Murphy. His injury had been more severe than Nate's as the bullet traveled around destroying muscle tissue in his back and rotator cuff.

"Captain," said Murphy extending his hand.

"Murphy," said Winters as he met his hand and leaned in for a slight hug.

"Heard you were here."

"Oh?"

"Sadie. She visits me all the time."

"She is something, isn't she?"

Murphy nodded. "She said you came here with more girls?"

"Oh, yeah," said Winters as he took a seat on a bench. He waited for the physical therapist to leave before he briefed Murphy.

Murphy shook his head throughout. "I'm sorry about your daughter, Captain."

"Thank you. I'm doing better with it. Helping all those girls really helped."

"Yeah, I get that. You know, had I not seen the party house, it'd be almost unbelievable a whole town could fall for that."

Winters nodded. "How's your therapy doing?"

Murphy raised his arm up halfway. "It's getting better. I should be able to straighten it next few weeks or so. You say Nate got shot in the shoulder?"

"Yeah, in the front," said Winters pointing above his chest, "and right out the back. Not as bad as yours, but still, he should have come here. He refuses to leave though, and now that Elliott's been shot, he won't leave his side."

"It's got to be driving him crazy missing the action."

Winters let out a laugh. "Oh, yeah, you know Nate. What about you?"

"Can't wait to get back."

"Yeah, me too."

"When you leaving?"

"Tonight. I got three trucks full of supplies."

"Butler and his crew helping you?"

"Yeah. You've met them?"

"I have, and I can't say I trust 'em, especially Fowler. I get a bad vibe from him. He seems a bit on the creepy side to me."

Winters gave him a concerned look. "Really?"

"Yeah, why?"

"It's just that we're taking two of the girls back home first."

"Is that wise?"

Winters shrugged his shoulders. "I've got 'em with Hicks for the whole day."

Burns smiled. "Sergeant Hicks will fix 'em right up."

"Exactly."

"Still, keep 'em with you on the drive back."

"I will and on that note I need to go."

"Captain, thanks for stopping by and tell everyone I said, hey."

"I will," said Winters as he gave Murphy another hug.

Winters would have liked to spend more time with him, but he wanted to check on the girls' progress and tie up some loose ends with the supply sergeant.

He headed to Sergeant Hicks' domain and was surprised to see Sadie in one of the lanes shooting a pistol. Her back was to Winters as he approached the window, so he took a seat and watched her empty a magazine at a target ten yards away. The gun looked big in her little hands but it didn't have too much of a kick, so he figured it was a 9mm.

The instructor brought the target back. Her shots were in a tight grouping but just to the right of center. The instructor held up his trigger finger to show her how to better place it on the trigger. The little things made all the difference when on a target twenty feet or more away. She tried again and took the lesson to heart, as her grouping was dead center.

She noticed Winters and smiled while waving him inside. He grabbed some ear and eye protection before joining her.

"Shouldn't you be in school?" asked Winters jokingly.

"I am in school, aren't I, Mike?" she answered looking at Sergeant Spencer.

Winters rolled his eyes and shook Spencer's hand. "How she doing, Mike?"

Sergeant Mike Spencer was a Canadian soldier and an expert in small arms. He had been working with Winters this morning and had instructed all the Shadow Patriots.

"She was one of my best students."

"Is she now?"

"Seriously, she really is. She actually listens and doesn't have an ego like a lot of guys do. I'm getting ready to move her up to .45's."

Winters put his arm around her shoulder. "I'm glad to hear that."

"You wanna take a turn?" asked Sadie.

"No, no. I just came down to check on the girls. Where're they at?"

"Sergeant Hicks has them in the Urban Warfare Course. I had them for a while after you left."

"How they'd do?"

"They both did good, especially Laney. She took right to it. Collette took a bit longer, but she came around. Both are quite competent and comfortable with weapons now."

Winters let out a sigh. "Good. I'm happy to hear it."

"Believe me, by the time Hicks is done with them, they'll be able to defend themselves. Last time, I checked, they were knocking down the right targets and not freaking out about hitting the wrong ones. And like Sadie, they listen."

Winters remember going through the course and how much it taught him about tactics, leading a squad, what to look for, speed and time management. Hicks ran them through the course multiple times a day over a month's time until he was satisfied with their performance. The girls won't need as much in-depth training but will come away with valuable skills to keep themselves and their families safe.

CHAPTER 34

DETROIT MICHIGAN

The 747 shut down its engines as the aircraft-boarding ramp was pushed to it. The Detroit Metro Airport like all the other airports was closed down after the fall of the government. The only people who still flew were the well connected or government officials. Mordulfah was the only person who used this airport with his private jet. His uncle Faisal owned the big jet that had just landed. Inside were five hundred experienced fighters who would be helping Mordulfah clean out the upper Midwest but more specifically the Shadow Patriots.

The men disembarked and gathered their stowed gear and weapons. Everyone wore light camouflage fatigues and had a confident manner about them. They were orderly and didn't hesitate to load their equipment into the charter buses Mordulfah had provided.

Colonel Khan watched off to the side with his captains pleased with this assignment. He stood to make a lot of money from Mordulfah and whatever else his men managed to loot from the various towns they would raid. He promised his men riches and plenty of virgins.

He was aware of Mordulfah penchant for young girls and shared the same notions. All he was asked by the prince was to give him first choice to fill his harem back up. After that, they could have as many as they needed, which would be a lot. Besides his men, he had to consider Mordulfah's men who had been fighting in Jackson.

These men had drifted in from the surrounding areas and were not trained fighters but still would want a piece of the action. It would be better to give them something rather than have a mutiny on his hands. Despite their lack of training, they were still fifteen hundred of them, more than enough to hamper his efforts.

He also had to consider the local cops. He had heard about the girls that were taken from them as well. No doubt, they wanted to refill their storehouse as quickly as possible. The cops didn't impress him, but it was another entity that had to be pacified. Because they were locals, they would come in handy in providing support.

Khan had been making plans with his captains while in-route and had decided the sooner they attacked, the better before word got out. He was to meet with Mordulfah's military leaders and the cops as soon as they got to Grosse Pointe, which would be in another thirty minutes.

The buses pulled into Mordulfah's place, and Khan was the first to get off and was greeted by the prince.

"Colonel Khan, I trust your trip was uneventful."

"It was thank you."

"My man Wali will direct your men across the street. We have prepared food for them and facilities."

"Excellent."

"Come inside," said Mordulfah escorting Khan into the smaller house on the grounds. Work on the big mansion hadn't begun yet as materials hadn't been gathered.

Mordulfah introduced Khan to his captains, which included Vatter who was visibly nervous being there. He hadn't seen Mordulfah since the rebels attacked the mansion and wondered if Khan was there to replace him.

Everyone took a seat at the rectangle table with Mordulfah on one end and Khan on the other end.

"Gentlemen, I want all of you to give Colonel Khan your assessment of the rebels and what you've seen them do."

Everyone blinked nervously at each other unsure if they would be losing their heads.

Khan removed his hat. "I'm not here to judge. I only need to find out their tactics and capabilities."

They let a sigh of relief and one by one began to report all they had experienced in fighting the rebels. Throughout the next hour, Khan asked questions to get better details of their answers. None of these captains had military experience and as such, what they thought was important wasn't always the case or vice-versa.

After they finished, Khan leaned back in his chair and thought for a few moments. The rebels were well trained and used good tactics. They were also well equipped, and more than likely had night-vision optics since they like to operate at night. There was only one way to overcome that advantage, and that was to fight them during the day.

Khan got up and looked at the map of Jackson, which was filled in as to where all of their men were currently stationed and where they thought the rebels had guard post. It was really a simple thing. The rebels were outnumbered and wouldn't be able to thwart a quick full-on assault. Any of the locals who volunteered to fight would fold as soon as they saw what was happening. Especially now that he had brought more munitions than Mordulfah had provided to his men.

Khan turned back to the men. "We will attack first light."

Everyone looked at each other with excited eyes.

"I will divide my men into two companies," said Khan as he picked up a pointer. "They will enter here," pointing at Ann Arbor Road. "Here on Page Road. Now, I need Captain Vatter to keep his police on US 12, that way we can squeeze them together. And all the men on Highway 60 will come across on McCain Road. We will do this all at the same time.

We will set fire to the houses as we go to squeeze them south where they will meet their fate. By doing this, we will avoid as much block-to-block resistance as we can. Anyone seeing what is happening will run away right into our funnel.

We will strike the hospital first, where many of their men sleep. This is where we will be able to take out most of their force. This will also divide them up into smaller groups making them less effective. It will only be a matter of time before we snuff them out.

Khan looked around the room and saw the excitement in their eyes. These rebels may have had success, but they hadn't been up against an organized, trained army such as the one he brought. His men were battle-hardened and loyal to Allah. With His blessing, they will have a quick victory and destroy the infidels. Perhaps a higher blessing was in store for him with the capture of their leader and a proper beheading.

CHAPTER 35

JACKSON MICHIGAN

Reese pulled into the eight-stall garage where Bill Taylor had been using to service all the vehicles while in Jackson. It was also the staging area for the evacuation of citizens across the border. He and Nate were the car experts, but since Nate's injury, it fell upon Taylor and a couple of other mechanics to take care of all the vehicles.

This afternoon's visits to the border revealed troubling signs the Jijis were going to attack soon. Scar received other reports of meetings being held by a commander where a map had been spotted.

This raised alarm bells in his head, so he decided to have Bassett beef up security tonight. He didn't want to take any chances especially since they hadn't had any success since Winters left. The fact they were moving citizens across the border was not lost on him. The last thing they needed was to fail at something they had been doing many times.

They spotted Badger at a workshop bench drinking a bottle of water.

He waved and then came over to them.

"How's my honey badger?" asked Taylor referring to their on-going joke about how there can only be one honey badger.

"Am I officially a honey badger now?" asked Reese as she hopped out of the truck.

"Honey, you've always been a badger…consider yourself a honey badger in training."

"Oh, I am on my way. I'm so excited," said Reese as she gave Taylor a hug.

Taylor looked at the truck up and down. "Did you actually wash this thing?"

"Yeeess," said Reese in a defensive tone.

"Hmph. Well, anyway, I got your new tires right here."

"And rims?" asked Reese looking at the new wheels.

"Yep. Don't have the time or energy to take the tires off the rims, so you get new ones."

"I love 'em."

"Good, cause you're gonna put them on.

"I've never changed a tire before."

"I figured that. But every girl needs to know how to change a tire."

"Did you teach your daughters?"

"Damn right I did. Hell, they can change their own oil too."

Reese's grin grew excited since she never had a father around to show her anything mechanical or anything else for that matter.

"C'mon, we're going to do it with the jack that comes with the truck, so you know how to use one of those as well."

Taylor grabbed the bottle jack from the back seat. She nodded each time he gave her the next set of instructions. She first loosened up the nuts by stomping on the lug wrench with her foot before jacking the truck up. By the time she finished the second wheel, she was able to do the last two without his assistance.

Scar watched and was impressed she didn't complain about her injured leg even though she struggled at times to lift the wheel onto the hub. He also was impressed the way Badger handled her with kid gloves. Something he didn't do with many other people.

He didn't talk about his family and Scar didn't even know he had daughters until Reese had just mentioned them. The way he got along with her, it was apparent he had raised daughters and not sons.

Taylor stood by Scar. She'll never get stranded with a flat."

"No, she won't," responded Scar.

"So, what's the latest?" asked Taylor. "Nordell came by earlier and said we're taking out a convoy."

"Yeah, I wanna lighten the load on the food supply."

"Good idea. I figure with the short-buses he's bringing over and the gas we siphoned, we can do right around a hundred people."

Scar nodded with a troubled expression.

"What's wrong?"

"There seems to be activity around the borders. I think the Jijis are up to something."

Taylor raised an eyebrow. "Think they're getting ready to attack?"

"They can't wait forever."

Taylor scoffed. "Let them. I'm sick of waiting around for them anyway."

"Yeah, I hear ya. I'm about tired of this myself."

"Well, I wouldn't worry about the convoy. They won't fight us at night anyway."

Scar gave him a dubious look. "There's a first for everything.

"Yeah, I suppose so."

"Either way, I'll send Meeks and Amber over to Hanover Road and reconnoiter the area before we move them across."

"What about Bassett and Burns?"

"They're headed out early in the morning to scout out the supply line again."

"Good luck on that."

Scar let out a sigh frustrated with that quest.

Reese stood up holding the tire iron. "All done."

"Let me check those lug nuts," said Taylor grabbing the tire iron. He squatted down to tighten them. He could barely move each one a quarter turn. "Not bad, honey."

"I can still give a good kick," beamed Reese.

"Yeah, I can see that," said Taylor as he picked up the front wheels and threw them in the back of the pickup. "Now you got a couple of spares. They still got good tread on them." Taylor then grabbed a five-gallon gas can and poured it into her tank topping it off.

Reese wrapped her arms around Taylor. "Thanks so much."

"Your welcome, kiddo. You coming out tonight?"

"No, I promised Nate I'd hang out with him and Elliott."

"You're not playing poker with them, are ya?"

"Yes, we are."

"Well, you just be careful around that Nate."

"Don't worry. We're just playing with chips."

"Alright," said Taylor squinting his eyes.

"I'll see ya in a couple of hours," said Scar getting back into the old Chevy.

Taylor nodded and waved to them as Reese backed the truck out of the big garage. She cracked a mischievous grin before slamming it into drive and squealing the tires.

"I had to break them in," she said with a coy look.

"But of course you did," chuckled Scar.

Reese sped down the road and glanced over to see Scar smiling. "What?"

"I didn't say anything."

"You're smiling about something. You care to share?"

"I was just thinking that I've never seen Badger treat anyone better than you. He's usually quite the grouch."

"Oh, he's harmless. He's like a squishy marshmallow."

Scar let out a belly laugh. "A marshmallow, huh?"

"A squishy marshmallow," Reese corrected him.

"Aren't all marshmallows squishy?"

Reese thought for a moment. "Not if they're stale."

"Well, that would fit him perfectly," Scar quickly responded.

"Okay. That, that was a good one," said Reese holding out a closed fist and opening it to drop an imaginary microphone.

Scar laughed proudly at his retort. Still, he wouldn't say anything to anyone as he didn't want to ruin Badger's reputation. He liked having that attitude around the guys because it helped keep some of the newer guys stay in line.

Since being in Jackson, they'd picked up quite a number of them, and they didn't have too much history with them yet. They lacked discipline and training and didn't always listen.

Once, they were done with Jackson, he'd take them up to Winnipeg and get them trained. They also needed to get up there to get more supplies. Thankfully, they still had plenty of ammo but could use more RPG's and whatever else Nordell wanted. He had mentioned the other day while they were in Sarnia he had some weapons in mind that would make their job easier.

CHAPTER 36

WINNIPEG

The Canadian supply sergeant grabbed the chrome handle on the back of the twenty-six-foot box truck and jumped on the bumper to pull the door down. He then handed Winters a list of supplies each of the three vehicles contained. The former rental moving trucks were loaded with food, medicine, weapons, ammo, and fuel.

"Here you go, Captain," said Sergeant Armstrong. "I've even added a few surprises for ya."

"Oh?"

"You'll have to wait till you get back though," said Armstrong who turned to the girls. "And I've got some gifts for you girls as well."

"Us? Gifts?" asked Laney.

"Can't let you girls leave here without a little something," said Armstrong as he walked over to a table that had a couple of backpacks sitting on it. He handed each girl a black backpack. "We didn't have pink, but they're filled with toiletries and such."

"Oh my God, I love it," said Laney. "Thank you."

"I love black," said the black spiky haired Collette. "Thank you so much."

"I've got some other things in there as well like some granola bars and chocolate, a first aid kit, a tactical knife."

The girls started squealing as they began pulling items out of the bag as if it was Christmas morning. In many ways, it was since they hadn't even seen some of these things in a long time.

Armstrong saddled up next to Winters. "I've got a couple of other things to give them as well."

Winters gave him a sideways glance.

"It just doesn't sit well with me what these girls went through," said Armstrong.

"Nor me, Sergeant."

"Besides the M4s we've already given them, I've got a couple of Glock 17's to give them and their own night vision goggles."

"Oh?" asked a surprised Winters. He had hoped to get more goggles but wasn't able to because of a delayed shipment to the base.

"Word got around the base what these girls went through, and a couple of the guys…let's just say…found a couple of pairs currently not being used."

"They'll love 'em."

"No sense letting someone sneak up on them at night."

The girls plowed through their bags setting everything out on the table and continued to squeal as they emptied the contents.

"Thank you so much," said both girls as they hopped over to give him a hug.

"I've got two more things to give you," said Armstrong.

The girls looked at each other wide-eyed as he reached into a cabinet and pulled two Glocks 17's out, each in a black nylon holster.

"Yes, I love it," said Laney as she took the magazine out of the pistol.

Armstrong pulled out some loaded spare magazines and said, "One more thing." He handed each girl a pair of ATN PS-15-WPT NightVision goggles.

The girls' mouths went slack-jawed as they took hold of the goggles knowing how special they were.

"Do me a favor," said Armstrong as he looked around. "Put those in your bags and don't let anyone know that you have those. Okay?"

"Oh, we won't say a word," said Collette. "Thank you so much."

"I put some solar chargers in there so you can charge the batteries," said Armstrong who then turned to Winters. "I got a little something here for you too." He pulled out another nylon holster with a Glock 17 pistol and a Silencerco Osprey suppressor in a side pouch. "There's ten of these in the back of one of those trucks, but I wanted to give you this one."

Winters grinned at his new weapon. "We've needed suppressors."

Armstrong took the weapon and threaded the suppressor onto the barrel of the Glock before giving him instructions.

"I can't thank you enough," said Winters.

While the girls were repacking their bags, Winters took his jacket off and strapped on the new holster. He took the suppressor off and slipped it into the side pouch. He liked the fit and gave Armstrong a nod of approval.

He then looked inside the cabs of the three trucks. Only one had a bench seat, and he told the girls to put their bags in that one.

Afterwards, Winters got the girls back to the infirmary to say goodbye to everyone. He didn't look forward to it because goodbyes were never easy. Thankfully, Sadie has a new friend, who will make the goodbye easier than usual, at least he hoped.

They reached Finley's room, and everyone stopped talking when they walked inside.

"It's time?" asked Sadie.

"Afraid so, kiddo," said Winters.

She got up and wrapped her arms around Winters' waist as he expected she would. He soaked in all that she had to offer, even more so now that Cara was dead. She had become his surrogate daughter, and he cherished the special bond they shared.

He fought to control his own tears as hers began to run down the sides of her face. This started the tear fest as all the girls started crying as they said their goodbyes to each other. Even, Collette's mom shed tears as she hugged her daughter

Winters leaned down to give Finley a hug. "I'll be seeing ya."

"You promise?"

"Absolutely. I want to see what those scars are gonna look like."

"Oh me too! I mean, like, they're gonna be so badass looking, I can't wait to, like, watch 'em heal up…"

Winters let out a chuckle as she started talking a mile a minute again.

She realized what she was doing and put her hand to her mouth. "I'm doing it again."

Winters nodded.

"Oh, Cole, here's all my cards," said Sadie as she handed him a large envelope stuffed with homemade cards.

"I'll be sure to give them to everyone."

It took another five minutes before he was able to pull Laney and Collette out of the room and back to the garage. It was just getting dark, and he wanted to be on the road sooner than later. It was going to be a long night driving the five hundred miles to Iowa, which he expected to reach by morning.

They would be driving with their headlights on, which wouldn't be a problem. All the times Winters had made this trip, they never once ran into anyone on the road, but still, their cargo was valuable, and he needed to be wary of hijackers.

Winters entered the garage and nodded to Armstrong who was still there keeping an eye on the trucks, as he was responsible for them until they left the premises.

"Girls, I got your rifles in the truck," said Armstrong. "Remember, you never leave 'em behind. Always be armed and never hesitate. Understand?"

"We won't forget," they both responded as they gave him a final hug.

"Your weapons are loaded so just remember your training, and you'll be fine."

The girls got into the cab, and Armstrong shut the door. He walked over to Winters who was standing in front of the truck. "They'll be alright, then?"

"They will now, thanks to you."

"Got two of my own, you know, about their age too. I just can't imagine it."

"Yeah, well, I couldn't either. But they're strong."

"Still, they're just kids."

Winters didn't respond. He was right they were just kids but had been forced to grow up in a hurry. No longer would they be able to enjoy their lives without a jaded attitude, which will affect everything they do for the rest of their lives.

Winters let out a silent sigh thinking about all the young lives this war has affected. The sad reality of war is that no one escapes it. A door opening in the back snapped Winters out of his thoughts as his three new recruits entered the garage.

"We all ready to go?" asked Butler.

"Just waiting for you guys," said Winters.

The third volunteer approached Winters and stuck out his hand. "I'm Pete Cochran. Sorry, we haven't met yet."

"Glad to have you aboard," said Winters.

"Which truck is mine?" asked Cochran.

"Well, I'm taking the first one so you guys can decide on the other two," said Winters.

"Where are the girls?" asked Fowler.

"Sitting in my truck," said Winters remembering what Murphy had said to him.

"They'll be driving with you then?" asked Fowler.

"It's got a bench seat so yes, of course."

"Okay, cool," said Fowler as he turned to Cochran. "I got dibs on driving."

Cochran shrugged his shoulders.

Winters cleared this throat. "So, listen up guys. I've done this route several times and have never had any problems so we'll be running with our headlights on."

"Is that wise? Shouldn't we have some kind of night-vision wear?" asked Butler.

"I'm afraid that's not an option. But, like I said, we'll be fine," said Winters. "We should make Iowa by early morning, and we'll rest up there before we continue to Jackson. Any questions?"

Everyone shook their heads, so Winters jumped into his truck and looked at the girls. "We ready?"

"We're good, Cole," said Laney who sat in the middle.

"Alright, well let's get this show on the road," said Winters as he started the truck. He saluted Sergeant Armstrong as he pulled out of the garage.

CHAPTER 37

JACKSON MICHIGAN

Reese decided to check on Amber before she left with Meeks for the night. She hadn't seen her since this morning and wanted to know how she was holding up after last night's incident. She hoped this morning's crying session did the trick but wasn't so sure. Amber was smart and stronger than she knew, but still, anytime you have an up-close fight it affects you, especially if they're trying to rape you.

She knocked on her door and heard her say it was open. Reese pushed the door open and found her checking her backpack.

"Hey, how's it going?" asked Reese as she went in for a hug.

Amber squeezed her hard. "Good, good. Just huh, getting ready for tonight."

"You doing okay, then?"

Amber moved her bag and sat down on the bed. "I am. Cried a couple more times, but I think I got it out of my system."

Reese sat next to her. "Don't be surprised if it sneaks back up on ya."

Amber turned to her and nodded. "I won't but like I said, I think I'm good."

"Glad to hear it. Did you go see Doctor Lunsford?"

"I did. Everything is good. No concussion to worry about. I took another Motrin and a long nap. What about you? What have you been up to?"

"Oh, I was out with Scar. We washed my baby and then checked in on the borders."

"Wait, what? Your baby?" Amber asked in a confused tone. "That…that truck?"

"Yes, my truck."

"You washed it?"

Reese raised her palms up. "Yes. Why does everyone have the same response?"

"Cause it's a piece of junk, sweetie," said Amber putting a hand on Reese's shoulder.

"Well, that may be, but she's my piece of junk now and besides, I first made-out with Cole in it."

"Ooooh, okay. I get that now."

And may I say, that it looks pretty darn good too. Badger even put some new tires on it."

"Now that, I understand," snickered Amber.

"Yeah…it kinda needed them," said Reese looking up at the ceiling embarrassed.

"Well, I'm glad to see you've got that taken care of. So, Nate tells me you're going to hang out with him and Elliott tonight."

"Yep. Gonna make it a game night."

"Good. Poor guys are getting frustrated they can't help, especially Nate. He's like that Tasmania devil cartoon guy wanting to destroy something."

"A knock came on the door, and Amber got up to open it. "Hey,

Meeks."

"You ready?" he asked.

"Just about. Just chatting with Reese."

"Reese?" asked Meeks as he walked into the room. "I heard you washed that beast of yours today."

Amber put a hand to her mouth to hide her laughter as Reese threw up her hands in frustration.

"Alright, I'm done," she said as she got up. "I'm out of here."

"What? What did I say?" asked Meeks.

"Everyone's been kinda making fun of her for washing that truck," said Amber putting her arm around Reese's shoulder.

"Well, that's because it's a piece of junk," joked Meeks.

"Yes, I know. Ha-ha," said Reese crossing her arms over her chest.

"Oh, c'mon now, Pieces. If we didn't love ya, we wouldn't be razzing ya."

Reese tilted her head to the side and drummed her fingers on her arm.

Meeks stared her down in an attempt to break her knowing full well that she was pretending to be mad. He'd been married long enough to recognize that look she was giving him. He broke out in a disarming smile, which finally did the trick.

She let out a scoff. "Boys. You guys suck, you know that?"

"Yep. We do. And I'm a juvenile at heart."

"Duh."

"Come here," said Meeks putting his arms out and stepping forward to hug her. "You know we're big kidders around here, but that still doesn't negate the fact that the truck is a junker."

Reese thought for a moment. "Yeah, I got nothing."

"Of course you don't," said Meeks letting her go. "But it is your junker, so we'll leave it at that."

"Thank you. Now, if you'll excuse me, I have a date with two other boys."

"Nate and Elliott?" asked Meeks.

Reese nodded.

"Cool. They could use the company," said Meeks.

"You guys be careful."

"We will," said Amber as she gave Reese another hug.

"You want me to wait up for ya?"

"No need. You look tired already," said Amber as she ran her hands down the sides of Reese's head.

"Yeah, I am," said Reese who then turned and walked out into the hallway. She let out chuckle thinking of Meeks. She wasn't mad at him at all, she was madder at herself for not having a good retort for him. Usually, she could keep up with him, but couldn't think of one because the truck was a piece of junk.

She turned the corner to Elliott's room figuring they would make fun of her as well. She stopped at the door to try to think of something but still didn't have anything. So, she thought the best defense was a good offense and would have to bring it up first. She tapped on the door before turning the knob. Inside, Nate was sitting in a chair next to Elliott's bed.

"Before you guys say anything, yes, I'm an idiot because I washed that piece of junk I've been driving around."

Nate turned to Elliott and then turned back to her. "I'm sorry, you did what?"

Reese groaned knowing she just busted herself out for nothing. She just couldn't win today.

CHAPTER 38

ON THE ROAD TO SABINE IOWA

The drive back to Iowa was going smoothly, and Winters was enjoying the girl's company. They'd been on the road for a few hours, and they chatted about everything and nothing like teen girls are want to do. He would miss them as he had grown close to them in only three days. It was easy to bond with people when you share life or death experiences. All three girls had impressed the hell out of him. Despite living through a nightmare, they had kept positive attitudes.

Of course, not all the girls involved were like this, but from what Laney and Collette had told him, everyone supported each other emotionally. They would get together and give each other pep talks about surviving their ordeal. What a fantastic thing it is to help your fellow man. Not only did it help receiving the pep talks, but also, it was just as helpful if not more to give them. Sharing themselves spiritually was their greatest strength, and it had kept them going.

Helping someone was always good for the soul. Winters knew this first hand, as it was what had been keeping him going these last few months. Especially this week when he needed it the most, he was able to feed off that diet of helping his fellow man to help fight off his own insanity. Winters took a deep breath and glanced at the girls he had the good fortune of meeting. Had they not met, he had no doubt he'd still be battling Mister Hyde and going insane.

"Whatcha thinking about, Cole?" asked Laney.

"Oh, nothing."

"Excuse me, but I can see it on you. You're, like, in deep thought."

Winters scrunched his face at her perceptiveness.

"Come on," said Collette, "Do I need to keep reminding you of road rules?"

Winters took another deep breath. "I was just thinking how fortunate I was to meet you girls and how much I'll miss you."

"Ohhh," said Laney putting her arm around his. "You're gonna make me cry."

"Me too," said Collette. "Oh, dang it, here they come."

"We're going to miss you too. I mean, like, how will we ever be able to thank you?" asked Laney.

"That's the thing, you'll never need to. Your plight was my salvation. It is what saved me. So, it's me that should be thanking you. You're the ones who were living in a nightmare. I just happened by and was able to do something about it."

"Then we all, like, saved each other," said Laney as she squeezed his arm again.

Winters looked at her. "That we did, girls. That we did."

"You'll see us again though, won't ya? You'll come back home, right?" asked Collette.

"I will now."

"So, we'll have a big party when you get back," said Collette.

"Yeah, that'd be awesome," said Laney.

"Listen, I hate to break this moment, but I have to go," said Collette.

"Yeah, me too."

Winters shook his head because they were literally out in the middle of the prairie with very little foliage. He looked to the right and saw they were driving next to railroad tracks. He began coasting before coming to a full stop. He didn't bother pulling over to the side since they were the only ones on the road.

"Where can we go?" asked Collette.

"Just over that hill are railroad tracks."

"How can you tell?" asked Laney.

"I've been on this road many times."

Both girls grabbed their new Colt M4 rifles as they jumped out of the truck.

"I'll escort you guys," said Winters bearing in mind Murphy's comment about Fowler.

"You don't need too."

"I insist, so wait while I go tell 'em what we're doing," said Winters not caring if he sounded like an overprotected parent.

He walked back and gave a head nod through the glare of the headlights before coming to the driver's side window. "Hey, just taking a quick pee break."

"No problem, Captain. We'll just stretch our legs out," said Fowler who then turned to his friend with raised eyebrows. They'd been waiting for an easy opportunity to take the trucks and finally had the chance.

Winters powered his night-vision goggles while he walked back over to the girls. "Alright let's go."

Laney was the first to hit the tall grass that covered the small hill and slipped. "Ah, it's wet."

"Careful girls," said Winters who stayed behind them as they climbed the small hill.

They reached the top, crossed over the railroad tracks, and started down the other side toward a set of trees. Winters stopped halfway down and scanned the area before the girls reached the trees. He kept looking around for any kind of movement. A couple of minutes later, he realized he needed to go as well. He moved over to the left and just as the girls broke out of the trees to start back up the hill.

"You coming, Cole?" asked Laney.

"Give me a minute," replied Winters.

"Alright guys, this is it," said Butler.

"We wait," said Fowler.

"Wait for what?" asked Butler.

"I want those girls," said Fowler.

"To hell with the girls. We got the trucks free and clear right now, so let's just go," argued Butler. "I don't really care about the girls."

"Yeah, but I do," said Fowler as he turned to Cochran. "You're with me aren't cha?

"They are cute."

"We'll just shoot Winters," said Fowler.

Butler shook his head. "Did you not see what the girls were carrying?"

"Oh please," said Fowler in a dismissive tone.

"I told you I didn't want to get into a gunfight with this guy. Besides, he has night-vision goggles on, so we can't very well sneak up on him. Hell, we can barely see twenty feet."

"Twenty feet's all I need," said Fowler. "I'll get up on the hill, and if I think it's good, then we'll take the girls. If not then we'll drive off."

"Fine. Go for it," relented Butler.

Fowler scooted across the road and up the hill. He squatted down and let his eyes adjust from the glare of the headlights. Before too long, he heard the girls coming, and one of them turn to yell at Winters. Fowler's heart pounded in his chest when he heard Winters was still down the hill. He let the girls walk past him. He gave them a few strides before he got in behind them. As they got closer to the lead truck, they came in view of the headlights. Fowler pulled a knife out and rushed at the girls just as they came to the door.

He pushed Laney into the door, wrapped his arm around her and put the knife to her throat. "Either one of you scream, and I'll slice her throat."

Laney's skin turned clammy as the blade cut a layer of skin. She looked at Collette whose eyes were bulging.

"Drop your weapon and get in the truck," said Fowler as he slid Laney's rifle off her back. "Do it now. If you don't hurry, I'll have to kill Winters."

Collette nodded and dropped her weapon before hopping into the truck.

"Slide over and drive," ordered Fowler as he pushed Laney into the truck.

Cochran rushed over, grabbed both rifles, and shut the door after Fowler climbed in. He then ran back to his truck and watched Butler pull away first. He then waited for Fowler to go before falling in behind them.

CHAPTER 39

An explosion of energy burst through Winters as he saw the trucks begin to leave. He raced down the hill as he swung his rifle off his back. He lifted it up and was about to shoot but thought better of it. He wasn't sure which one was carrying the fuel and didn't want to blow it up. Besides, he saw a better way once he hit the asphalt. These trucks were loaded down with supplies and not the fastest off the line, which gave him one small chance. He dug deep and kicked his legs as fast as he could.

Thankfully, he was in much better shape these days and silently thanked the Canadians for training him. He had lost weight over the last few months and had built up his endurance.

He could see the chrome handle on the back of the truck as he closed in on it. His weapon bounced off his chest with every stride making him tug on the strap. He lifted his right arm to reach for the handle. The stinging exhaust from the muffler choked his breathing as he stretched his arm to grab the handle. The cold metal was reassuring as he pulled himself onto the bumper, which was six inches wide giving him plenty of room to stand on.

He began cursing at himself for being duped by these three guys. Murphy had been right about the creepy vibe he had detected. Winters shook his head at the negative thoughts because there was no way of knowing these guys had ulterior motives. Bringing up Taylor as a reference was what sold him on their trustworthiness.

He then began counting his blessings they decided not to have a gun battle. No telling who might have been killed in a shootout. He suspected the girls were doing as they were told and hopefully were keeping their minds clear. No doubt, these guys would keep them alive, which gave him the time he needed to kill the bastards.

The wind kicked around Winters as he kept a vice-like grip tight on the chrome handle. He thought about pulling the cargo door open and crawling in but decided to wait. They weren't but ten miles away from Detroit Lakes and the first major intersection. A turn meant they would have to slow this heavy beast down before taking it. If this happened, then he would rush the cab and climb in.

He gave his new Glock 17 a confident pat. His new toy would come in handy. Not only would the suppressor tone down the report but it would also help hide the muzzle flash.

The anticipation of which direction they would head grew as the truck began to slow down. They were making a turn but which way? If they went right, he would need to come in on the driver's side to keep hidden from view from the other two trucks.

Was that window open? The air conditioner wasn't working in the truck he drove.

He rocked back and forth ready to pounce on either side. It didn't matter to him which side. If the door were locked, he'd shoot through the window. The fully loaded truck was coming to a complete stop. He peered through his goggles to the right side and saw nothing but could hear the engines roar in the dead air. They were going left.

He let go of the handle and stepped off the bumper. He pulled out the suppressor and threaded it on the Glock as he peered over to the left side to see Butler driving the first truck. He kept watching and saw Collette driving the middle one. Good to know. He racked the slide on the Glock before sweeping around to the passenger side. He grabbed the door handle as the truck started to move and found it unlocked. He jumped inside pointing his pistol. Cochran's eyes grew wide knowing he was in trouble.

"Keep driving," yelled Winters.

Cochran didn't respond but continued with the turn.

"So, where are we headed?"

"Duluth I think."

"You don't know?"

"I swear I don't."

"Got a buyer for this stuff do ya?"

"Butler does."

"Who are they?"

"I'm not sure."

Winters shook his head. "You don't know much do ya?"

"I swear I don't know them. It's some gang. Butler's dealt with them before. Scary bunch is all I know."

Winters leaned back in the seat. He knew gangs were roaming around and paid tribute to the National Cops. They had never run into them but knew they were some in Ohio where a booming sex trade was developing. He had no doubt that's where Laney and Collette would be taken and sold off.

"When were you meeting them?"

"As soon as we arrive we're gonna go find 'em."

"Anything else I should know?"

"No, sir."

Winters scoffed at the man's newfound respect. "Do want to live?"

"Yes, sir."

"Well, it's your lucky night," said Winters as he turned and placed his legs between the bucket seats. "Open the door and jump."

"What?"

"You heard me," said Winters as he pointed the gun at his head. "Now, either jump or take a bullet, it doesn't matter to me."

Cochran hesitated before opening the door.

"Remember to roll," said Winters as he took control of the steering wheel and shoved him out the door.

Winters looked in the mirror and watched him hit the ground. He bounced on the road rather than roll. Idiot. Not that he cared, but he didn't feel like shooting him. He didn't want it on his mind because he had more important things to think about like what his next move was. These trucks have fifty-gallon fuel tanks and get about ten miles to the gallon. This was plenty to make it to Duluth without stopping. He could only hope they would pull over to take a break.

CHAPTER 40

ON MN 34 PAST DETROIT LAKES

The suspense in the cab was gut-wrenching as Collette dropped a hand from the steering wheel and gave Laney a reassuring pat on the leg. Laney's muscles tightened, and she took some deep breaths to calm down remembering what Cole said about never panicking. The reminder helped calm her nerves down enough to better access the situation.

First off, these guys were not going to kill them, granted, they were going to rape them, but then, what's new? So, they had a chance at some point to escape. The best way to enhance that opportunity was to cooperate. It would throw them off balance if they gladly had sex with them. This was easy since they had been doing that for the last six months. Once they had their trust, they could make their move.

She started gaining confidence, which then made the situation transparent. They had guns in their backpacks. Thank you, Sergeant Armstrong.

Both bags sat on the floor, each with a Glock sitting snug on top. She took another deep breath to keep the nerves in check. She always jumped into the fray because of a compulsion problem. This was not a good trait right now. That wasn't how Cole operated. When he was getting ready to climb in her bedroom window, he asked if there were any creaks on the floor. That was the type of thinking this predicament demanded. She needed to come up with an excuse to dig into her bag without arousing suspicion. It had to be something so innocent that Fowler wouldn't give it a second thought.

Then the perfect opportunity arose.

"You know it's a long way to Duluth and I need to relax," said Fowler. "Why don't you get over here and help me relax."

Laney rolled her eyes knowing exactly what he wanted. "Well, it wasn't innocent, but it's a perfect distraction," she thought.

"What did you have in mind?" asked Laney.

"Oh, I think you know what I want. Hell, you're both prostitutes, so I don't think I need to spell it out."

Collette squeezed Laney's sweaty hand as she turned to Fowler and let out a dramatic sigh. "Fine. Get it out."

"Now that's more like it," said Fowler as he unzipped his pants.

Laney was grateful it was dark in the cab and wouldn't have to look at it. She'd seen too many over the past few months and wanted to forget them. She started to move down to the floor when he ordered her to just lean over to him.

"Honey, who's the professional here? Let me get situated and I will rock your world."

Fowler laughed. "Well, alright then."

Laney let out a quiet scoff at his stupidity. Fighting to remain calm, she reached for her bag and pretended to be moving it out of the way while unzipping it.

She grabbed the cold polymer grip of the Glock, which instilled confidence even as her racing heart increased ten-fold. Coughing loudly hid the sound of the slide racking, which didn't take much effort despite the sweaty hands.

Laney placed a hand on his bare thigh and said, "Okay, I think we're all set, so spread your legs,"

"Come on already," demanded Fowler.

Lifting the pistol Laney's face grimaced knowing she had only one chance. There would be no hesitation and no regrets.

She shoved the pistol into his gut and squeezed the trigger. The report exploded in the enclosed cab. Collette jumped as Fowler hollered in pain. He wasn't dead yet.

Laney squeezed the trigger again and yelled, "Die you son-of-a-bitch."

Fowler stopped moving as blood began to spill down his stomach.

"Friggin bastard," yelled Collette.

Laney moved back up on the bench seat shaking because of her super-hyped nerves. "Prostitutes my ass."

"Oh, my ears are ringing," yelled Collette.

"What? I can't hear you."

Collette nodded and pointed to her ears.

The closed windows kept the loud gunfire inside the cab, and it took a few minutes before they were able to understand each other.

"Damn, I so knew you were gonna go for your Glock."

"Stupid idiot," said Laney between hurried breaths trying to calm down while still fidgeting in her seat.

Collette handed her a bottle of water and Laney gulped the water spilling some down her shirt. She looked over at Fowler and nodded in satisfaction.

"So, now what?" asked Collette.

"We're gonna take out the one behind us and go back for Cole."

"How do you wanna do this?"

"We could slow down a little at a time and, like, let the one in front get ahead of us," said Laney.

"Then stop and rush the one in back of us," finished Collette.

"Ya. Whaddya think?"

"I like it. Get my gun out," said Collette.

Laney reached into Collette's bag and pulled the Glock out. She also grabbed some granola bars needing to reenergize. The power bars Cole had given them the other night did the trick, and it was most needed right now. She tore the wrapper off before handing it to Collette.

"Oh, this so good," said Collette between bites.

"Oh, my God, yes."

So far, the girls had it handled, but the one behind them would be more difficult. They needed to run on either side of that truck and open fire without hesitation.

Collette began slowing the truck down. Over the next ten minutes, little by little, the one in front of them got further ahead, and then it disappeared around a bend in the road. They looked at each other and nodded.

"I'll go first," said Laney. "Give me, like, a second to climb over this idiot. Remember, run in and don't hesitate."

"Okay. Got it. You ready?"

"Do it."

Collette pressed down on the brake as Laney climbed over the corpse before they came to a stop. Laney opened the door and jumped to the ground holding the Glock with one hand as she raced towards the back unaware she was opening fire on Cole Winters.

CHAPTER 41

ALEXANDRIA VIRGINIA

A nervous Green was driving behind Stormy as she headed to one of the storage units he had rented. They had just picked up her white BMW and weren't too far away from their destination. They had waited until it got dark and the mall was just closing as they pulled out among all the other traffic blending in with all the other cars and keeping to the speed limit.

"Just a couple of more miles," Green said aloud.

He had taken the rest of the day off and stayed with Stormy at home. Green let out a small laugh at his mom. He thought she was even more excited about having a girl in his life than he was. Of course, she wanted grandchildren like anyone else but had to wait. She was used to waiting on a military man since she had been married to one.

Green's nerves subsided as they pulled into the self-storage lot. He had chosen this place because it was a Mom-and-Pop operation on a quiet road without a lot of traffic. It didn't have any staff workers after hours, and you used a passkey to open the gate.

Driving the lanes between the rows of buildings, he came to his two units that were side by side where he had another vehicle stashed here. He would take it tonight because of the phony tags.

He wasn't sure about this artist they were meeting, and he would take all of the precautions he could. It included using a fake name tonight and dressing as casual as he could, which included wearing a ball cap. It seemed silly, but he tended to dress conservatively and needed to dress down. So blue jeans, a t-shirt, and ball cap was the way to go. It was dangerous to meet new people who were going to help you bring down the government. You never knew if they would turn you in or if caught rat you out. It was one thing he already knew Stormy, but he couldn't allow anyone to be able to identify him.

He got out to open the garage door. She backed her BMW into the empty one as Green drove the spare car out. It was an older Toyota Camry, which was as dependable as you could get. It was one of his requirements when he purchased these vehicles. He didn't need any of them to break down on him while on an operation.

He then backed his newer Toyota Camry inside. Stormy stood off to the side while he shut both garage doors and padlocked them.

He shoveled around the passenger side and opened her door.

"Why thank you."

Green received a kiss for his efforts. He could get used to this.

"So, this place we're going to, does he live there?"

"Yes."

"Does he have any roommates?"

"No. At least I don't think so."

"Listen, it's important that he doesn't know who I am."

"I know…I know. Oh, and I've decided on a new name for you."

"Oh? I thought that…"

"No. I got something much cooler than the Bob Smith you came up with. I mean, c'mon, Bob Smith."

Green turned to her in anticipation.

"I'm dubbing you Rick Case."

"Rick Case, huh?"

"Yep. Whaddya say, Rick?" asked a smiling Stormy.

"I like it.

"So, where are we headed?" asked Green wanting to refocus."

"It's down on New York Ave in Ivy City."

Green winced at hearing the location. It wasn't in a great neighborhood, but artists were typically attracted to those areas because of the cheap rent.

"What's wrong?"

"Nothing. It's a bit on the seedy side."

"Good. The seedier, the better to keep the cops away."

Green liked her thinking. The more remote they were, the better. Especially, now that there was an arrest warrant for Stormy. It was dicey enough to be out here with her, to begin with. He would have to see about getting her a fake id or passport. His friend Sam could probably help with it. He had been the one to get all the counterfeit documents and tags for his new vehicles.

The drive to the artist place didn't take too long, and Green parked in front of a small building that was jammed in between two larger ones. It was on the fringe of one of D.C.'s more inhospitable neighborhoods. The area was strewn with garbage. A shopping cart with a broken wheel was abandoned next to a dirty mattress. None of the streetlights weren't working, and it was difficult to see anything. It was a perfect place to come to. No cops in their right minds would bother to come down here unless it was to pick up a dead body.

"What's his name?" asked Green as he turned the car off.

"Julio Vasquez. He's like early-twenties."

They got out and banged on the front door of the windowless façade. It took a few moments before Julio answered.

"Stormy!" he said as he gave her a big hug. Julio stood about five-six and sported mid-length hair with a shadow of a beard he desperately tried to grow. His smile was infectious as he reached out to shake Green's hand.

"This is Rick, Rick Case," said Stormy.

"Pleasure to meet you, sir," said Julio.

"The pleasure is all mine," said Green.

"Come in, come in," said Vasquez pulling the door open.

It was an open-air type of interior with a workbench off to one side with carpenter tools lying about. An artist easel stood next to a table with various tubes of paint and brushes. A copying machine sat adjacent to it. In the very back was a closed off area where Vasquez slept.

"I've been anxiously waiting for you guys. I've got some great ideas that I've already put together."

"Oh?" asked Stormy.

"Yeah, man. I got real excited when you told me what you had in mind and why."

Green looked at Stormy wondering exactly how much she'd told him. Not that he was too worried about this young man. He had a way about him that immediately put you at ease.

Vasquez led them to table with rolled up tubes of paper lying on top. He grabbed a four-foot wide one and asked Stormy to hold the end. He then walked backward as he unrolled a six-foot caricature of Perozzi as a frail old man being held up by two bikini-clad, busty ladies, one of who was holding a colostomy bag.

Green's mouth dropped open.

"Oh my goodness," laughed Stormy. "That's friggin awesome."

Vasquez turned to Green. "You like it, Rick?"

"Wow! You are talented," grinned Green.

Vasquez rolled it up and grabbed another. This was of Perozzi as a puppet master holding the strings of the President as a marionette. Another painting showed Perozzi looming over the President and his Vice-President with the words "bought and paid for" on a receipt.

"Julio, these are fantastic," said Stormy. "Didn't I tell you this guy was good?"

"They're outstanding," said Green.

"I've got a ton of ideas and a few people to help me put them up."

Green shot him a concerned look.

Vasquez recognized it. "It's all good. Look, a lot of my artist friends have been changing their minds. You know, we thought things would be better with the government controlling everything, but they're worse. A lot worse. We got no freedom to say or paint what we want, and we're pissed off about it. It isn't right what they're doing, and it's time to change it. Artists can make a huge difference, and we're gonna paint this town and show them that."

"I'm glad to hear it, Julio," said Green pulling a wad of hundred dollar bills out of his jacket. "Will this be enough to get things rolling?"

Vasquez's eyes widened. "More than enough. I've got some supplies already, but this will buy us everything we're gonna need and then some."

"Take some and pay these friends of yours," said Green.

"Thank you," smiled Vasquez.

"When can you get started?"

"Oh, we're going out tonight. Got some bus stops to hit up, and these big ones are gonna be wheat-pasted up high. It'll take them at least a day to take 'em down."

"Okay. Now, I'm sure I don't need to tell you not to get caught.

"Oh, yeah. We've all done this type of thing before, so we know what we're doing."

"Just make sure your guys understand that if you get caught, they'll torture you for any info so they can round everyone up."

"We understand that."

Green and Stormy chatted with Julio for a few more minutes before leaving. Green was impressed with him and his enthusiasm. He was like a lot of people that thought the government was there to help but only found out later the harsh realities of total control. Thankfully, it wasn't too late to change things.

Green smiled because he had just hired some Shadow Patriots, though they didn't know it. There were thousands of potential members across the country and easily outnumbered the government. They just needed a spark, and with some luck, this art would help do that here in the district.

CHAPTER 42

ON MINNESOTA 34

After running to catch up with his stolen truck and taking out the driver, Winters liked his chances of rescuing the girls. As always, he would rely on the element of surprise. He had used this tactic to great effect over the past few months. It was how he was able to defeat larger forces with his much smaller army.

Up until an hour ago, all he could think about was getting back to Jackson and see his small army again. He hoped they would forgive him for taking off in the middle of the night. It wasn't his best moment, but at the time, he wasn't thinking clearly. He was confident Reese hadn't given up on him. She of all people knew what he was going through. He tapped his fingers on the steering wheel thinking about her and fantasized about what he would do when he saw her. He would grab onto her and kiss her regardless if anyone was around.

He was yanked out of his fantasy when he noticed a flash of light on the side mirror of the truck in front of him. He leaned forward when another flash happened.

"Those were gunshots," he said aloud to no one.

He let go of the gas pedal and backed off for a second, but then maintained his speed. Something has happened. Was it the girls? It was two shots. Did Fowler kill them? But Collette was driving. He slowed down some more to see if a body was going to tumble out of the truck. Did the girls kill him? His mind was racing trying to come up with an answer. Collette didn't jam on the brakes in sheer panic. She was driving as if nothing happened.

Over the next ten minutes, Winters' mind hadn't stopped thinking about what happened in that cab. However, as the lead truck slowly drove away from them, it dawned on him that Collette was slowing down a little bit at a time. Then it hit him. Fowler was dead.

At first, he nodded his head at how proud he was of the girls, but then he realized he was in trouble. His two innocent shadows were going to come after him thinking he was Cochran.

This was Laney's style. Impulsive, only this time she was thinking in advance. They let the lead truck get far ahead so he wouldn't see the muzzle flashes. No doubt, they'll charge in and shoot first then ask questions.

He let off the gas to put a little more space between them. His palms began to sweat when he saw the lead truck hit a curve in the road and disappear into the darkness. This was the perfect place, and they knew it.

He jammed on the brakes just a couple of seconds before Collette did. He had one option. He saw their brake lights just as he pulled the door handle. He jumped to the ground just as Laney came rushing in on the other side firing her pistol inside the cab. Winters tripped when he landed and fell into a full roll to the other side of the road.

Collette sprinted to the truck and fired her Glock through the windshield. The girls kept shooting while Winters tumbled into the tall grass. He tried to count the shots but lost track. He didn't dare yell out until he thought they emptied their magazines.

Finally, the shooting stopped.

Winters lifted his head and saw them looking confused.

He put his hands to his mouth and yelled. "Don't shoot girls. It's me. Cole."

Both turned in his direction with their pistols raised.

"Don't shoot me, girls," yelled Winters again. He got up and raised his hands high in the air. "See, it's me."

"Cole Winters!" yelled Laney.

Collette squealed.

They both charged in and threw their arms around him.

"You didn't think, I'd let these fools get away did ya?"

"Well, ya. That's why I killed Fowler," said Laney as she let go of him.

"We were, like, going to come back and get you," said Collette.

"Good going," said Winters.

"Oh damn, we, like, almost killed you," exclaimed Collette.

"Yes you did, but luckily, I figured it out just in the nick of time."

Oh, my God. Thank God you did," said Laney. "That would have sucked big-time."

"But, like, how did you get here?" asked Collette.

"As soon as I saw the trucks leaving, I hauled ass and was able to jump on the bumper. I got in the cab when we made that turn."

"Wow," said Collette.

"Look we need to get going, so Butler doesn't think anything is wrong," said Winters.

"We're going after him?" asked Collette.

"Damn right, I need that truck back."

Laney pumped her fist in the air. "Yes, I love it."

"Besides if we take off now, he might come looking for the trucks in Sabina."

They nodded in agreement.

"Is Fowler still in the cab?"

The girls nodded.

"Okay, let's get him out, and I need you guys to hurry. As soon as Butler stops, I'll come around and take him out. Okay?"

Winters pulled Fowler out of the truck and dragged him into the tall grass. He told Collette to go before slamming the door. They were out of Butler's sight too long, and he didn't want to miss an opportunity if he stopped to wait for them to catch up. It was imperative to take him out before they got to Duluth. No telling if he had people waiting for them.

Winters picked up speed and began to laugh as the wind blew through the holes in the windshield. There were three of them and had a nice tight grouping for someone running. Considering the tense moment, Collette's aim was damn good. Neither of them panicked and charged in without hesitation. That was an incredible moment for them. No longer were they innocent shadows but determined fighters.

He turned on the interior light and saw the bullet holes through the passenger door and a couple in the seat. He nodded in approval. Good thing he figured out what they were up to, otherwise, he'd be dead. That would have haunted them for the rest of their lives.

CHAPTER 43

Winters was behind Collette as they drove on US 2 and she was staying about a hundred feet behind Butler, who they were following. It didn't appear he had stopped to wait for them because it took quite awhile for them to catch up to him. They had been following him for over two hours and had already gone through Grand Rapids, Minnesota. They were closing in on Duluth, which was the last place Winters wanted to go with three trucks loaded with valuable supplies. People still lived there and were probably just as desperate as the rest of the Midwest. It would be too dangerous to show up with loaded trucks, two of which driven by teenaged girls.

Collette tried to signal Butler to stop, but he was either ignoring her or was aware it wasn't his friends. They could have had a coded signal and was leading him into a trap.

Winters pulled the map off the dash to decide on a red line they wouldn't go over, and if crossed then the third truck would be forfeited. Not knowing who was meeting Butler, it wasn't worth it to put themselves in danger. The problem was they weren't a lot of roads to take before they got to Duluth. There were only two decent options, one was State Road 73, which was coming up fast, and the other was State Road 33. He had decided on the latter giving Butler one more chance.

He ran his finger over to Wisconsin, which was just east of Duluth. They would be at the very top of the state with a straight shot into the UP of Michigan. This was ideal because it would be just less than three hundred miles across the UP and then another two hundred miles down the state to Jackson, Michigan.

It wasn't appealing to take these girls to a war zone, but driving back to Iowa before going to Jackson would make it a twelve hundred mile trip. Of course, the girls would do whatever he asked of them, so that wasn't the question. He just didn't want to get them involved, but at this point, it would be foolhardy to not keep going.

They flew by the State Road 73 exit and had just another twenty miles to try to get Butler to pull over. Deciding to get ahead of the girls, Winters swerved into the other lane and waved as he passed by them. Winters turned his lights off and on a few times to no avail and stuck to his red line decision to abandoned the third truck. The loss would hurt especially since it contains most of the food supplies.

The exit to State Road 33 was just a couple of miles away, and Winters let off the gas to put some distance between them but not enough to raise suspicions. Little by little, they were falling further behind. Winters would turn the headlights off before turning and then disappear into the night.

The overpass was just up ahead, and Winters let out a scowl when Butler's brake lights lit up the dark. He was slowing down to take the exit.

"Well, there goes that plan," thought Winters. They weren't going to Duluth after all. The third truck was back in play but so was his initial concern over meeting other people. The nearest town was Cloquet, Minnesota, which was five miles south. It was a small town and most likely deserted. There was nothing to do at this point but see where Butler would take them.

Ten minutes later, Butler was finally pulling over by taking a right into a parking lot in front of a closed down office building on the outskirts of Cloquet. The building measured a hundred and twenty feet and had an entrance in the middle. The parking lot in front of the building was only two lanes. One was for parking and the other as a right-a-way with an entrance and exit.

Winters took his time turning into the narrow lot and wanted to keep some distance between the trucks. Butler stopped after passing the entrance, so Winters parked at the end of the building. Collette smartly followed suit and stayed behind him.

Winters pulse quickened waiting for Butler to get out of the truck. Was this his place? Did he live here? Or was this Fowler's place and he was supposed to get out and open the door? Butler then started beeping the horn. Winters was unsure what this meant. Was Butler beeping at him or was there was someone in the building and if so, how many?

Deciding it was best to keep the headlights on to blind anyone approaching, Winters jumped out and ran back to the girls.

"What's going on?" asked Collette in a nervous tone.

"Not sure. Listen, turn the headlights off, put on your goggles, and grab your gear. Slip around the corner of the building and be ready."

The horn beeped a few more times convincing Winters that this was a meet. He jumped back in his truck and powered his night-vision goggles on before taking out his new Glock. He threaded the suppressor onto the barrel while keeping his attention to what was happening in front of him.

Butler remained in the truck and beeped the horn a couple more times. Whoever was here wasn't expecting him. These people could either be friends of Butler's or his buyers. Cochran said the buyers were a bunch of scary people.

The headlights behind him went dark, which meant Collette and Laney were out of the truck.

Winters kept staring at the door when it finally opened. Four shirtless men exited the building carrying weapons. They belong to a street gang, as everyone had what could only be described as gang tattoos covering their bodies. They talked to Butler for a moment before one started coming his way.

CHAPTER 44

CLOQUET MINNESOTA

A shirtless man came up and banged on the door. He was a lean, muscled man with a tattoo on each side of his face and host of others covering his body.

"Are you Cochran?"

These were the buyers, and this one didn't know who Cochran was. Winters answered in a muffled tone while pushing the door open to climb out.

"Yeah, I'm Cochran," said Winters as his body tensed.

Tattooed started towards the back. "Where are them bitches you got?"

Hitting the pavement, Winters kept the door open and flipped his goggles down before catching up to him. He took a quick deep breath to try to slow down his heart rate.

"Where are they?" he asked in a frustrated tone.

"Got in 'em in the back, man. They're tied up and ready to go if ya want a turn," said Winters playing on the man's desires.

"Good. Cause I got a train waiting for them inside."

Running a train was slang for when a group of guys stood in line to have sex with the same girl. Winters knew the term but didn't know how many it meant. "Cool. How many are ya?"

"There's eight of us. Think these girls can handle it."

Winters jerked his head back. His job just went from doable to more difficult. "Are they asleep or something?"

"Yeah, man. Hell, we were all sleeping till you guys showed up."

Winters heard enough and raised the suppressed Glock pointing it at the back of Tattoo's head just as he went to pull the cargo door open. He depressed the trigger once, and it bucked in his hand followed by a muffled spit. The front of the man's head exploded splattering blood and flesh onto the cargo door as it rolled up. Winters let the body fall to the ground unconcerned where it landed.

He was satisfied with the suppressor. The report had been minimal and further disguised by the cargo door opening. It was louder than you'd hear in a Hollywood movie.

The sound of footsteps caused Winters to turn around to find Collette and Laney rushing in wearing their night-vision goggles. Neither of them spoke and breathed in measured paces while shouldering their weapons. He motioned them to follow him to the front of his truck.

Another man had appeared outside as they began looking at the supplies in the back of the truck. This left three more inside who would be able to barricade themselves, which meant an extended gun battle. It wasn't ideal, but he didn't have the patience to wait for the others to join them.

He turned to Collette and Laney. "I want you guys to swing around to the other side of the road till you're in the middle of the trucks and get on the ground. Don't fire until I signal you. Once you fire, your position will be exposed, so you'll need to move to another one."

"What's the signal?" asked Laney.

"I'll turn the headlights off."

"What about you?" asked Collette.

"As soon as you guys are in position, I'll open fire and take out what I can. The ones I don't hit will scatter. There's three more inside. That's why I want you to stay hidden. You'll have the perfect line of sight. Got it?"

They gave short jerky nods.

"Remember girls, we own the night," said Winters tapping on his goggles trying to give them a confidence boost. "Now, go."

They took off and swept around before falling on the asphalt in the middle of the road. Winters pulled his M4 into his shoulder and stepped in front of his truck. He flipped the weapon to full auto and applied pressure to the trigger.

The parking lot lit up with muzzle flashes and a deafening barrage of rifle fire. Two guys instantly fell to the ground dead, both taking multiple rounds to the chest. Another in the truck turned around with a pistol. The pistol jumped twice in his hands with one bullet whizzing by Winters, as he emptied his magazine on the gang-banger. He took numerous hits before dropping dead.

The one managed to run back inside while Butler jumped into the cab of his truck and started to drive away. This was an unexpected move, one that he didn't have an answer for. Losing that cargo would make this gun battle a useless endeavor and a waste of time.

Winters ejected his empty mag and fished out another. He slammed it in and started for Butler but was cut off by gunfire from inside the building. It was time to get the girls involved, so he turned the headlights off.

Collette opened fire at the building firing in full-auto shattering all the windows. Winters nodded in satisfaction and was pleasantly surprised when Laney took off after the escaping Butler. She ran right up to the driver's door and started shooting inside the cab. Seconds later, the truck's movement began to slow down, and she hopped on the running board to open the door. Butler's body tumbled onto the asphalt. She then crawled inside and threw the truck in park.

All that was left were the four men barricaded inside the building. Collette continued to keep them at bay, but she had nothing to hide behind, and they would soon fire on her position.

Winters thought of a quick solution and ran to the back of his truck finding just what they needed. He grabbed a long carrying-case before jumping out of the truck and running out to the road. Laney had just begun to suppress the enemy fire from her new position while Collette moved to a different one. Winters reached her just as she was about to open fire again.

"Wait. Don't expose yourself," ordered Winters as he put the case on the ground.

Collette bobbed her head at him. "What is that?"

Winters opened the case.

"Is that what I think it is?"

"It is indeed," said Winters just as the men inside began to return fire at

Laney's position. He could see the muzzle flashes from their rifles. Winters hoisted the RPG to his shoulder but then remembered when they fired one at the police station in Detroit. They were further away than this and still felt the concussion. "Let's back up a bit," said Winters.

He looked over at Laney and waved her back. She saw the RPG and scurried away. Collette was first across the road and into another parking lot. Winters saddled up next to her and put the launcher back on his shoulder. The men inside were firing blindly as Winters pulled the trigger. The rocket flew out with a swoosh and fire entrails lit up the night as it zoomed towards the building. It took a couple of seconds before impacting into a massive explosion.

Debris began raining down on the road and bouncing off the asphalt, so Winters dropped the launcher and got on top of Collette to protect her.

After it stopped raining down on them, Laney came running over yelling.

"That was friggin awesome. Look at it. It's, like, all gone."

Winters helped Collette up and turned to see the building partly demolished and on fire. There would be no survivors. The flames began reaching the two trucks.

"C'mon let's get those trucks out of the way."

Collette reached hers first and began backing it up out on the street. After moving them, Winters checked for damage only to find paint burned off the front of his.

"Did you see me stop, Butler?" Laney asked in an excited tone.

"That was impressive," Winters said putting put an arm around her shoulder.

"I knew I had him. He, like, never even saw me coming and I fired right into the truck."

"Both you guys did great. Collette, you moved to a new position just when you needed to."

"Sergeant Hicks trained us on that," said Collette.

"Did he now?"

"Oh, yeah. We ran those courses a bunch of times."

"It shows. Now listen, I need to ask you guys a favor."

"Yes, we'll drive the trucks to Jackson," said Laney.

Winters raised his eyebrows.

"You want these trucks, and you need drivers," said Laney. "Of course, we'll help you."

"We'll do anything for you, Cole," said Collette.

"Well, alright then. What do ya say we get the hell out of here? No telling if there are any more bad guys around. Laney that truck's yours," said Winters pointing to the one she shot at. "Keep the headlights off."

Winters didn't stop worrying until they were through the town of Cloquet and on State Road 210. He wanted to get as far away from Duluth as possible before the sun came up. They would need to pull over and get some rest before they went much further. Their adrenaline would be waning, and fatigue would set in after such a long and eventful night.

A tattooed gang-banger crawled away from the burning building and got up on his feet dizzy. He was shaken and not thinking clearly but knew enough to go for help. He took a few steps and had to catch himself from falling over.

The sound of engines revving in the air snapped his head back to reality. He aimed toward the end of the building but found his coordination floundering. If he didn't know any better, he would have thought he was drunk the way he stumbled around the building. He was just in time to see three moving vans pulling out onto the street and head east.

"Who the hell were they? Was it those bitches that Butler kidnapped?" he asked aloud.

Whoever they were, they were stealing a payday and making their escape. He needed to get to his squad and stop them. He fell into his white Caddy and fired it up. It took all his strength to pull down on the gearshift. He floored the gas pedal and squealed the tires as he swung onto the road. Help was five miles away, and he would have to hurry if they had any chance of catching up with them. If anyone could do it, it was their leader, Big Mike. He was the baddest among them and tenacious as hell.

CHAPTER 45

HANOVER MICHIGAN

The temperature hadn't dropped much since the sun had gone down a few hours ago and Meeks was glad he'd worn his tactical chest rig rather than a vest. It was hot, and he was out of breath after jogging across empty fields for the last fifteen minutes. He flipped up the thermal goggles and grabbed a bottle of water. He took a few gulps before offering it to Amber. She shook her head and grabbed her own. Meeks chuckled knowing she didn't want his cooties.

They were on the other side of the border, way past Pulaski Road where they usually brought the convoys across. They'd been out for over an hour and was surprised the separation between the Jiji guard post was much broader than usual. They had never seen it like this before and thought something was up. They hoofed it up and down the field on both sides to see if they could spot any hidden Jijis. It would have been impossible for them to hide from them since Meeks was wearing the thermal goggles, which picked up the smallest of heat signatures. Not finding any, the concern was the enemy had changed tactics. Meeks had decided to jog a couple of miles west to make sure they hadn't moved into a different position.

"So glad we came this far," said Meeks sarcastically.

"You're not tired are ya?" kidded Amber.

"Not enough to not keep up with you."

"Oooh. I sense I've challenged your manhood."

"Ya damn right, you have."

"Well, the way I heard it from Reese, is that she beat you that night you guys were on the run."

"That there girl, is a speed demon, let me tell ya."

"Yes, she is," said Amber remembering her own little run-in last night when she plowed into a Jiji face first. She won't soon forget it, if ever. She was glad she came out tonight because she needed to get back-in-the-saddle and put it past her.

"You know, if ya didn't know any better, you'd think the Jijis have given up."

"It is weird that they're not in their usual places."

Meeks looked at his watch. "We better get back to the border."

"Are we racing or pacing."

"C'mon now, we're not in that big of a hurry."

"Alright…wimp-dog," laughed Amber as she started jogging back toward Pulaski Road.

Meeks wasn't ready and took another sip of water before he started running to catch up to her. She set the pace for the next fifteen minutes faster than he would have liked but as soon as he saw the border up ahead, he took off in a sprint. He was feeling confident, as the empty road was not more than fifty yards ahead. As he got closer, he kicked it up a notch knowing she was doing the same. He was just about there when Amber pulled past him and reached the border first.

It was a couple of minutes for them to catch their breath and settle down. Meeks took the ribbing from Amber in stride having enjoyed competition. It was the one thing he missed most from his football days, competing with others. He didn't mind being beat by a girl, as she was younger and a former athlete like himself.

Meeks grabbed the radio and called out to Scar who had been waiting on Main Street in the small village of Hanover. Ten minutes later, the convoy arrived and started moving across the border, unimpeded.

The last short-bus crossed the border, and Meeks turned to Scar. "How many did we get across?"

"A hundred and twenty-five."

"Nice."

Nordell stood on the other side of Meeks. "How far away are those idiots?"

"About a half-mile on either side of us."

Nordell turned to Scar. "Something is going on. I think we should check them out."

That notion had been gnawing on Scar too since earlier while he was out checking the borders with Reese. Add to it that the western border guards had separated more than usually told him they should investigate. "Let's do that then. Gunny, you and Badger, take half the guys to the south. Meeks and I will take the north."

"C'mon Badger," said Nordell.

"We jogging there?" asked Amber half-kidding.

Scar turned toward the SUV. "You can if you want, but I'm driving."

"I'm with Scar," said Meeks. "But hey if you want."

"Wimp-dog," whispered Amber as she passed Meeks before hopping into the front seat.

Scar looked at Amber and then back at Meeks. "I take it winners sit up front?"

"Ya darn right they do," stated Amber.

Scar kept the speed at a snail's pace through the empty fields not wanting to arouse any attention as they approached their enemy. It didn't take too long before they were a hundred yards away from the Jiji border directly across from them. Scar got out of the truck and led his team of fifteen toward the Jijis.

He took out the Night Optics D-321B-AG binoculars and observed the Jijis leaning on cars. They were at ease and chatting with each other seemingly bored of guard duty. None of them were paying attention to the field in front of them. Scar could easily walk right up to them before they'd know he was there. The thought appealed to him and suggested it to Meeks.

"Don't see why not," whispered Meeks.

"What's further up?" asked Scar.

"We didn't go up that far."

Scar thought about it for a minute before pulling his radio out to call Nordell. His main apprehension to attacking the Jijis was they had been using this area to bring convoys through and didn't want them to post more men out this way. They've had much success in using this area and didn't want to spoil it. However, his fear that something was amiss overrode the concern.

"I'm thinking the same thing," said Nordell. "I want to see their response."

"Roger that. I'm sending a squad north to cover our flank."

"Will do the same. Call me when you're ready. We'll synchronize our attack."

"Roger that."

Scar sent a squad north and instructed them to only engage if they tried to flank them. He waited ten minutes before leading his team closer to the border. The crunching of grass underfoot was the only sound they made as they closed in on their prey. Sporadic clouds kept the light from a crescent moon to a minimum as the twelve Jijis stood in a couple of groups yakking and laughing oblivious to their impending doom. Scar sent Meeks and Amber around the north side of them while he lined up with the others. They were fifteen yards away and could hear the Jiji voices carry across the field.

Scar pulled his radio out and whispered into the mic. "We're in position."

"Copy. We're ready," said Nordell.

Scar looked to his left and right signaling his four men before he opened fire. Muzzle flashes lit up the darkness as gunfire rained in on the twenty Jijis. A group of eight leaning on the side of the car fell dead taking the brunt of the fire. Scar emptied his magazine and threw in another before aiming at the other group. They scrambled and took cover behind a car but by doing so exposed themselves to Meeks and Amber.

Meeks was in a kneeling position with Amber next to him waiting for them to make this very move. As soon as they did, they opened fire on the defenseless Jijis. There was an abject look of terror in the Jijis eyes as he and Amber swept their Colt M4's back and forth. Bullets slammed into them and the cars behind them. It was over in under a minute. All twelve Jijis were dead or dying.

Scar began walking toward the carnage while listening to the echo of gunfire from Nordell's men finishing their job. He didn't detect any other type of weapons being fired, which meant these Jijis didn't return a single round.

Scar's radio came alive from his squad in the north to report the Jijis piled in their cars and drove away from the gunfire. They weren't going to help their friends. Scar put the radio away confused as to why they responded this way. He suspected something was going on, either that or they've gotten lazy.

CHAPTER 46

GROSSE POINTE MICHIGAN

Floodlights lit up the parking lot where fighters were preparing to board their assigned buses. There was an eerie ambiance as the men moved around in silence with an occasional acknowledgment to a superior. The rustling of clothing and the clanging of weapons only added to the eeriness.

Off to the side was a table with a large map of Jackson. It was marked with the areas of Mordulfah's men and the National Police. Red lines had been made where they would enter the town.

Mordulfah watched with his arms crossed over his chest to control his natural instinct to be in command. He was heeding his uncles' advice and allowed Colonel Khan to take charge of the invasion he had planned while in route to Grosse Pointe. It was a solid plan, and he was sure of its success. By afternoon, he would have Winters and the rest of his rebels either killed or taken prisoner. His one demand was to capture Winters, alive. A picture of him had been passed around to help with the request.

Khan signaled his captains to join him at the table along with Captain Vatter of the National Police.

"As you all know we have sent advance strike teams to sneak across the border and clear out a path for our main forces. Since Prince Mordulfah's men were attacked here yesterday," he said pointing to the Proving Grounds, "it is only natural that we would still have men in the area, which will camouflage our advance strike team and not raise alarms. They will take out their guard post here and here, eliminating their advanced warning system.

They will then proceed to the hospital and start a covert attack just as we are taking our positions. Khan looked up at Vatter. "This is the route that Captain Vatter's men took when they attacked the hospital."

Vatter nodded. "As long as you come in from this field you'll be alright."

"The hospital is where their men sleep, and it will be our first target. A surprise assault will throw them into chaos and scatter their forces. Our second strike team will come down Lansing Road where the rebels have been using the men stationed there as target practice. We will take out their guard post and cut off another escape route. The third will come down Business 127. Once we hit the hospital, we will then flood the town with our men from the north and the west forcing them to the south where Captain Vatter will be waiting for them."

All eyes turned to Vatter who forced himself to control his joy. He had hoped not to be included in the main assault but rather be waiting in the wings. He had already given his men strict instructions not to put themselves in any unnecessary danger. Despite his hatred for rebels, he had a profound respect for their capabilities, so had taken some precautions.

Too many of his men had already died at their hands, and he couldn't risk losing too many more. He would rather have his men be in a defensive position than going house to house. That was risky for his untrained men. Besides, he could get first dibs on any women that came through there. He already had plans to move any capture women out of the area as quickly as possible.

Khan looked at his captains. "We strike hard and fast. Remember, we have superior numbers and with our grenade launchers, the day will be ours. Praise be Allah."

"Praise be Allah," they responded.

Thomas watched in vain, as the vehicles began pulling out of the parking lot to head to Jackson. His stomach turned in knots because he didn't expect them to be leaving so soon. He had figured wrongly that he'd be able to sneak out today to go warn the Shadow Patriots. As it was, Mordulfah needed him to be at his beckon call and wasn't able to slip away.

He turned to see the prince with a small smile on his face. He had never seen him smile before and it sent a shiver down his spine. The prince was confident of success. He wished he hadn't waited and should have known better they'd leave right away. Colonel Khan had insisted because he wasn't sure if the rebels were spying on them. Of course, he was right, but not in the way, Khan thought he was. He was afraid that they had spies watching the grounds and would notice new fighters coming in. Little did they know they had a spy in their midst.

Unfortunately, he wasn't a good spy because he failed at raising the alarm. Perhaps, he could still help the Shadow Patriots if any of them became prisoners. For now, all he could do is pray for their safety.

CHAPTER 47

JACKSON MICHIGAN

Bassett rolled out of bed ready to cross enemy lines once again. Only this time, he would take one of their police cruisers and plenty of gear. Yesterday's fiasco was an embarrassment that unfortunately happens in war. Not all missions can go your way. However, it was the second mission that had failed over the past few days. He could only laugh at himself. He'd make up for it with this next one. He and Burns were going to spend the day looking for those supply trucks and hijack them.

He headed to the cafeteria and found Burns sitting with Scar and a fresh pot of coffee.

"Didn't think you'd be up," said Bassett as he grabbed the coffee decanter

"Yeah, I didn't think so either," said a worried Scar.

Bassett sat down and took a sip of coffee before biting into a muffin. He washed it down with another sip. "How'd it go last night?"

Scar caught them up on the successful crossing and the taking down the Jijis. Bassett nodded in satisfaction but showed the same concerns about why the Jijis would take off as they did.

"They had no problems coming after us in the Proving Grounds," said Bassett.

"Yeah, they were all over the place," said Burns.

"Something has changed that's for sure."

Burns took a sip of coffee and said. "Pretend inferiority and encourage arrogance."

"More Sun Tzu?" asked Bassett.

Burns nodded.

Scar leaned back in his chair. The quote made a lot of sense considering the way the Jijis ran away after they opened fire. Perhaps Mordulfah was using his defeats as a way to lull his enemy into arrogance and a lax attitude.

"You think Mordulfah has given up?" asked Bassett

"No, I don't think so. This guy is too proud for that," said Scar.

"He can't be used to losing," said Bassett.

"No, he can't."

"He'll probably go and hire experienced fighters," said Burns.

"Yeah, maybe. Hopefully, Thomas will be able to report in soon," said Scar.

Bassett took the last sip of his coffee and stood up. "As soon as we cross over, we'll radio in, but it'll be hours before those supply trucks come by."

Scar nodded. "Are you going to hit the drivers before they deliver or find out where they come from?"

"Not sure yet," said Bassett.

Burns stood up. "I'd kinda like to see where they go to get more supplies. Could be a bigger score."

Scar nodded in agreement. "Push come to shove you can at least hit the evening delivery."

"Exactly," said Burns.

"We need to get going," said Bassett.

The three walked out to the parking lot where their cruiser was waiting for them. Bassett had packed it last night with everything they would need for their extended mission.

Bassett and Burns shook Scar's hand.

"See you guys later tonight," said Scar.

"Hopefully with a rack of lamb," smiled Burns.

"Just don't forget the mint jelly," retorted Scar.

Bassett started the car up and pulled out of the parking lot. They were at the border within ten minutes and checked in with Craig Robertson. He and his brother, Rick, were the ones who told them about the supply deliver schedule. Usually, they kept watch on top of a building, but today they would be hiding out nearer the border.

Bassett parked the cruiser so they could reconnoiter Manchester Road. It had only been a day since their encounter with the Jijis, and he wasn't sure if they had tightened their security.

They broke through the foliage and Bassett raised the night-vision binoculars to find the Jijis hadn't moved their guard post closer together. Bassett shook his head and handed the glasses to Burns.

"You'd think they'd be changing their strategy," said Burns.

"You'd think."

They got back in the cruiser, crossed the Jiji border on Manchester Road, and headed to Parker Road in Dexter, Michigan. This road went over the interstate but didn't have an exit or an on-ramp. It was an ideal place to keep an eye on the delivery trucks at a distance and be able to leave to catch up to them down the road.

Bassett parked the squad car on top of the overpass not too worried about being spotted seeing how it was a cop car. Burns had been dialing around with the police radio band to see if he could pick up any chatter from the cops but heard none. It wasn't too unusual, as it was early in the morning and they didn't start using the radios before the sun came up. Ever since they confiscated the squad cars, they had been monitoring their radios for any morsel of information. Everyone once in a while they'd catch a gem, but for the most part, it was boring stuff. The cops knew they had the radios so they didn't use them as they typically would.

They'd been sitting there for nearly an hour when Burns spotted a set of headlights coming from the east.

"Heads up," said Burns.

"What do we have here?" asked Bassett lifting up the binoculars. "There's just one."

"Yep."

It took a minute before a passenger van drove under the overpass. They immediately scooted over to the other side to look at it.

"Whaddya think?" asked Burns.

"I don't know. Maybe replacements."

"Strange hour to be replacing men," said Burns

"Yes, it is."

Bassett picked up the radio to call out to Craig Robertson but got no answer.

"We're too far away," said Burns.

"Yeah, I know. Just thought sitting this high up and the night air might improve its range."

"It's probably nothing."

"Yeah, but still, I've never seen them moving around at this hour before."

"Nor have I, but it could be because we had a firefight with them."

"Maybe," said Bassett. He let go of the binoculars unsatisfied with guesses but had no choice. They had a mission to complete and needed to concentrate on that. If all went well, they'd be able to bring back needed supplies.

Over the next hour, they kept watch as the skies to the east began to light up as the sun was just breaking over the horizon. Bassett put away the night vision binoculars and broke out the regular ones. He handed Burns a pair and reached into his bag for a couple of power bars.

"Oh damn," yelled Burns.

Bassett's heart started racing when he raised the glasses and saw a convoy of vehicles coming toward them. Bus after bus came in his vision as well as pick up trucks filled with armed uniformed men. These men were different, and they were not coming to guard the town. They were going to attack it. Bassett's mind flipped into hyper-drive thinking of his options. They were too far away to warn Scar. There was just one option left.

"Our mission has changed. Let's get 'em out," ordered Bassett.

to begin.

CHAPTER 48

DEXTER MICHIGAN

Bassett grabbed the M4's sitting in the backseat and handed one to Burns. While he would have liked to give Scar a heads-up, it was more important to take out what they could to lighten the load on the town.

"Let's take out what we can and get the hell out of here," said Bassett.

Burns checked his weapon. "I'll take the other side. Let the first two buses pass through."

Bassett nodded as Burns scooted across the other side. Bassett leaned against the concrete barrier and peeked over to see the massive convoy getting closer. This was it. This is what they had been expecting all week, and it was finally here. He had been warning all the guard posts to stay alert. He just hoped they had paid attention and did what they were supposed to do.

Bassett figured the convoy was full of soldiers from the Middle East. Soldiers was a bit of a misnomer when it came to fighters from that part of the world. He'd seen them before when he fought in the Middle East. Most weren't the best fighters, but some of them were quite good having filtered in from the many different armies. There was no reason to think

Mordulfah would import more incompetent fighters like the ones he'd been using. He'd spend the money and bring in the best.

The noise from the engines grew louder as they closed in on the overpass. Bassett rose his head up as the first bus drove under the bridge and then the second.

"Here they come," he yelled.

The third bus was closing in when Bassett stood up brandishing his Colt M4. The driver's eyes zeroed in on him, and his face betrayed a split second of surprise. Bassett gritted his teeth and pulled the trigger.

The staccato gunfire echoed in the crisp morning air. The big windshield on the bus spider-webbed with cracks splitting off in a hundred directions as the rounds blew holes through it. Blood splattered on the glass as the bus swerved toward the median picking up speed. It crashed into the guardrail shooting sparks into the air as it plowed through the metal barrier. Bassett lost sight but heard it crash into the pylon.

Bassett lit up the next bus, but it had slowed down giving him more time to take out the driver and anyone else sitting in the first few rows. He slammed in a fresh magazine and sprayed the top of the bus peppering it with holes. He wanted to do as much damage as he could before they organized and returned fire.

The convoy came to a stop as men began to pour out the back of the buses and took up positions. Bassett watched their movements as he popped in his third magazine. These guys weren't panicking but were methodical with their positioning. These guys were the real deal.

On the other side of the bridge, Burns lit up the two buses with an initial salvo. He then began moving down the overpass to get a better angle on them, as they continued on the interstate. He sprayed the sides of the two buses ripping bullets into them unsure of how many he was hitting. His goal was to make as many holes in the bus before it got out of range.

Down below a Jiji carrying an M320 Grenade Launcher ran from the relative safety of the bridge to get an angle on the men above. The launcher was a single-shot 40mm and had an effective range of 150 meters. It could do significant damage if used correctly. Holding the launcher at his waist, he stopped and pointed it up at the overpass. Burns recognized the weapon and dropped to his knees as he yelled at Bassett to get down. The grenade flew up and over the bridge dropping down to the interstate on the other side. The explosion took out everyone who had climbed out of the crashed bus. It was an ill-advised desperate move as the grenade took out the wrong people.

Burns jumped up to see the man reloading the weapon. He raised his own and shot him dead. He cautiously looked down to see men bleeding out on the ground.

Bassett continued firing as Burns hunched over to join him.

"Some have already peeled off into the woods," said Bassett. "We got maybe another thirty seconds before they've flanked us."

Bullets began hitting the bridge throwing rock chips up in the air. Both kept their heads down as the rounds continued pounding the bridge. Burns motioned to the car, and Bassett nodded. They crawled toward it when they heard the distinctive firing sound of an RPG. This would be aimed better and much deadlier than the previous grenade. They hurried to the cruiser and reached it as the round hit their last position. The thunderous explosion shook the bridge as debris shot out in different directions raining down on them.

They climbed into the car and Bassett started it up. He looked in the rearview mirror and didn't like what he saw. There was too much debris scattered across the road, and he didn't want to risk a blown tire. Not here. Not now. So, he threw the car into drive and stomped on the pedal. The car zoomed across the overpass to the north.

Going this way was putting them further out of radio range and away from Jackson. Bassett knew the area having driven the roads over the past couple of weeks. He liked to familiarize himself for such occasions. The route he had in mind was longer but safer.

"Bastards have stepped up their game," said Burns

"Yeah, they have, and these guys are professional. They moved into position in quick order and didn't panic."

"Except for the one dumbass that tried to lob up a grenade. It took out half a dozen of his own guys."

"That was stupid."

"I'm sure I took out close to half of them in those two buses."

"We slowed the bastards down," said Bassett.

"Where're we headed?"

"Up and around the town of Chelsea. This beast needs big roads so we'll stay on the main ones and then come down Lansing Road where Eddie is at."

Bassett didn't want to take chances on any of the smaller roads, many of which were dirt roads with rocks, which could penetrate a tire especially at the speed he was pushing the cruiser at. The route he was taking was out of the way, but the speedometer was topping a hundred, which would make up for the longer distance. They would still be behind enemy lines, but that could be a tactical advantage, at least he hoped.

CHAPTER 49

Colonel Khan looked up at the smoldering overpass and saw a car pull away. His nostrils flared at the thought of those cowardly infidels leaving without giving his men a chance to fight them. Like vermin, they struck while hiding behind a concrete barrier. They didn't dare come face to face with his men.

He looked around at the carnage. Men were bleeding and sobbing for help. Dead bodies lay near the crashed bus. He stepped toward the back of the second bus and looked inside to see more of his men dead.

He began cursing himself and pleading to Allah to help him in this desperate hour. This was a devastating setback, but he needed to keep moving. His advance team should be well on their way to taking out the enemy guard post. Those infidels that just attacked would warn the town of an impending attack.

He needed to hurry.

His radio came alive from the first two buses reporting they had lost half their men during the attack. They were either dead or wounded. Khan ordered them to keep going. He put his radio away, yelled for one of his captains, and commanded the remaining convoy to get moving. There was not a minute to lose. He instructed his medics to stay behind do what they can before proceeding to Jackson.

He hopped on the next bus and looked at his men. He swept his arm around. "Those cowardly infidels will soon pay the price for attacking us.

We will release our vengeance on them, and it will be a glorious battle for Allah."

The men shouted back and cheered as the bus began to pull away. Khan looked through the window as he passed by mangled bodies. He didn't have a count of the dead or wounded but figured at least a hundred were not going to join them. It was a severe blow but not enough to stay the attack. He kept standing for the remainder of their journey wanting to show his men strength.

It took only fifteen minutes before they got to Manchester Road. Once they arrived, Mordulfah's men on the interstate piled into vehicles and started to line up behind them readying for the quick strike.

Khan reached for his radio and called to his advanced team.

"Achmed, have you completed your mission?"

"Yes, Colonel, we have taken out the two guard post with ease. We are now proceeding to the hospital. We'll be in position in about ten minutes."

"Have they been alerted?"

"No sir, they have not."

Khan nodded while glancing up to thank Allah for the help. They still had the element of surprise. He pressed the button again. "Wait for my command."

"Yes, sir."

Khan climbed on top of the bus to get a better view of his men. With his thrust-out chest and shoulders back in perfect posture, he looked taller than his five-foot-eight frame. The sun was just above the horizon, and he put his hand to his forehead to shade his eyes. His men stared up at him as he turned around to inspect the men. He nodded and allowed himself a slight grin. Things were looking better. Close to a hundred vehicles full of men, were now parked on Manchester Road ready to go.

He climbed down and ordered the driver to proceed.

The buses pulled out and the long convoy of vehicles fell in behind them. It was fifteen miles to the hospital, which will take approximately twenty minutes. The men on the bus readied their AK-47's.

Khan and his men hadn't seen a battle in three months after taking over a small territory in Afghanistan. It had taken several weeks to defeat his enemies, and it had cost him dearly. He'd lost close a hundred men, but the victory was worth it as it was a strategic piece of land.

He left the Middle East at the behest of his longtime benefactor Prince Faisal who he had known since childhood. Khan's father served in the kingdom as a leading general and was often invited to gatherings where he would bring his sons.

Khan studied with Faisal in Great Britain before joining the military. He had never visited America but had longed to come and help with the take over of the country. He had heard about the plans to bring down America a year before implementation and offered his services to Prince Faisal.

It was a month ago Faisal had flown him and his men to America. Faisal had been waiting patiently for Mordulfah to finally come and seek his help. The man had lost five hundred men in Minnesota a couple of months ago and knew he'd eventually need help. Mordulfah may be a sharp businessman, but he was no general.

The buses made the final turn and Khan looked at all the abandoned buildings as they came down East Michigan Avenue. His heart skipped a beat when he saw the hospital on the right. He grabbed his radio and ordered his advance strike team to move in through the emergency room. He tapped the driver on the shoulder to take the next right. This would lead them to a parking lot.

As they passed the hospital, Khan saw his advance strike team storm through the emergency room. The battle had begun, and he praised Allah..

CHAPTER 50

JACKSON MICHIGAN

Sandy the nurse who had taken care of Reese had just gotten to the hospital and carried a thermos from home filled with her own private stash of coffee. It had become a commodity around town, and she needed it to get through her day of seeing patients.

However, as of late, she saw less, and less of them as the town's population dwindled. She reached the nursing station in the emergency room and saw an older couple waiting to be seen by Doctor Lunsford who hadn't arrived yet. She smiled at the couple and told them it wouldn't be too long.

She sat down, took the thermos cap off, and poured a cup. She took a sip and looked up to see ten gun-toting men burst through the doors. She didn't recognize them but realized she was in danger and froze from fear.

Khan's advanced team shot her before turning on the elderly couple, as they embraced each other before the bullets ripped through them.

Scar sat with Meeks in the cafeteria drinking coffee. He didn't get much sleep last night and saw Bassett and Burns off earlier. He had decided to go back out to the borders to see what he could do to tighten up their perimeter. Meeks had offered to go out with him and told him Amber wanted to join them as well. They had been waiting for her for about fifteen minutes when she finally came through the doors ready to go.

"Was about to give up on you," smiled Meeks.

"Were you really?" said Amber grabbing a cup of coffee.

"Yep. Thought maybe you were going to sleep in."

Amber sat down across from him. "Are you saying I need more beauty sleep?"

"Oh no. Perish the thought, my dear. Why too much more of that and I won't be able to control myself around ya."

Amber shook head before taking a sip coffee.

"Nice one, buddy," laughed Scar.

"Well, I mean, look at her."

"Okay, down boy," said Amber.

They stopped talking as gunfire echoed upstairs.

They stared at each other in disbelief for a split second before jumping out of their seats. They swung their Colt M4's chest level and charged toward the stairs. Meeks was the first to hit the steps followed by Amber.

Scar keyed up his radio and yelled, "We're under attack. I repeat the hospital is under attack."

Meeks hit the top of the stairs first and rushed toward the emergency room. He saw Jijis marching down the hall toward them. He pointed his weapon and laid down a hail of gunfire.

The wide empty hallway reverberated into an earsplitting tone of gunfire. Two bad guys fell backward from the rounds punching through them. The enemy returned fire as Meeks led the team around the corner to another hallway.

"Eddie do you read me?" yelled Scar into the radio.

"I read you Scar. They just started attacking up here."

Scar lowered the radio. He had been right that something was off with the borders. They were going to attack all at once. Somehow, they got past their border guards and came in unseen.

He raised his radio again. "I say again, we're under attack. The whole town is under attack. You know what to do, now do your duty."

A chorus of "Roger that" began flooding the radio as men began springing into action.

Winters with the help of Nordell and Bassett had laid out a solid plan on where they should hold defensive positions and assigned everyone to one. It wasn't helping that a large portion of the men was still upstairs sleeping. With the exchange of gunfire, that problem would remedy itself.

Meeks came around the corner and fired again to stop them from advancing. He turned to Scar. "What's our play, boss?"

"This is a small contingent. The bigger one will be in the parking lot. C'mon."

Scar ran down the hall with Amber on his tail. Meeks fired off a three-shot burst before falling in behind them. They reached the side door to the parking lot and saw buses coming in.

"Let's go before they can get off," ordered Scar. "Meeks keep our six clear."

Meeks nodded and stayed at the door while Scar and Amber headed outside.

Scar and Amber split up and aimed at different buses.

Both emptied their magazines within seconds. The rounds hit the bus forcing it to keep driving to get away from the gunfire.

Scar ran further into the parking lot to see vehicle after vehicle trying to enter. He made a quick decision and yelled for Amber to join him. They had to strike before these bastards got organized.

Amber ran to him, and they started firing at the street that was jammed pack with vehicles. So far, the Jijis hadn't been able to return fire. That didn't last too long as Jijis began emptying their rides and firing wildly at Scar's position.

"We can't get trapped here," said Amber.

Scar surveyed the situation. She was right. They needed to get back to Meeks.

As he turned, he saw the convoy of vehicles go around the jammed up intersection and turn on Waterloo Street. This road gave them access to the rest of the parking lots out back. This was where he'd strike next.

Meeks opened the door as Scar and Amber dove through for cover as lead began pelting the entrance.

"We need to get over to the other lot," said Scar.

By now, more Jijis had entered the emergency room, and the sound of non-stop gunfire bounced off the walls. More and more M4's were in the mix of gunfire as the Shadow Patriots began to fight back.

Meeks led them down the hall and over to the exit where they parked most of their vehicles. It was a big lot capable of handling all the vehicles that were pouring in. Scar stopped at the entrance to answer a radio call. Meeks pushed the door open and ran down the sidewalk keeping to the back of an outer building with Amber behind him. He came around the corner and saw a Jiji pointing a grenade launcher. Meeks turned and jumped onto Amber taking her to the ground as the grenade flew over their heads.

CHAPTER 51

Landing hard on Amber, Meeks kept on top of her as the explosion shook the ground. The thunderous blast blew out the main back entrance three hundred feet away. Meeks thanked God he decided to take the side entrance. An outcrop of a building kept most of the concussion away from them but still, the blast dazed them.

He pushed up on his hands and looked down at Amber. Her eyes were blinking fast, and she started mouthing something to him. Their ears were ringing from the blast, and neither could hear the other.

Scar came running toward them and was yelling at them. He took a quick look at them and then zipped around the corner to fire on the approaching Jijis killing the one who launched the grenade. He turned back and yelled again.

Meeks rolled off Amber and sat up. The ringing in his ear started to subside, and he turned to Amber who stopped blinking rapidly. She hit her head with the palm of her hand a few times trying to regain her senses.

Meeks got off the ground and held his hand out to her. He pulled her up and waited to let go as she regained her balance.

Scar continued to fire at the approaching Jijis. He wanted that grenade launcher, and all he needed to do was kill his friends who were growing in numbers.

He turned his head. "You two okay?"

Meeks joined him and started firing. "Damn blast knocked out my hearing a bit."

Scar motioned to the dead Jiji still holding the launcher. "I want that launcher."

"I can see why. If these guys got more of these…" said Meeks.

"Exactly," interrupted Scar.

Amber came up beside them. Scar turned to her. "You okay?"

"Yeah. I'm, I'm, good. What the hell was that?"

"Grenade," said Scar. "And it's laying right there."

Amber sensed what Scar wanted to do. It was about seventy-feet away. A little bit more than running to first base. "Give me another second, and I'll get it."

"You sure?" asked Scar.

"I'm the fastest here."

She grabbed her canteen and took a sip of water before splashing some on her face. The water cooled her down and flushed the remaining haziness away. She offered it to Meeks who grabbed it. He took a big gulp and handed it back to her. He gave her a firm nod. Today there was no such thing as cooties.

"Okay. You guys ready?" asked Amber as she dropped her backpack to the ground.

"He probably has it on a strap, so be ready to cut it away," said Scar.

Amber nodded and patted the knife on her belt. After the other night, she now carried two knives, one in her boot, the other on her waist. She checked the magazine on her weapon; satisfied it was almost full, she said, "I'm ready."

Scar and Meeks turned the corner and started laying down a barrage of rounds at the Jijis. They scattered trying to take cover behind cars.

"Go," ordered Scar.

Amber took off in a full sprint and cleared the seventy-feet right at three seconds. She fell to her knees keeping low to the ground. Scar had been right. It was strapped to him.

She rolled the bloody corpse over and found his glassy eyes staring at her. She pulled her knife out and cut the nylon strap making quick work of it.

A bullet whizzed over her head making her flinch as she pulled on the launcher. She hated that sound because it meant danger was close by. Too many times over the past couple of weeks, she had heard the eerie noise.

She looked around and saw a Jiji had snuck around the corner of a car off to her side. He was moving up to get a better angle on her position. She lifted her weapon and fired as he peeked around the corner.

He moved back to take cover.

She didn't have much time before he'd try again, so she yanked the launcher free and was about leave when she remembered it needed ammo. A black nylon bag was strapped around his waist. She opened it up and saw the spare grenades.

Movement over by the car caught her attention again, so she kicked her legs out into a prone position. She rested her M4 on the corpse using it as cover and carefully aimed at a pair of boots sticking out from the front tire.

She took a breath and held it before gently squeezing the trigger. The loud snap of the gun was followed by the man rolling over to grab his bloody foot.

Big mistake.

Amber kept her aim and fired again. The bullets ripped into his thigh rolling him over exposing his head. The next volley exploded the head blowing one side of it away.

She then grabbed her knife again and cut through the belt. She scooted up on her knees and looked over to Scar and Meeks.

He waved her over, and she raced back over to them.

Scar let out a sigh of relief. He adored and respected Amber as a valuable member of their team. She and Reese had proven themselves many times over. However, what she had just done was beyond risky, and he would have hated himself forever if she had been killed.

He grabbed the handheld grenade launcher. "This baby is an M three-twenty single fire launcher."

"Ever used one?" asked Meeks.

"Oh, yeah, ones similar but they all fire about the same."

Scar looked in the bag and was pleased to find ten grenades.

"Got a lot of cars coming in," said Meeks flickering his eyebrows at Scar.

"Then let's welcome them," said Scar as he loaded a grenade into the launcher. He turned the corner and found a string of cars at the entrance. He hadn't fired one of these in quite a while, but it wasn't something you forgot. He took aim and pulled the trigger. The launcher thumped as the grenade took off in an arc through the air. Scar scooted back around the building and waited.

It took a couple of seconds to sail right into a Suburban and detonate in a blinding explosion. Glass and bodies erupted through the air as black smoke rose in all directions.

They looked around the corner at the chaos. Jijis ran away dazed by the impact. Some were in full panic mode, but others were not. Those were the seasoned fighters, and they yelled at the approaching vehicles to keep driving up the street.

"Those guys are good," said Scar. "Look at 'em keeping order."

"Hit 'em again," said Meeks.

Scar threw in another and aimed at them. The grenade launched toward the soldiers and hit a smaller SUV right at the entrance of the parking lot throwing another fireball into the air killing a few of those soldiers.

Amber stayed behind Scar and Meeks as they came around the corner to inspect the damage. She looked back over to where she retrieved the launcher and saw two men further back in an adjoining parking lot. He had something on his shoulder, and she realized what it was just before he fired. An RPG was headed their way.

CHAPTER 52

Reese woke up thinking she had just heard gunfire. As she slowly shook off the fog of her deep sleep, she wondered if she dreamt it. It wouldn't be the first time she heard gunfire in her dreams. It was the downside of being around it all the time. You sometimes had flashbacks of past gun battles or dreamt of future ones. So, sleep became a challenge for her with some nights being good and others, not so much.

Last night she had gotten to bed later than she would have liked having played cards with Nate and Elliott. It had been a fun night because she actually won some hands of poker. Both of them were quite good at it with Nate coming out on top.

More gunfire rang out.

The hairs on her arms stood straight up as if an electrical charge shot through her body. She threw the sheet off the bed and grabbed her jeans. The gunfire multiplied and became louder as she pulled her pants on.

The hospital was under attack. Was the whole town?

She laced up her boots while thinking what she needed. If it were a full-on assault, then she would not be coming back here. She shoved the knife down her boot, strapped on the Velcro holster holding her Taurus 9mm before grabbing her M4.

She looked around the room and decided to take a Motrin. She'd be running today and fighting off the pain. She took a tablet before throwing the bottle into her go-bag and putting her arms through the straps. She was about to grab her crutch but decided to leave it.

She burst out into the hallway to find several of the guys running toward the darkened stairwell. She followed them not questioning why they were going this way. She had absolute trust in these men and knew they would be heading towards the battle.

Because of her bum leg, she was slower than the others were as they descended the stairs. Gunfire echoed through the halls as she reached the first floor. She was last one through the door as the rest disappeared around the corner.

She came to the corner, but her heart was caught in her chest. Screams mixed in with the gunfire echoed in the hallway. Her friends were taking bullets, and one fell backward tripping her to the floor. She had to shove him off her before crawling to the corner on her hands and knees to see the whole group dead.

She flicked her eyes up ahead and could see why. At least twenty Jijis had the advantage. Her friends didn't stand a chance.

Images of Robinson Road flashed through her mind. They had been outnumbered that night and lost a lot of good men. If the whole town was under assault, then they were going lose even more. Nate had been wounded that night, and he would need help moving Elliott. She had to go and help him.

A few rounds flew over her head, so she turned and moved back to the stairwell, which was dark because of a lack of electricity. She opened the door and began taking the steps two at a time.

She heard footsteps below but couldn't see anything through the dark. They were down there. It sounded like several different footsteps. She pointed her M4 down and squeezed the trigger. Muzzles flashes lit up the darkened stairwell with a blaring assault on the ears. She didn't have time to see if she hit any and stormed through the door. She raced down the half-lit hallway with the morning rays spilling through the windows.

She ran into Nate going to Elliott's room. "What the hell, Nate?"

"It's a full-on assault. The bastards snuck in here before they attacked. Our guys are fighting 'em everywhere."

Nate shook Elliott. "Elliott, wake up. Wake up."

Elliott struggled to open his eyes. "What's going on?"

"We're under attack, brother."

"Oh damn."

Reese kept watching for the Jijis that had followed her up the stairwell. She shouldn't have come here, but it was too late for regrets. She heard a door close down around the corner and moved over to inspect.

Her heart pounded like a piston, and a wave of sweat broke across her forehead as she peered around the corner and spotted four of them. She pointed the M4 and squeezed a couple of three-round bursts. She waited for it and wasn't surprised when they returned fire. The bullets ripped through a door behind her to the empty room next to Elliott. She ducked down to fire another burst.

She turned her head and yelled. "We need to get Elliott out now."

There was no way Elliott could walk, and Nate couldn't carry him. He turned back to Reese. "Go get a wheelchair. At the end of the hall."

She threw down more cover fire before bolting down the long carpeted hallway. There were a few wheelchairs in a storage room at the end of the hall. Her heart was already pounding against her chest, but not out of fear but frustration. They should have had a wheelchair ready to go for Elliott.

She reached the storage room just as Nate laid down his own cover fire to keep the advancing Jijis at bay. They just needed another minute before they could get Elliott out of there. She grabbed the wheelchair and struggled to maneuver it out of the room.

She cursed aloud as she yanked it through the doorway and started running back down the hall pushing it. Her M4 hung down from its sling bouncing between her and the wheelchair. She was twenty feet away from Elliott's room when a grenade flew into it.

She didn't have time to react before the explosion rocked the whole floor blowing out the entire wall into the hallway. Reese felt the impact to her left shoulder before it threw her against the opposite wall like a freight train.

Several Jijis stormed over the fallen wall through the smoky debris into the hollowed out room. They fired their AK's riddling Elliott and Nate's already bloodied bodies until they emptied their magazines.

The thick smoke and dust swept around their jerky movements making it difficult to see through as they looked around for anyone still alive. Satisfied with the results, they turned and headed back to their friends to kill more infidels.

CHAPTER 53

IRON RIVER WISCONSIN

The sun was starting to come up, so Winters took his night-vision goggles off. It had been a long night made even longer with a firefight. Killing those gang-bangers had taken its toll on him. He figured the girls were getting tired as well. They'd been driving all night with the excitement surely wearing off.

They were on US 2 going through Wisconsin where the landscape would change from woods to open fields and back again. There wouldn't be anybody out on these roads, and it would take them right into Michigan.

They'd been on the road for a couple of hours and far away from the gun battle. It was the girls' first real battle, and their performance was quite impressive. Sergeant Hicks would be proud of them. He had trained them just for the day, but apparently, they caught on real quick. Collette stood her ground suppressing the enemy gunfire while Laney, who was always impulsive, acted decisively by taking out Butler. The poor bastard probably didn't know what hit him. Winters hoped he did know and had a WTF moment before taking his last breath.

The thought made Winters smile. He had immense respect for the girls with what they went through and how they had helped him the other night. However, now he saw them in a different light and felt better about bringing them into a war zone. They had proved themselves to be just as good as some of the guys he currently had in his group. They didn't run away and wanted to get into the fight. They did what they were told and stood tall while doing it.

A lot of guys had come through the ranks didn't get anywhere near that. Some had talked a big game, but when the fight started, they ran away. Not that he blamed them. Hell, he had done the same thing himself at the train station. He ran away as soon as he could and didn't turn around until his guilt got the better of him. It wasn't something that was easy, and a lot of the guys died trying it.

Winters saw a barn up ahead with its roof partly gone. It sat at the end of a field about five hundred feet from the road and backed up to a wooded area. A demolished house sat across the road, and it didn't look like anyone had been around here in a long time. It was an excellent place to hide the trucks and get some rest. He slowed down and then turned onto a grass-covered roadway. The two-story barn was eighty feet long and forty feet wide giving them plenty of room to park the trucks. He got out and directed the girls where to park.

There were old bales of hay still stacked against the south wall, and an old hay baler was buried beneath the collapsed roof. It looked like a tornado came through the area destroying the house across the road and damaging the barn.

"This is a neat place," said Laney as she hopped out of the truck. "Think it'll hold up while we're here?"

"Damn well better," said Winters. "We need some rest.'

"Tell me about it. My eyes were starting to close."

"Yeah, I figured."

Collette climbed out of the truck. "I hope there's, like, no spiders. I hate spiders."

Winters laughed. "It is a hay barn, so yes, probably so."

"Ewwe."

"C'mon girl," laughed Laney, "look at all this hay we can make a bed out of."

"But the spiders."

"You just fought off gang-bangers, and you're afraid of spiders?" laughed Laney.

"Ah…yeah."

Winters shook his head and pulled his knife out. He grabbed a rectangular bale and moved it across the floor before cutting the twine. He then began pulling it apart and spread it around.

"See. No spiders," said Winters. He repeated it on four more bales and piled up a nice bed for the girls.

Laney let out a laugh while falling backward on it. "This is comfy."

"I don't know," said Collette.

"You can rest in your truck then," suggested Winters

"Nah. It'll get too hot," said Collette as she joined Laney in the hay. "It is comfy."

"It's the best," said Laney.

Winters broke out the boxes of food and found some MRE's to prepare for them. They gladly ate the food before collapsing back onto the hay. He told them he'd take the first watch and let them sleep for a few hours. Both girls fell asleep within minutes, so Winters grabbed his rifle and headed down the driveway. He wanted to fluff the grass back up on the roadway to hide any indication they were there.

The tall grass came alive with every step as grasshoppers and ladybugs scurried out of his way. The morning dew soaked his pant legs by the time he made it to the road. He held the binoculars up and looked in both directions before fixing the grass at the entrance. It took some doing as it was still wet, but he added a fallen branch to finish off the deception.

He wasn't going to take any chances with these trucks especially since they had been in a gunfight with a gang. He had no idea how big this gang was but didn't think it consisted of just eight members. More than likely, it was part of a much bigger group, and they could be out looking for them. They were a couple of hours away from the battle, but there weren't too many roads out of the area.

He had grown more paranoid recently, which helped him avoid some of the mistakes he'd been making in the past. Keeping watch while the girls slept was a more recent habit. He hadn't always done that it and he had paid the price with the lives of some of his men.

He went out on the deserted country highway to take one more look before heading back up to the barn. He put the binoculars to his eyes and scanned the horizon. Then a shiver shot through him when he spotted an object way in the distance. He stepped over to the side but kept the glasses fixated on it. A car was approaching, and it was moving fast. Winters ducked down behind a bush and waited for it to pass. He didn't have to wait too long before a Cadillac flew by. He barely had time to see the passengers but could make out that they looked like the ones he had killed earlier. He was about to get up when another Caddy sped by.

They were out looking for them and would have caught up with them in no time. Thankfully, he decided to pull over to get rest because there was no way they could have outrun them in those slow trucks.

CHAPTER 54

JACKSON MICHIGAN

Having retrieved the grenade launcher, Scar fired it twice at the vehicles coming into the parking lot to stop their advance to the hospital. While inspecting the damage from the second grenade, Amber spotted two bad guys launching an RPG from across an adjacent parking lot.

Amber screamed. "Over there."

Scar turned to see a Jiji holding a launcher and the rocket start to take off. He had a split-second decision to make as to which way to go. They couldn't outrun it, and it was coming straight at them. He had only one option, and it was to head into the line of fire.

"This way," said Scar grabbing Amber's jacket.

Meeks followed them around the corner toward the Jijis who kept firing at them. Scar laid down cover fire as he pushed Amber around the other side of the building. The rocket flew behind them and missed the building they used as cover but hit the side entrance they had exited from. The explosion ruined any chance of using it again.

They were vulnerable and exposed, and the Jijis took advantage by cutting them off from getting between two buildings for cover.

Scar was losing patience with the situation, so he decided to waste another grenade on them. It was more to put the fear of God into the men who were gaining confidence to charge them and to force them to keep their heads down.

Scar aimed it at a group who were using a van for cover. The grenade hit the parked van. The explosion gave Scar enough time to go back to where they were before. He then decided to vacate the area. There was too many to handle, and their position was becoming vulnerable. The guys who fired an RPG would try again.

"This way guys," said Scar as he headed through a small grassy area between trees past the main back entrance that had been obliterated. Up ahead was the F150 pickup that Scar had been using and knew the keys were in it. As much as he wanted to get back in the hospital, it wasn't going to happen. He would have to trust his men still in there to do their job. He needed to regroup and figure out a new strategy. If the Jijis were attacking the whole town, then there were plenty of opportunities to engage them. He needed to know their numbers and where they were. More importantly was getting the citizens to safety.

Scar got in the truck and started it up as Amber scooted in the passenger side with Meeks sliding in next to her. He threw it in drive and tore out of the parking lot as more Jijis poured into it. He took a left on Ellery Avenue and hit the gas pedal.

Scar took out his radio that was alive with chatter from all who had them. Reports crackled in from the hospital that it was crawling with Jijis. Scar glanced at Amber and Meeks, both of whom were staring at the radio in a cold silence. Neither wanted to bring up who might already be dead but only hoped the best for all of them.

Scar keyed the radio. "Break Break. This is Scar. I'm with Meeks and Amber. We took out a number of them from the north side parking lot. But there is still a large number coming in from that side. You should abandon the hospital and get to your stations. Boys, they have grenades and RPG's. I repeat they have grenades and RPG's. We managed to get a grenade launcher and ammo."

"Bassett here."

Scar's eyes widened. He wasn't expecting him anywhere near Jackson. "Where are you at, Corporal?"

"I'm up on Lansing Road on the other side of the interstate. Eddie is holding firm, but the bad guys seem to want this bridge. We've got them pinned down but could use those grenades."

Amber turned to Scar. "They're trying to cut off escape routes."

"We better get up there then," said Scar.

It wasn't too far away, and if they could control the bridge, then they'd have an escape route if they needed one. He keyed the radio again. "Eddie, we're coming in, I repeat, we're coming in, confirm."

"We hear ya. It's getting dicey up here. Park at least a block away. They're trying to flank us."

Scar put the radio back in his jacket. "How much ammo you guys got?"

Meeks patted his chest rig counting the magazines. "I've only got four mags left."

Amber had just loaded her bag last night. "I've got ten."

"We'll reload at Eddie's," stated Scar.

Eddie Perlee's men had plenty of ammo. Guarding the Jijis made for excellent target practice, and he always made sure he was fully stocked.

Scar made a right onto Lansing Road squealing the tires. It reminded him of Reese doing the same thing. He let out a breath hoping she was okay.

The worst part of being under a surprise attack was that you didn't know where everybody was or how they were doing. It also made it difficult to get everyone rallied to different spots. Everyone was assigned an area, but not all would be able to make it. They would do the next best thing and get to the nearest rallying point. Lansing Road was one of those places.

As they pulled in, they could see Eddie's guys shooting into the foliage on the left side of the road. The thick foliage ran down an embankment to the interstate. The Jijis were climbing up the hill to flank them. At the entrance of the overpass, Eddie had parked a car sideways and was using it as cover from the Jijis on the other side who had done the same thing.

Scar pulled the F-150 into a lot behind a building. He grabbed the launcher and bag of grenades. "Alright guys, let's go."

They hopped out and ran toward Eddie. Gunfire was going off sporadically around the area. More of it sounded in the distance from all directions as the whole town was under assault.

"How we doing, Eddie?" asked Scar kneeling down.

"These bastards were smart but not smart enough. We didn't suspect a thing because the ones on the interstate didn't make a move. So, we had no idea they had a team trying to sneak around us. Had Bassett not warned us, then we'd be dead."

Scar figured Bassett and Burns spotted the enemy coming down the interstate and hauled ass in.

"As soon as he gave us a heads up, I knew what they were gonna do. Hell, it's what I would have done. I sent my men around our flanks, and sure enough, we caught them. Killed a bunch too but then all hell broke loose. We started firing down on the interstate, and that's when the whole lot of them ran in different directions to attack us."

Scar tightened his jaw absorbing everything he was telling him.

Eddie took a swig of water and spat on the ground. "We're holding our flanks for now, but there's just so many of them. I just sent more men down the street to guard our six."

"We need ammo," said Scar.

"Right there on the porch. Help yourselves."

Scar and Meeks grabbed as many extra magazines as they could carry while Amber filled her backpack.

They moved over to look across the bridge. There was a whole nest of them waiting on the other side.

"We can clear them out," said Scar. He dug into the bag and grabbed a grenade. He loaded it and then asked Meeks to warn Bassett.

Meeks pulled his own radio out. "Corporal, fire in the hole."

"Roger that. We are good to go."

Scar rose up and peeked over the hood. He lifted the launcher and fired it. Everyone dropped to the ground, and a couple of seconds later the grenade hit the target. The car the Jijis were using for cover exploded in a fireball throwing shrapnel in all directions.

Meeks patted Scar on the shoulder.

"That is one badass weapon," said Eddie. "How'd you get it?"

Scar turned to Amber. "She got it."

Eddie nodded and flashed her a thumbs-up

Bassett came over the radio. "One more should do it. A couple degrees to the east, we've got a group taking cover."

Scar didn't want to waste the grenades and decided to take a quick look. He asked for binoculars, which Eddie handed to him. Hiding in the foliage was a group of twenty Jijis, a big enough group to justify using another grenade.

He loaded another one and aimed. The grenade shot up and landed on the group instantly killing everyone in a fifteen-foot radius.

"The coast is clear. The rest are running through the woods," said Bassett over the radio.

Scar wanted to fire into those trees but didn't risk it because he wasn't sure how many Jijis were still in the woods on their side. It would be better if they drove across the bridge and then fired from that side.

"Let's move this thing. Amber, go get the truck, we'll get across and then drive them into the open."

They pushed the car out of the way as Amber ran back to the truck. She again took off in a full sprint and as soon as she reached it, five Jijis popped out of the woods and took aim at her.

CHAPTER 55

The rapid gunfire was a sound Gunnery Sergeant Nick Nordell had been anticipating for the last week. He knew it wouldn't be too long before Mordulfah struck back. He had been outside talking to his friend John Hollis in his driveway when it happened.

Nordell had formulated a strategy with Winters and Bassett on where people should go, when, not if, this would happen. It was a solid plan, but like all plans, they could go from a solid plan to a disaster in an instant.

The gunfire echoed from the direction of the hospital, which was smart on the enemy's part. It was where the majority of the Shadow Patriots slept and the heartbeat of the town. By attacking the hospital, the Jijis would keep a significant portion of their enemy contained. Even if it took all day, it would allow their overwhelming numbers access to the rest of the town unimpeded.

Nordell had expected this and would now implement a plan to prevent this from happening. Without saying a word to each other, both headed back inside their houses to get what they would need. Within a few minutes, they started throwing their armament and supplies into the back of Nordell's pickup. He loaded up the M249 Squad Automatic Weapon, affectionately known as the SAW. The Shadow Patriots had been using two of these with tremendous effect and still had plenty of ammo. Hollis gently laid his Knights Armament SR 25 rifle in the back along with a steel box of ammo. This weapon had precision-fire on targets past a thousand yards, especially with the attached Schmidt & Bender scope.

Nordell's plan was simple. He was going to put his friend, Hollis on top of the old Energy building that had a good line of sight to the hospital. The building was just under two hundred feet high and looked right down East Michigan Avenue to the hospital. It was easy pickings for a sharpshooter like Hollis. To protect him, Nordell would set up teams across the street and around the high buildings to fire at any approaching Jijis trying to take out the sniper.

As he was backing out of his driveway, a truckload of Nordell's men pulled up. Ten guys were sitting in the bed of the truck armed with M4's that Winters had provided to them.

Nordell backed out of his driveway pulling up beside them. "We're going downtown like we planned. Now let's go."

He stomped on the gas and looked at his friend. "It's going to be a long day."

"Yep. I got plenty of food and water."

"Stick to the plan, and we'll be good," said Nordell trying to give his friend a confidence boost. Hollis had never served in the military and besides fighting out on Robinson Road had never been in a firefight. It wasn't an easy thing to acclimate yourself to and would test your mental readiness like nothing else would. Most of the guys with him were civilians as well or had served but never saw action.

They reached the intersection of Frances and Michigan Avenues just as more of Nordell's men showed up. He parked the truck in the middle of the street and got out to direct the vehicles where he wanted them.

The area had a natural border because of the Grand River. This narrow river was only thirty feet across but came from the north and ran right along the outer perimeter of downtown providing an ideal defensive border. He had already closed off the bridge on Mechanical Street last week by parking a tractor-trailer across the street and another on Business 94 effectively shutting down the whole intersection.

This left four other bridges to defend. There were others, but they were further south and were not an immediate concern. The ones the Jijis would use were right in front of them.

"I want those bridges blocked off and fortified. You know your stations now get to them."

"Bobby, get your truck over here."

Bobby was an old friend from high school and had been instrumental in getting everyone organized into different teams. He was a mechanic and had been helping Taylor with the maintenance of the vehicles.

Nordell wanted to clog up the area as much as possible to prevent the enemy easy access to the streets. He needed as much control as possible because it would be a primary route for the Jijis to come through. There were eight tall buildings in a four-block radius, and he was sending his men to the tops of each one.

Nordell picked up enough chatter on the radio to know the enemy's main assault was coming from the east and north. If they could control downtown, then it might be enough to prevent them from taking the whole town. The downside was getting his men trapped in those buildings. However, since the enemy surrounded them anyway, it was a risk he was willing to take, as it was their best option.

Hollis grabbed his equipment and led a squad over to the Energy building. He would have spotters on all four sides to give him protection. Others took off to their assigned areas, and Nordell stood watching and giving last minute orders.

He grabbed his radio and called Scar. "Scar, come in."

It took a few more tries before he answered.

"We're all set up downtown and ready," said Nordell.

"Gunny, they've got seasoned fighters with light armament."

"Copy that. We'll give 'em hell."

Nordell tucked the radio in his vest and picked up the SAW. He walked through the entrance of a five-story brick building on the corner of Francis Street and Michigan Avenue. It would be in the heart of the action and just the way he wanted it. He hurried up the flights of stairs to the rooftop. The air was starting to get humid, which meant it was going to be a hot one today. He looked down on the street satisfied with the placement of vehicles. Across the street was the Energy building and a spotter waved to him. He acknowledged him and drew out his radio.

"Hollis, you set up?"

"Just getting set up, Nick. There's a crap-load of them down there."

"Should be easy pickings then."

Hollis looked through the riflescope toward the hospital. The enemy was scrambling around in different directions, with cars lined up on Michigan Avenue trying to make a turn into the parking lot. Gunfire was coming out of the upper-level hospital windows as Shadow Patriots returned fire.

The hospital was just under a thousand yards, but the parking lot where the Jijis took position behind cars was right at seven hundred yards. He adjusted his scope before looking for his first target. His heart was racing from the twelve flights of stairs, so he took a couple of breaths to settle down. He pulled his ball cap down and took another breath. He decided to take out a driver in a van that was sitting on the street waiting to turn. Hollis lined up a shot and squeezed the trigger. The .308 round took two seconds to travel before it hit the window killing the driver.

Hollis allowed himself a slight smirk before lining up another. He aimed for a group hiding behind a Chevy Impala thinking they were protected. There were four of them, and Hollis started picking them off one by one. None of them suspected a sniper was bearing down on them.

CHAPTER 56

Amber raced to Scar's F150 so they could drive it across the overpass. As she reached it, five Jijis broke out of the woods fifty yards away. They raised their rifles and fired on her. She ducked down behind the front of the truck as rounds penetrated the side just as a group of Eddie's men racing in to take them out.

The automatic fire forced the Jiji head's down, so Amber rose up and fired a volley taking one out as he tried to run back into the woods. She didn't have time to worry about the rest and hopped into the truck praying it would start as it had taken some rounds.

She turned the key and smacked the steering wheel with her fist when the truck came alive. She threw it into gear and took one last look at the remaining Jijis. They were in panic mode as Eddie's guys had the advantage on them. She floored the gas and took off to the bridge.

Scar jumped into the passenger side while Meeks and Eddie hopped into the bed. She punched it and shot across the bridge praying the enemy wouldn't take pop shots at them from the other side. She came up to the smoldering car Scar had just hit with the grenade.

"Push at the end of it and spin it around," said Scar.

Amber hit the brake and let the truck coast into the backend of the car. She then pressed the gas and had a determined look on her face as the truck started pushing the car. The tires of the bombed out car started squealing. She then pressed the pickup harder, and the car slid forward before spinning to its side.

"Take it easy, Reese," smirked Scar.

"I know, right, kinda fun."

Up ahead Bassett and Burns waved them over, so she eased the truck over to them and parked it.

"Nice seeing you guys," said Bassett. "We got here as fast as we could."

"Where'd you see them?" asked Scar.

"On the interstate. We took out some but had to get out of there."

"How many you think?"

Bassett looked at Burns. "Good five hundred maybe more?"

"Right around there," confirmed Burns. "We had to have taken out fifty or more of them though."

"These guys are the real deal," said Bassett

Scar nodded. He already suspected it, especially with the firepower they brought. They had right around two thousand men attacking the city. Those were big numbers, and it meant they going to lose a lot of people today. They still had about nine hundred civilians in town, which included a lot of women and children. He was thankful they had moved a hundred of them last night.

"Where's the SAW?" asked Bassett.

"Nordell has one of them and Badger the other," said Scar.

"We could use it here," said Bassett pointing to Eddie's side of the interstate. "We need to light up those woods."

Scar turned to Eddie. "Tell your guys to keep their heads down."

The six of them rushed back to the bridge and split off into two groups on each side of the entrance. They navigated through the brush to get to the opening to see across the interstate below.

"Two magazines each," ordered Scar not wanting to waste ammo.

They started firing all at once, and the smoke floated around them as brass shell casings hit the grass. Across the interstate, tree branches snapped free, and leaves flew up in the air. A few Jijis began tumbling down through the thick foliage and screams could be heard through the non-stop staccato fire.

It took just under a minute before each finished emptying their two magazines. Bassett and Burns moved down the embankment to the interstate and hopped over the median wall to finish off a few lying on the ground. Satisfied they had the bridge under their control, they ran back up and joined the rest of the team.

Scar grabbed the binoculars, looked down the interstate on both sides, and didn't see any more Jijis. He let out a frustrated sigh. The enemy left no one else on the interstate, which meant their main assault, as far as he could tell, was from the north and east. He got a status report from the guards on the west that were starting to be overrun by Jijis going around their positions. The southern border reported no movement from the cops.

Scar looked at Bassett as it came across the radio and was thinking the same thing as he was.

"They're gonna push everyone south," said Bassett.

Scar gave him a firm nod. With their overwhelming numbers, they could direct the movement of people. All they had to do was start burning the town and make a big show of it, which wouldn't be too difficult. Scar had only so many people in too few places. Being everywhere today would be problematic.

The thought forced a reality on him that they could very well lose the town today. This presented two problems for him. Besides the obvious one of taking out the enemy as best as they could, he needed to evacuate as many people as possible. This was going to be difficult at best, and he knew they were going to lose a lot of them today.

He let out another sigh of frustration. He'd be lucky to get half of them to safety. Another quarter or so would hide as best they could while the other quarter would either be shot or captured while on the run.

He had no doubt they were on the hunt for young girls, which there was still plenty of in town. If he was right about forcing everyone south, then the cops were in perfect position to scoop them up. The more he thought about it, the more sense it made.

Still, the southern border might be their best option. If the Jijis were trying to force everyone to the south, then they'd be less resistance, that is until they ran into the cops.

The geography made better sense for refugees to go south. It was more wide open and didn't have any major roads to pass over until you hit US 12, but by then it was spread out more.

"Corporal, you think you could sneak us down to US 12 in your cruiser?"

"Don't see why not. What do you have in mind?"

"I want to come in from behind the cops and take some out."

Eddie gave him a concerned look.

"We need to open up an escape route. We still got close to nine hundred people in this town. Half of them are going to be running scared and right into the cops arms."

"What about our guys?" protested Burns.

"They're going to need an exit too."

Amber put a hand on Scar's arm. "Are we going to lose the town?"

"We have to be ready for that possibility," said Scar with a grimaced look.

CHAPTER 57

All of Nordell's spotters reported in that the coast was still clear. He wasn't expecting the enemy to be marching down from the north or the west anytime soon. He agreed with Scar that they were driving the population to the south. He'd just gotten off the radio with him asking for a SITREP.

A lot of his fellow citizens were starting to head that way in vans and the back of pick-ups. He had just instructed his Block Captains to barricade themselves in the old Jackson College down on Browns Lake Road. The facility consisted of a half dozen buildings with a couple of them tall enough to have spotters on the roofs to keep an eye on things. If the Jijis wanted to drive them south, then they would oblige them.

With the exception of the hospital, all the other gunfire was still in the distance and Nordell was thinking he needed to change his strategy. He hadn't considered the Jijis would take their time corralling everyone in one particular area, which he thought was an interesting strategy.

If the enemy created enough chaos by shooting into the first few houses, they came to and set them on fire. That would give everyone enough of a warning to take off running. In doing so, they'd have fewer people holding up in houses thereby corralling them in one area, which would save them time by eliminating the need to go house to house.

Nordell wasn't foolish enough to think this was the only thing they would be doing. If the Jijis saw anyone on the streets, they would shoot at them without hesitation. He entertained the thought of leaving this area to engage the enemy on the west side of town. If they were moving slowly, then they could take pop shots at them and harass them as they continued across town. The majority of their citizens were behind him and not in front of him.

He was growing anxious to get into this fight and had to fight off the temptation. There was fighting six blocks away at the hospital, and surely the Jijis would soon realize they had a sharpshooter plucking off their men. Hollis had been at it now for close to twenty minutes with great success. If these guys were real fighters, then they would know and would be planning something to stop it.

This notion gave Nordell pause. What would he do in their situation? He'd assign a team to sneak in to take them by surprise. Try to infiltrate the building and go up the stairs. This wouldn't work because he had ground forces all over the place keeping an eye out of this very thing. They were in pairs and in constant radio contact with those up top, who was keeping an eye on the fluid situation. It wasn't like in the movies where you could just sneak in. Then what would they do?

A flash of sweat popped up on his forehead. It is precisely what he would do, and it made sense. They would fire an RPG. He pulled his radio out just as all hell broke loose.

He watched in horror as a rocket raced across the sky and exploded right where Hollis was shooting. Nordell grabbed his binoculars to see if there were any survivors but there was too much smoke to see anyone moving. He called out to them on the radio. "Hollis, come in, come in." Nothing. "Can anyone see anything? Where did it come from?"

His old friend Bobby answered. "I see 'em, Nick. They're up the street on top of the building across from the train station."

Nordell knew the building. It was four stories high with a direct line of sight to where Hollis was stationed. "Take 'em out, Bobby. Take 'em out."

Gunfire erupted across the street from a building that was blocking Nordell's view of where the Jijis were. Nordell had to control his temper at Bobby and his squad because it was only six hundred yards away and they should have seen them. He then remembered the building had two levels allowing them to not only come in unseen but also be shielded from gunfire. These guys were smart picking this building and could now aim for

Bobby's position with little worry.

"Bobby get out of there. I repeat, get out of there," yelled Nordell into the radio. His rapid pulse was going to give him a heart attack. Then Bobby called back.

"We're out. We can't get at 'em anyway."

"Get out of that building and fall back."

"Ten-four."

Nordell ran down the stairs two steps at a time. He needed to take care of this personally. He ran out onto the street just as another RPG exploded. It was Bobby's location, which was a good sign because he had at least a ten-second head start. He reached for his radio. "You still with me, Bobby?"

"We're good."

"Everyone?"

"Yep."

"Meet me around back. I'm coming in. We need to take these guys out."

It was four hundred yards to where the Jijis fired the RPG and Nordell wanted to save his strength. So, he hopped in his truck and after finagling his way through one of the blocked off bridges drove over to Bobby's position. He looked up at the Energy building and saw the smoke had cleared. He didn't see any of his guys, so he tried calling out to them again.

"I'm here, Nick," said Hollis. "Saw 'em just in time."

Nordell let out a sigh of relief. "You all right?"

"Yeah. Just a little shaken up is all. Their shot was off, which helped."

"Are you still up top?"

"Yep."

"Get out of there then. Go to hide two."

"Copy that." Nordell entered the parking lot and saw Bobby's team. They jumped in the back of his vehicle, and he headed toward the train station. It was right across the street, and he would drop off half of Bobby's team. Nordell wanted to keep the enemy busy while he flanked them.

After dropping them off on Hupp Avenue, he raced back around the Jijis before coming in from behind them on North Park Avenue. He kept his foot on the brake, as he got closer to the intersection. He grabbed his binoculars and looked down the block. There was a van parked next to the building, which allowed them easy access to the roof. A couple of Jijis stood by the van keeping watch. Another two were still up on the roof. They wore fatigues, which meant these were the real fighters. He'd find out just how good they were.

He picked up the handheld radio called out to Bobby across the street. "Bobby, light 'em up and keep 'em busy."

He waited for the shooting to begin before letting off the brake. He ordered the men in the back not to fire until he signaled. He didn't want these guys to escape, and if they could surprise them, then they might be able to get their hands on an RPG.

The two Jijis keeping guard heard the gunfire across the street and began to return fire at Bobby's men. Nordell sneered at their stupidity for not checking their six.

He rolled the truck until he was a hundred feet away and then yelled at his men to open fire. He threw the gearshift in park as the boys in the back laid waste on the two on the ground. Empty shells tinkled in the bed of the truck as Nordell came around the front. He aimed at the two exposed Jijis up top. Nordell emptied a magazine and dropped them both before they could return fire.

He ran toward the dead Jijis and looked inside the van to see three RPG's sitting in the back. All he needed was a launcher. He climbed on top of the van and navigated his way on top of the roof where the other two Jijis lay dead. Nordell smirked when he saw the launcher and another grenade next to them.

Bobby called in on the radio just as he reached down for it. "They're coming in, Nick, get out of there."

CHAPTER 58

Bassett drove the cruiser while wearing a police hat as they drove down the center of town. He tightened his grip on the steering wheel as he passed by the Jiji line, which was spread out across a few streets on either side. They were setting houses on fire as they marched through the neighborhood. Pillars of smoke billowed up into the air and spreading a nauseating smell through the town.

It didn't matter too much up here because Winters recommended to Mayor Simpson that everyone should evacuate the north side of town.

"Look at 'em," said Burns who was sitting up front next to Bassett. "They seem to be enjoying themselves."

"Yeah, for now, they are," said Meeks in the back. "Wait till they hit our lines."

Meeks turned to Amber who was squashed between him and Scar. Between their rifles and backpacks, there wasn't much room in the backseat. "Anything?" referring to her attempts at raising Reese or Nate.

She shook her head.

"They'll be alright. I'm sure Reese is watching over them," stated Scar. He had too many people to worry about and orders to give to concentrate on just one person. He was worried for sure, but his mind was on bigger things.

He had an exit to get open. Opening it wouldn't be much of a problem, it was holding it open. He didn't know how many cops they had down there and if they were reinforced with the Jijis.

They continued south while listening to the radio chatter. The boys at the hospital were still defending it from all sides. They hadn't given up yet and regained control of the back wing of the hospital. The enemy had ceased firing more RPG's into the building, which could mean they had only so many of them.

"Scar, come in," said Taylor over the radio.

Scar had been trying to locate him for a while. "Badger, where the hell are you?"

"I'm over at the garage. I got young Hadley with me. Soon as I heard what was going down, I hightailed it over here."

Scar let out a breath of relief. "Tell me you got the SAW."

"The what?"

Scar was about to scream into radio but was cut off by Taylor.

"Why do you think I came way the hell over here?"

"Of course, Badger. Foolish me."

"Yeah, I'm just giving ya shit, Scar, thought you could use a little Badger humor."

Scar shook his head while looking at Amber and Meeks. Usually, he was full of smart-ass responses but not today.

"I thought it was funny," said Meeks.

Amber shot him a "now is not the time," glare.

"Can you sneak across US 12?"

"Sure as hell can. I've got a few boys that can come along with me."

A load just lifted from Scar's shoulders hearing Badger's voice, especially, since he had the SAW. They needed all the firepower they could get if they were going to take these cops on. There were too many of them and too few of us.

Bassett stopped the cruiser on Emerald Drive, two hundred yards away from the US 12 where the cops guarded the border. Burns peered through the binoculars and saw they had the intersection blocked. They also had cars lined up every hundred yards or so making it impossible for them to go across unnoticed, even in the cruiser. The cops were aware they had confiscated a few of their cars and would be watching for them. Strangely, the cop's radio was in complete silence. Vatter must have given verbal instructions to his men beforehand.

Bassett made a right and cut across the flat fields to the Jiji line on the western front. His passengers kept their heads low while he boldly approached the Pulaski Road border with his cop lights flashing. He acknowledged the Jijis with a wave as they parted the way for him. None of them wore fatigues, which meant the hired guns weren't in the area.

As soon as he was across, he hit the pedal to the metal and tore down Route 99 toward the town of Jonesville. The small town had already been abandoned a couple of months ago, with some of their residents coming into Jackson.

After blowing through the town, he took a left and covered the fifteen miles back to US 127 in record time. As he hit the road, Scar keyed up the radio and called out to Taylor to see their progress.

"I'm already here. Been waiting for ya. What the hell took you so long?"

Scar jerked his head back. "How did you beat us?"

"Over by the Michigan Speedway. Those idiots think the whole thing is fenced off, but it ain't."

Taylor had a knack for finding an alternate way of doing things. He never was one to tow the company line. He liked to do things his way, and he was right more often than not.

Scar put the radio down and thought for a moment on an action plan. It was essential to clear out a path for citizens to come down but he couldn't wait for a specific time to get them all across at once. Besides, to do that, they needed transportation, which would make it more difficult. Those without rides would have to make a run for it and hope for the best. All he could do for now was open up an exit.

"I need a map," ordered Scar."

Meeks unfolded a map out and placed it on Amber's lap.

"Where's that college, everyone is going to?"

Amber pointed it out.

Scar didn't like what he was looking at. Other than 127, there wasn't a single road that ran straight down and across US 12. You had to take a right or left on US 12 to pick up another road. This meant they had a wider area to control and more cops to take out.

He ran his finger down South Jackson Road and like the others, it ended on US 12, but it was the most direct route from the college. Just to the west of it was a neighborhood where Waldron Road came down to US 12 but picked back up a couple hundred yards to the east.

Scar began nodding his head. It was the smallest area he could find, and it was their best option because this country road ran straight south to the Ohio border. You could get to it by taking a left off Jackson Road before you hit US 12. Perfect. If they could take out enough cops, then this would be the ideal place to open up an escape route for the fleeing citizens.

Scar looked up at Bassett who was waiting for orders. "You say the cops are about every hundred yards?"

"Affirmative. What do you have in mind?"

"There's a country road about a half mile west of Jackson Road in Somerset."

"I know that road."

Of course, Bassett knew where it was. The man made it a point to remember every nook and cranny of the area. It had served them well over the last couple of weeks.

Scar keyed up the radio and ordered Taylor over to them. With a cushion, it would be approximately six hundred yards. This meant six cop cars to take out before they could establish a stable hole in their lines. It was doable, but for how long could they hold this position? That was the more significant question.

CHAPTER 59

Having just taken out the four Jijis who had fired a rocket grenade at his friend Hollis, Nordell bent down to pick up the RPG-7 shoulder-fired rocket-propelled grenade launcher just as Bobby screamed a warning across the radio. The Jijis were racing up Michigan Ave toward his position. He turned to see two vehicles coming at them guns blazing from the back.

The retired Marine calmly reached over the corpse he had just killed and grabbed the PG-7VL grenade laying next to him. The High-Explosive, Anti-Tank grenade can penetrate an armored vehicle and would have no problem taking out a pickup truck.

He loaded the launcher and mounted it before taking a knee. He sighted in his target and squeezed the trigger. The rocket took off at the approaching vehicle now just fifty yards away. He watched as the RPG sliced through the air at hundred and fifteen meters per second. It struck the truck dead-on. It exploded in spectacularly fashion as it lifted off the ground. Bodies flew out the back in different directions. The pickup behind it veered off and did a U-turn to avoid the same fate.

That was the great thing about these types of weapons. They put the fear of God or in their case, the fear of Allah in anyone around. It was a devastating weapon used to great effect by small armies around the world.

Nordell stood up and jumped back down from the roof to the van below. He ordered his men to grab all the weapons and throw them in the van. He could use another vehicle to block off roads. Besides, it already had three more grenades in the back and no telling what else.

Nordell strode back over to Michigan Avenues and raised his Vortex

Crossfire 10 x 50 wide-angle binoculars. He held them rock steady as he looked down past the smoldering truck and towards the hospital where the gunfire was still echoing through the air.

He scanned the area and was surprised to see an older man wearing fatigues holding a pair of binoculars looking at him. Nordell recognized the emblems of a Saudi Colonel.

"Interesting," said Nordell aloud.

"What's interesting?" asked his friend Bobby who ran up to him.

Bobby was Nordell's age and had known him since first grade. He still had most of his hair, though it was entirely gray bordering on white. He was surprising fit for a man who liked to drink beer and play pool.

"I'm staring at their field commander, and he's a Saudi Colonel."

"Too bad Hollis isn't still up top."

"Which is exactly what this colonel is thinking right now. C'mon, we need to get back. They're going to attack us."

"Ya think?"

"Yep. They have to. They can't let another sniper get the drop on them, besides they'll want their RPG's back."

Nordell ordered everyone back before climbing into the van he just confiscated. He turned his head at the grenades in the back. Not only was this a good catch, but he had also forced that Saudi Colonel to move against him, which would lighten the load for the guys still defending the hospital.

Knowing he just lost control of an RPG was going to gnaw on him and he would do whatever it took to get it back.

Nordell threw the van into gear and got on Michigan Avenue hoping the colonel was still looking his way. Driving the man's white van was a good screw you pal. Now come and get me.

The retired Marine tipped his head from side-to-side thinking how many men the Saudi would use. It would be a hurry-up operation, one they wouldn't have prepared for, so he'd probably send a Company of at least a hundred men maybe more depending on how many he can spare.

Nordell didn't worry about not knowing the number because he had spotters everywhere, and would know as soon as they made a move. They were perched high in all the surrounding buildings. Most were decent shots and would be able to slow down the enemy's progress toward their fortified position.

Nordell had been itching to get into this fight, and the enemy was obliging by coming to him. Killing those four Jijis had opened a reservoir of dividends.

He parked the van in the middle of the street, tightening the access to their position. He wouldn't trust his guys to properly use the RPG, so he grabbed his new weapon and carried it back up the steps to the four-story brick building he was using as a command center.

He keyed up the radio and called out to Hollis.

"I'm here Nick."

"You in position?"

"Just setting up now. Damn those stairs, though."

Nordell snickered. His friend was across the street in a ten-story building. If you're not in shape, those stairs had a way of knocking the wind out of you.

"Okay, listen up everybody. We just confiscated one of their RPG's, and they're gonna want it back. I expect at least a Company will attack us."

Nordell remembered he wasn't talking to Marines or Soldiers and needed to speak in layman's terms. "That's one hundred men. These guys will have to find us, which will leave them exposed. It's to our advantage so choose your targets carefully and take your time."

Nordell let off the mike key. He could only pray his guys were ready. Most had never been in a firefight, though some were involved in the Robinson Road battle. However, they were motivated because everyone had someone they knew murdered in the churches.

Thankfully, the Shadow Patriots happened upon them. Even though most of those guys weren't former servicemen, they had been trained by the Canadians and were now seasoned fighters having been in many firefights over the last few months.

Unfortunately, most of them were down at the hospital fighting for their lives. Nordell shook his head knowing it was going to be a bloodbath. He still had faith in them to put a hurting on the attackers.

CHAPTER 60

Scar got on the radio and ordered the guard post across the road to get up to the college and get them ready to move. They needed to find transportation and hightail down here. He wasn't sure how long they could keep this area open before the cops tried to outflank them or get organized and pursue the fleeing citizens.

Taylor and his ten-man team would take out the cops east of Waldron Road while they attacked the west side.

Bassett drove up that road towards US 12 and parked the cruiser in a dirt road by a cemetery. Everyone grabbed their gear and began skirting the graveyard in total silence.

Within a few minutes, they came to a house at the edge of the woods. Scar tapped Bassett on the shoulder to join him and to clear out the house in case any cops were still in there. He didn't think it was likely because the siege on Jackson had started, but you couldn't take anything for granted today. Murphy's Law tended to make an appearance in these situations.

Everyone stayed in the woods as Scar and Bassett reached the back door, which was covered in chipped white paint. Scar turned the handle and was surprised to find it open. A shiver shot through him as the door creaked as he pushed it.

It was an older home with worn out hardwood floors. The place had a moldy odor to it as if water had seeped through a leaky roof and into the walls.

Bassett grabbed his tactical tomahawk and ten-inch blackened steel knife before he came through the entrance. The door led to a laundry room and then the kitchen. Scar came in behind him Bassett with his M4 shouldered. They were halfway through the kitchen when a flushing sound came from an interior bathroom.

Scar felt a chill sweep over him. They weren't in a good position to take him out in silence. If any of them fired a weapon, it would expose their operation and make it much more difficult.

A door opened, and heavy boots clomped on the wooden floors. Bassett moved over to a red Formica counter. Scar joined him just as the cop turned to go back outside.

Scar exhaled a deep breath.

Bassett checked the bedrooms before coming back into the living room where Scar was looking through the picture window.

"We're clear," said Bassett.

"Got one right out front and three to the left."

Bassett moved to the window. "Yeah. It looks like they got two cops per car. Nice to see they have their backs to us. This shouldn't be a problem. Burns and I can take the last two, but we'll need help holding the line once we get it cleared."

Scar nodded. Ambushing the cops was the simple part, controlling the area afterward was going to be troublesome. The cops had the manpower not only to flank their position but also surround them. This is why Scar wanted Taylor to join them with the SAW. After they took control of this area, Taylor would send a team away from the action to keep an eye on the cops in case they figure out what they should be doing. It wasn't a guarantee they were smart enough to do this, but he wasn't going to take any chances.

"As soon as we take ours out, we'll run to your position."

Scar grabbed his radio and called out to Meeks. "We're clear here."

They had some time before they would initiate the ambush. The people at the college still needed time to get ready. He looked at his watch. It had been thirty minutes since he sent some men to get up there and get them moving.

He leaned on the dusty kitchen table worried about the men at the hospital and how they were doing. The last he heard, they were able to clear out a path for an exit after some of the Jijis left in a hurry.

Scar grinned knowing Nordell had something to do with this as he heard what had happened downtown. He had a lot of confidence in the retired Marine to handle the situation, and now that he was in possession of three RPGs, the odds increased in his favor.

Amber came through the back door first followed by Meeks and Burns. She slipped off the heavy backpack and put it on the kitchen table. It was loaded with spare magazines and had to weigh close to thirty pounds with all the ones they took off Eddie's porch.

Scar looked at everyone. "Is everyone fully loaded?"

Bassett and Burns patted their vest.

"I could use some," said Burns.

"Me too," said Bassett.

Scar motioned to Amber's bag. Each took four mags and stuffed them inside their vest. Amber then passed some power bars around. They stood in silence as they eagerly ate. The waiting was the hard part because everyone had the same things on their minds. No one dared say it, but everyone thought it. Not if, but how many Shadow Patriots have they lost? And why haven't they heard from Elliott, Nate or Reese? Were they dead?

Finally, Scar got the call he been waiting for on the radio. There was a convoy of vehicles coming down from the college loaded with citizens. They could begin their ambush.

Scar radioed Taylor. "You get that Badger."

"10-4. Let me know when."

Scar looked at Bassett and Burns.

"Give us ten," said Bassett.

They scooted out the back door and disappeared back into the woods. Scar motioned Meeks and Amber to the picture window.

"Meeks you take out this one. Amber and I will take out the one on the left. As soon as we take 'em down, we need to get over to Bassett's position and help hold the line."

Meeks gave a firm nod and slipped out the back door swinging to the left. Scar followed Amber out as she headed west. They hustled the sixty yards through the woods towards their target. They had a more demanding task because they had about thirty yards of open ground to their targets. Once he gave the signal, they would break from the trees and fire while on the run.

Coming to the tree line, Amber squatted down behind a tree. Scar stood over her and could hear her breathing. She was as nervous as he was, which is the way it should be right before a battle. Fear is good. Fear makes you cautious. It helps prevent you from doing something stupid. The secret is acting completely normal. Calm. In control, as if you're a person who knows no fear. So quickly conquering the fear allows you to become more focused on the task-at-hand.

Both Amber and Reese had that talent in spades, more so than some of the guys that came through their ranks did. While Reese had an insatiable appetite for killing the cops who raped her, Amber had an inner strength that had blossomed over the last couple of weeks. She was also intelligent but didn't over think things and only offered sound ideas to the group.

Scar crouched down next to her. "Look at 'em. They're not paying much attention, are they?"

"No, they're not."

"We'll be alright. Stay right by my side. I want you on full auto. Empty that mag fast and swap it out. I'll zero in on them with controlled fire."

Amber nodded.

After what seemed like an eternity, Bassett and Burns were in position.

Scar stood up, as did Amber.

He keyed the radio. "Okay, here we go. On three, two, one."

Gunfire broke the silence of the quiet road as everyone began firing at once. Scar flipped around the tree with his weapon at the ready. He aimed and pulled the trigger. He felt Amber's presence before she opened fire.

They charged across the open field firing as they went. Amber emptied her magazine in short order. The rounds went wide at first, but she got them under control taking down one of them. A couple of shots exploded his head painting the side of the cruiser with blood.

Scar aimed at the second cop and sunk a round in his leg making him drop to the ground. The cop was in full panic mode and crawled on his hands and knees to the front of the car. He then rose up and fired his AK-47 in full auto. The shots were high and out of control. He emptied his magazine and disappeared behind the car to reload.

Amber grabbed a magazine from the small of her back and slammed it in while sweeping around the front of the car to flank him. She stopped firing but kept the rifle against her shoulder as she moved with purposeful steps.

Scar closed in and squatted down to see where the cop was. He was behind the front tire and still on the ground. He looked over at Amber and motioned where he was.

She moved in a broader arc as Scar turned to see how Meeks was doing. He had already taken down his targets and was now jogging in to help. Scar signaled him where the other one was.

Meeks swung over and saw the cop lying on the ground. He was too far away to get a clean shot but fired a couple of pop shots to distract him while Amber continued her sweeping arc.

The cop responded as expected and fired at Meeks.

Amber then picked up her speed to get into position. The cop was still firing at Meeks as she came around the corner. She fired on full auto. It was sloppy but did the trick. A few rounds went into the side of his face blowing out the other side making him unrecognizable. The others ripped through his chest. Air hissed out from the tire as it also had taken some lead.

Meeks came running in and stared at the bloody corpse. "Eewwe, Amber, don't let me get on your bad side."

"I know right, that's disgusting."

"Hell, you even took out the tire. We could have used this as a ride."

"Couldn't be helped, but you know, you're more than welcome to change the tire."

Meeks chuckled. "Yeah, like that's gonna happen."

Scar spoke up. "Ah, if you two are done, we need to get up to Bassett."

CHAPTER 61

The closer Scar got to Bassett's position the lower he crouched down as bullets whistled by them. Amber and Meeks were close on his tail as they scooted around the dead bodies Burns' had killed. They reached Bassett and Burns who were returning fire on the cops further up. A bunch of cops had already congregated and repositioned a couple of their squad cars. They certainly didn't want to be ambushed like their friends just were and fired wildly, slamming rounds into the car Bassett and Burns were using as cover.

"Looks like a Mexican Standoff," said Scar and he reached them.

"Yeah, it didn't take 'em too long to get their act together," said Bassett.

"Well, hopefully, they won't get too brave," said Scar.

He pulled the radio out and confirmed the exit was opened for business. He turned and wasn't able to see the convoy of vehicles. There were too many trees bordering the road, and it had a slight incline, high enough to keep their activity a secret. This was ideal as it would buy them more precious time giving the fleeing citizens a better chance of escaping.

While the woods kept their convoy hidden, it invited an ambush by the cops, which would prove devastating. It wouldn't take a genius to figure it out, so Scar decided to give them more protection. Despite Badger sending a team to monitor their flank, it was too big of an area to patrol adequately.

"Meeks, those cops you took out, was the car damaged?"

"No, that one is in perfect condition," responded Meeks while smiling at Amber who had just flattened a tire.

She gave him the finger.

"You and Amber take that car down there and go get it. I want to set up a perimeter around us."

"You got it, boss. "C'mon kiddo, you got shotgun."

Meeks jumped in the driver's seat and started the car. He threw it in drive and squealed the tires as he forced a U-turn. He had to stop up ahead as the convoy of vehicles was now starting to turn on US 12.

"Damn, more than I thought there would be," said Meeks.

"Thank God," said Amber. "Let's get out, so they don't think we're cops."

"Good idea."

They got out carrying their rifles and walked toward the vehicles that were having to drive around the immobile cop car with the flat tire. Some of the passengers waved as they passed by them.

An SUV stopped, and the passenger window came down. Amber recognized the women and approached it.

"Amber, thank you so much," said Kelly as she held her arms out the window. She was a mother of two teenaged daughters who were in the back with their grandmother.

The daughters had looked up to her and Reese and wanted to join them. Reese had handled the situation by sharing some of her story. After listening to the horrific details, they stopped pestering their mother.

Amber leaned in and gave her a hug. "You guys get as far away as possible and stay safe."

"We will," said Kelly who began shedding tears.

From the back, the teen girls yelled, "We love you. We'll never forget you."

"I won't forget you guys either. Now, go, get going."

The grandfather stepped on the gas, and the convoy continued with more waves from passengers.

"Makes it all worth it, doesn't it?" said Meeks.

"Yeah, it does."

The last vehicle to go by was a pickup truck pulling a flatbed trailer loaded with the elderly and mothers holding their children. All with anxious faces but relieved to be getting away from Jackson.

"That was a lot but not enough," said Meeks.

"I know. That was what, maybe a couple of hundred."

"If that."

"Still leaves, what, about seven hundred or so."

"Yeah…about that. C'mon, let's go," said Meeks heading back to the squad car.

Meeks dropped Amber off at the cop car he took out, and she followed him back up the road.

Scar kept his head down as the cops continued firing on their position. They were wasting their ammo as none of the shots was doing anything. They were amateurs at best and certainly not trained as real cops. They only paraded around as ones taking advantage of their position.

He saw Meeks and Amber break over the horizon and once they were parked on either side of them, it suddenly released some pent-up stress he didn't realize was there. Amazing what a fortified position can do to bolster your confidence.

"Sorry it took so long," said Amber getting out first and ducking down. "We had to wait for the convoy to pass through."

"No problem. How did it look? How many?"

"Close to two hundred, maybe."

Scar nodded. "It's a start."

Meeks joined them. "How many cops you figure are up there?"

"Can't say for sure but the longer it goes, the more will join them."

"Why don't we waste one of those grenades on them?"

Scar considered this for a moment. "Might not be a bad idea. Whaddya think, Corporal?"

"I'm always up for some boom-boom. Besides, it'll scare the hell out of them. How many you got left?"

Scar agreed with him. "Got five."

"Mine if I had the honors?" asked Bassett.

Scar handed him the launcher and Bassett rose up to take aim. The grenade took off in an arc and sailed through the air before hitting the squad car on the hood. A big fireball began consuming the car. Smoke poured out and wafted through the gentle breeze.

"Damn that thing really is awesome," yelled Meeks. "Look at that damn car burn."

Scar laughed to himself. He remembered training with grenades in boot camp. The first few times he had the same reaction as Meeks did. It was something of a big-boy-toy to a civilian.

The gunfire from the cops ceased, and they could see why as the smoke blew away. Every cop was dead. Scar was starting to re-think his strategy in that they might be able to leave fewer people down here to handle the cops. Undoubtedly, more would come this way, but how many would dare get close to them after seeing one of their cruisers blow up. This would let him get back into town and start taking out the Jijis again.

He pulled his radio out and called down to Taylor. "How's it looking down there Badger?"

"We got things under control here. What was that I just heard?"

"Launched a grenade to clear them out."

"Well, perhaps you could send one down my way, make my job a bit easier."

Scar looked at Bassett. "Think you boys could hold down the fort?"

Bassett looked at Burns. "We can do that."

"I'm thinking if we cleared out Badger's position, we could send a couple of his men up this way while we go back into town."

Bassett nodded.

Scar turned to Meeks and Amber. "Let's go."

CHAPTER 62

WASHINGTON D.C.

Green drummed his fingers on the steering wheel as he drove to work. The traffic was heavy and was making him late, but he was in too good of a mood to let it bother him. A smile broke across this face as he thought about kissing Stormy. It was a thrilling surprise and one he'd never forget. He thought she liked him but could never be sure because of their crazy situation. It threw off all the normal signals you'd use to pick up the interest from a girl. He wasn't bold enough to just come right out with it because he didn't want to make things awkward for the group if she had no interest in him.

The other reason he was in a good mood was their meeting with the artist last night. The young man's ideas, talent, and enthusiasm had been another surprise that Green wasn't expecting. He had no doubt that they were going to make an impact on the city.

His mind drifted to Lawrence Reed, who he still had not heard from since the assassination attempt. He hadn't shown up in the office, and no one else had seen or heard from him. He had to be plotting his revenge on Perozzi and hoped it involved an attempt on his life.

Green pulled onto 18th Street NW and patiently waited in the traffic. He again found himself tapping on the steering wheel when he saw a small crowd of people on the corner of G Street. He slowed down as he came to the intersection and passed by the World Bank where a large poster was pasted on the corner of the building. It was the one Vasquez had shown them.

His mouth dropped when he saw people taking pictures of Perozzi being held up by two bikini-clad beauties. It was the one with the colostomy bag, and it looked absolutely brilliant.

Green couldn't park his car fast enough at work so he could trot down and observe everyone's reaction. He wondered how many they had plastered around town and how long would they last. Vasquez had told him that wheat pasting wasn't an easy thing to remove. You needed a pressure washer to get it off cement walls. You couldn't just peel it.

After parking, he hurried back down the three blocks and couldn't believe the number of people who stopped to stare and laugh. Some people even dared to have their picture taken standing beside it. This was a bold thing to do in this current political climate, as you never knew who was watching you. He stood off to the side and watched building maintenance come outside trying to decide what to do. One of them tried to peel a corner of it off but was only able to get a small piece. The people's reactions were priceless and ranged from glee to fear. Some had a healthy dose of caution knowing what could happen to the artist or those celebrating it.

Vasquez couldn't have picked a better location than the World Bank. This one would be seen by lots of influential people in the banking community.

After seeing enough reactions, Green headed back to the office where his secretary, Grace asked him about the posters.

"Did hear about the posters making fun of Mister Perozzi?"

Green nodded. "I just passed by the one on the World Bank."

"There's a lot more than that one."

"How many you think?" asked Green.

"I know of at least six others."

Green acted surprised.

"There's one at the top of a building. I just don't know how they got up there," said a confused Grace.

"That is weird."

"I wonder who did them?"

"Oh, I'm sure we'll find out."

"They better hope not," whispered Grace. "You know what happens to people like that."

Green didn't answer her but only nodded.

Grace took a quick look out the office door and said in a low whisper. "They're pretty funny if you ask me."

Green nodded again. He didn't want to continue talking to her about this. He did find her response fascinating because she worked for the man who would give the orders to "black-bag" everyone involved. Regardless, even she had let her guard down to her boss and confided her approval. She was taking a risk doing that, but the shock of the whole thing must have released some repressed frustrations of some sort to allow herself that one moment.

This is what Green found fascinating. If she reacted this way, then many more people around town were going to do the same thing. It would spread like wildfire, frightening some and giving hope to others, perhaps starting some dialog. That's what was needed. Dialog. Bold dialog.

After grabbing a cup of coffee, he entered his office and sat down. As soon as he did the phone rang. He heard Grace answer it and looked up when she came to his door bugged-eyed

"Mister Reed is on the phone."

A shot of excitement burst through Green's body knowing he must have heard about the street art. He took a sip of coffee before reaching for the phone.

"This is Major Green."

"Major Green. How are you?"

"Sir, I'm very well, thank you, but I've been worried about you. How are you?"

"I appreciate your concern, Major, but you have nothing to worry about."

"So, what can I do for you?"

"I heard some artist put up some interesting pieces of art last night."

The question gave Green pause. That was a strange way of describing vandalism. He needed to tread lightly here because Reed obviously was enjoying the negative art at the expense of his new nemesis, Perozzi. Green couldn't let on even the slightest of approval. Otherwise, he might catch on that he knew it was Perozzi who made the attempt on his life.

"Yes, sir. I happened by one that was pasted on the World Bank."

"Tell me about it."

"Well, after driving by, I walked over to it."

"What was the picture?"

Green purposely hesitated to pretend not to want to tell Reed. The old man was without a doubt enjoying this.

"Go on, Major.

Green described the piece to him in full detail.

"What was the people's reaction?"

Again, Green continued haltingly but made sure to relay to him how lots of people were laughing and taking pictures. Green could sense Reed's elation through the phone.

"All very interesting," said Reed.

"What are we going to do about it?" asked Green.

"I think we should let the people have a little fun so they can blow off some steam. It'll be good for morale, don't ya think?"

"Yes, sir. I suppose so, sir."

"I'm instructing the National Police to back off for awhile, and we'll see how this thing plays out."

Green had to fight off his impulse of a celebratory scream. "Is there anything else I can do to help you, sir?"

"No, I think that will do it for now. I appreciate what you did the other night, and I'll not forget it."

"Yes, sir. Thank you."

"Goodbye, Major."

Green put the phone back in his cradle shaking his head in disbelief. He silently thanked himself for instructing Vasquez to concentrate on Perozzi. Not many people even knew who Reed was, so they wouldn't have been as effective anyway, but if they had, then Reed's response would have been entirely different.

CHAPTER 63

JACKSON MICHIGAN

Nordell raised the binoculars and looked across the road. He couldn't see them yet, but his spotters just reported troop movement on several streets heading toward Francis Street and East Washington Avenue.

Colonel Ali Baba as Nordell was calling him, was sending fighters in from two different directions. No doubt, they'll come in from behind them as well.

He called out to Bobby who was hiding on top of a warehouse building down by the railroad tracks on Washington Avenue. He was one block away from the side street Colonel Ali Baba would have to use to get on Washington, as it was the next best road with direct access to downtown from the hospital. He wouldn't use Michigan Avenue as it would be too obvious.

"Nick, they're turning onto Washington right now. There's a bunch. I count fifteen vehicles, so close to a hundred I'd say."

This piqued Nordell's attention. If he were sending a company one way, then he'd send another company the other way. This meant there would be two hundred fighters to engage.

Bobby's men were stationed in a warehouse area with plenty of long buildings to use as cover. "Bobby, I need for your team to light them up. Do not let them pass through Hupp Avenue. I repeat, do not let them get past that intersection."

"You got it, Nick."

Nordell then turned his attention to Francis Street. Again, an obvious choice for someone who didn't know the town like he did. There were three or four streets the man would try and use, but all emptied out onto either Francis Street or Mechanic Street both of which he had barricaded.

It was a residential neighborhood with plenty of houses to hide behind. He had placed thirty men throughout the area, and they would use guerrilla tactics of shooting and running to the next spot. The Jijis would suffer casualties before they'd be able to hit downtown and once they do, Nordell had his sharpshooters to finish them off.

Gunfire started erupting from Bobby's men, and after a few minutes of non-stop gunfire from M4's, he started to hear the AK's returning fire. Before long, that was all he heard for the next excruciating five minutes. It was punctuated with two different explosions that shook the ground each time.

Nordell's confidence melted away once he heard the first explosion. He strained his ears for any more M4 fire but heard none.

He yelled into the radio. "Bobby, what's going on?"

Nothing.

"Bobby, what the hell's going on?"

Finally, he answered. "Nick, we're about done for. They got most of us on the run."

Furious blood rushed to Nordell's head. When Murphy's Law visited, things went south in a hurry, and he had just paid him a visit, and as always, it wasn't pleasant. The Jijis would be able to flood downtown from all directions. This wasn't good, but it was still doable because not only did he have the bridges barricaded, he had shooters on top of all the buildings. He also had the SAW and three RPGs left. He wasn't done by any stretch of the imagination.

Sporadic gunfire from the north knocked him out of his thoughts. The shooting stopped for a minute before picking back up. Nordell nodded his head. That's what he wanted to hear. Off and on shooting. His guys were doing what they were supposed to do.

Vehicles in the distance caught his attention. He hustled to the other end of the rooftop and raised the binoculars. Three vehicles approached the barricade at Washington Avenue. He watched as his men started firing at them.

The Jijis took up defensive positions for a few minutes and returned fire. It looked like his guys stopped them in their tracks, but then Nordell saw a Jiji shoulder an RPG. It took off and hit the barricade.

The rocket punctured a hole into the side of the car before it exploded in a fireball. His guys didn't stand a chance as the concussion killed everything around it.

Nordell lowered his binoculars and let out a frustrated sigh. The enemy had superior firepower and was using it effectively. His only hope was that they didn't have too many rounds or enough launchers.

He looked down at his own supply. He had three and would have to use them sparingly.

The three-vehicle convoy moved through the smoldering remains pushing the vehicles aside as it rammed its way through.

This must be the first of the fifteen vehicles that Bobby had reported. He watched the first one start to come toward him on Washington Avenue.

"About damn time," he grumbled as he grabbed the SAW and racked the slide. He then ran back across the rooftop to other end and got down into a prone position placing the machine gun on the edge of the roof.

The big M249 fired 750 rounds per minute with an effective range of 870 yards and a maximum range out to 3900 yards. It was a beast in the right hands, and the retired Marine had the right hands.

The van stopped at Francis Street.

"C'mon, ya little bastard," Nordell said aloud. "Turn this way."

The van started moving again and continued up Washington, but the pickup behind it turned his way. It had two men in the back with AK's shouldered as the truck continued slowly on Francis Street. It stopped a half a block away when the driver saw the road blocked off.

Nordell took a deep breath and held it for a moment before exhaling. He lined up the shot and pulled the trigger. Bullets began slamming into the pickup truck. A couple of rounds hit a Jiji taking his head clean off while the next few rounds knocked his partner back into the bed in a bloody mess. The staccato fire punctured the windshield into a million pieces while taking out the driver and his passenger.

It didn't even take five seconds to take them down.

Nordell swung the gun over to the right. The van that had passed by was backing up on Washington and turned into a parking lot.

"Dumbass," said Nordell as he applied pressure to the trigger.

Hot shell casings flew out as bullets ripped into the van. The driver was no longer in control, and the wheels turned left as it shot forward crashing into a building. The side door opened up with men falling out. Nordell felled the first two with non-stop rounds into the van. Any other passengers inside didn't stand a chance.

Nordell stopped and grabbed his binoculars. The perforated van had no movement inside.

He scooted his body over to the left swinging the big gun to search for the third vehicle. He didn't see it.

Whether they had heard the SAW ripped into the first two vehicles or saw it torn to shreds, Nordell would never know. Either way, it was sitting safely behind the building waiting. Were they waiting for backup or preparing for an assault?

Nordell got a sinking sensation in his gut. These guys weren't waiting for backup. They were getting into position to fire a damn RPG. On a gut instinct, he grabbed the SAW and rolled over a few times before getting up to run to the other side of the building.

Just as he reached it, an RPG exploded in the very spot he just left. It shook the whole building with the concussion knocking him over.

CHAPTER 64

Nordell lifted up on his elbows and shook his head. His focus was foggy, so he rolled over on his back. He grabbed his water bottle and poured it on his face. The fresh water began to do its work helping him regain his senses.

Gunfire erupted across the street from his friend Hollis. This gave Nordell some relief that his guys were engaging.

The building was on fire, and the smoke wafted over his head. He used the smoke as cover and crawled over to the edge to take a quick look. Just as he expected, Jijis began pouring out of vehicles in various areas.

More gunfire from his guys up high kept the Jijis ducking for cover, but it wouldn't last forever. If they were willing to waste an RPG on him, then no doubt they'd start using them on his snipers.

The sound of both M4 and AK-47 was now echoing throughout the downtown area as his guys on the ground were getting into the mix.

With the fire consuming the building Nordell didn't have too much longer before he needed to vacate his position. Before he would, he'd continue to use the smoke for cover to look for another target he could take out. He'd only be able to do one more before that third vehicle figured out that their RPG didn't take him out.

He grabbed his binoculars and scanned the area. He wanted a target with multiple Jijis.

He finally found what he was looking for. Two more pickup trucks had just turned onto Cooper Street from Washington Avenue. They stopped in the middle of the street giving Nordell the ideal target.

The Jijis in the back were still sitting waiting for the trucks to move again not realizing they were sitting ducks.

Nordell grabbed the grenade launcher and loaded it up with one of his three he had left. He got into a kneeling position and mounted the launcher on his shoulder. He took a breath before squeezing the trigger.

The rocket bolted out of the launcher and sliced through the air leaving a trail of blue and white smoke. The round was on the money. It landed right in the bed of the first pickup tearing it off the truck while exploding the gas tank. The force of the explosion threw bodies out of both vehicles as the rolling fireball curled up into the sky.

Nordell studied the area and didn't see anyone looking in his position. Smoke from the fire was just over his head giving his complete cover. A slight breeze had moved toward his way blowing the smoke right at him making a hot day even hotter.

Keeping his head low, he grabbed the SAW deciding to take advantage of his vantage point one more time. He looked around for another large target but could only find small pockets of Jijis.

Better than nothing.

He took aim at three Jijis hiding behind a concrete building across the street. He fired a quick short burst. The first rounds hit high throwing rock chips at his targets. He readjusted and fired again. These shots took two out forcing the third to run. Nordell tried to follow but was too late before one of his guys hit him in the chest.

He wondered which of his snipers got him. Doesn't matter, he's dead.

The smoke was beginning to chock him. It was time to go. He got up and grabbed his gear.

Overall, it hadn't been too bad of a firing position. He knew he wouldn't be there for too long before he had to move. These types of positions are never long-term. You squeeze out what you can before getting the hell out of there. He successfully took out three vehicles killing an untold number of Jijis. Not bad.

Once on ground level, he scooted out the back door into a small alley and jogged back over to Michigan Avenue. So far, their vehicles blocking the street were helping, but he realized Jijis were everywhere now. He dumped the remaining grenades in his pickup and grabbed another box of ammo for the SAW.

It was about to get messy with up-close fighting. It would be block-to-block style and floor-to-floor.

He pulled his radio out to get a SITREP from his guys.

Not everyone reported in, which meant he had casualties. He looked up at the top of the building where Hollis was as he reported in.

"We've taken out a quite a few, but there's just so many of them."

"Tell me where."

"Cooper Street. They're trying to find ways to get across the river. They're jammed up there because we've got Francis covered. Get over there, and you'll find them starting to come in."

If the Jijis could cross Cooper Street, then they'd be able to get over to Washington Avenue, which was now open to them. That revelation hit him hard because the enemy will figure out they could come in from behind his guys. Bobby reported fifteen vehicles and only five had exposed themselves, one of which was the third vehicle still hiding. This one would soon figure out that they could come in from behind and take out a barricade.

Nordell looked down Michigan Avenue towards city hall. He still had shooters in those tall buildings that hadn't engaged yet. They had a nice size kill-box waiting to spring on the enemy. They would wait until they had a large number before firing.

He yelled for some of his guys to jump in the back of his pickup. He then hauled ass over to where the third vehicle was still hiding.

He turned the corner and saw it up ahead. He yelled for his guys to be ready. He slowed down as he closed in on it expecting to be fired on.

"Where the hell were they?"

He stopped his truck fifty feet away from the third vehicle. He jerked his head from side-to-side looking for them. Not seeing them made him realize they were already sneaking in on the barricade just up the street.

More furious blood rushed to his head as he let off the brake and floored the gas pedal.

"Hang on," yelled Nordell as he made a hard left-hand turn.

There they were. There were three of them, and one had the launcher on his shoulder getting ready to fire.

CHAPTER 65

Nordell floored the gas pedal to reach the Jijis before they could fire on the barricade but it was too late. The RPG took off before he reached them. It didn't prevent him from ramming the Jijis who were standing in the middle of the road admiring their handiwork. They were sitting ducks.

One managed to jump out of the way, as Nordell slammed into the other two. One flew up in the air before landing on the hood. His bloody corpse slid off the passenger side while the wheels on the driver's side bounced up and down as the truck ran over the second Jiji. The guys in the back opened fire at the third Jiji as he tried to run away. Multiple rounds dropped him like a sack of flour.

The celebration was fleeting as the RPG they fired had taken out all of the guys manning the barricade.

Nordell shook his head in frustration. His position was quickly becoming untenable. In no time, the rest of the fifteen-vehicle would be coming down Washington Street and would overwhelm them. On the other side of the burned out barricade, that other company would soon approach them as well. If he wasn't careful, he'd be stuck between them. His only option was to take out what he could from the approaching convoy and then get the hell out of there.

He stopped his vehicle and surveyed his surroundings. He looked to his left and liked what he saw. It was a three-level parking garage. It was a perfect place to take cover while firing at the enemy.

He hit the gas and did a U-turn. He swung two hard rights before entering the darkened garage. He stayed on the first level and parked in the middle after turning the truck around for a quick exit.

He had six men with him and told them his game plan. They ran and each lined up behind a cement barrier.

Nordell marched to the one nearest Washington and saw the remaining ten vehicles of the convoy coming. He popped a grenade into the launcher and shouldered it. He locked his legs while he followed the van as it slowly went around the still smoldering barricade. Nordell could see some of his men bloodied and dead from the explosion.

Just as the van, came around the barrier Nordell pulled the trigger. The rocket took off speeding through the air covering the seventy yards in mere seconds. It struck the van and turned it into a bonfire instantly killing everyone inside.

The convoy of vehicles stopped dead in its tracks. This is what Nordell wanted to happen. Make them flinch and throw them off guard. They may have superior numbers, but he would make them pay dearly for every inch of this town.

Nordell yelled to his guys to open fire.

The earsplitting gunfire echoed throughout the garage as a non-stop hail of bullets began hitting the convoy.

Some of the Jijis began pouring out of the vehicles while the ones at the backend of the convoy peeled off to get behind buildings for cover.

Nordell bent down and picked up the SAW. He racked the slide back and opened fire. The effects were devastating as rounds ripped into the vehicles puncturing tires, windows, and anyone still inside.

While the gunfire continued to wreak havoc across the street, no one noticed four Jijis coming in from the other end of the garage. They opened fire and immediately took down two of Nordell's men.

The surprise move caused panic in their ranks as the rest of guys fired back at them, but the Jijis had taken up defensive positions behind concrete pillars.

Nordell needed to recover from his mistake. He should have had that entrance guarded. He swung the SAW over at them and pulled the trigger. The rounds began chewing through the concrete throwing rock chips in all directions. Nordell marched toward the Jijis while yelling at his guys to fall back. The report from the big gun was so loud that he could hardly hear himself let alone his guys. They weren't paying attention to him but were still firing at the enemy. He had to stop for a second to get their attention.

Only three got the message before the fourth was cut down while trying to flank the enemy. Nordell could see he was dead and was forced to take satisfaction he still had three men with him.

At this rate of fire, there was no way, he'd be able to reach the enemy before running out of ammo. He began backing up. He looked across the street to see the Jijis from the convoy regrouping. This position was no longer advantageous. They needed to get out of there and fast.

"Let's haul-ass out of here," he yelled. "Get that launcher!"

Nordell still had one more RPG and wasn't going to leave the valuable weapon behind.

Once everyone was loaded, Nordell jumped in and peeled out of the garage. He half expected to see the exit blocked off but was relieved no one was around.

He came up to Washington Street and looked across the way. Jijis were coming across the Grand River in droves. Their superior numbers would soon overwhelm them, but he just needed to keep them off balance to give everyone time to get out of Jackson.

New gunfire echoed in the air. It was coming from the kill-box Nordell had set up. They had strict instructions to wait until they had a sizable number inside the box before opening fire.

He took a right and headed back to his original position. The building he had initially been using was engulfed in flames. The fire would jump to the next building, which would eventually spread throughout the whole downtown.

He came up to Michigan and pulled his binoculars out. He looked down at the kill-box. Jijis from the west must have hurried towards the fight because they were spread out all over the place. His guys in the tall buildings were firing down on them and doing their best to hold them off, but there were just too many bad guys to handle.

Nordell hopped out of his truck and got in the bed to scan his surroundings. He didn't like what he observed. The enemy was starting to close in on all sides.

He yanked out his radio and called out to Hollis.

"John, what's it look like?"

"Not good, Nick. They're everywhere with more coming up from the hospital now. Way I see it, we don't have much time before they have us surrounded."

Nick's mind raced around considering the situation. He had no doubt they were going to lose the town. It wasn't a matter of if but when.

Colonel Ali Baba had come up with a solid attack plan and had plenty of men to use as pawns to get what he wanted.

It has been just over a couple of hours since the attack started and the enemy began moving away from the hospital. This meant Colonel Ali Baba must be confident enough with the situation to send even more men up here. Then again, many of the Shadow Patriots had already escaped from the hospital. This drew down the number of targets the Colonel had to shoot at.

They needed to hold this area for just a little bit longer, so he keyed up his radio and called out to Eddie who was still up on the interstate.

"Gunny, what's your status?" asked Eddie.

"Not good Eddie. We're about to get surrounded. I need some help down here."

"No problem. I got a bunch of guys here from the hospital with more coming in. They want some revenge."

"Roger that."

Nordell's shoulders lightened hearing the news. Not only would this help give the citizens more time but also to get his sharpshooters down from their positions.

CHAPTER 66

IRON RIVER WISCONSIN

Winters sat at the edge of the woods about thirty feet from the entrance of the barn. He could see the girls sleeping on the hay while he kept an eye on the road. It had been three hours since he saw the two Caddies. They hadn't come back yet, which worried him. If they don't come back this way, then they might be waiting for him up the road. He'd have to take an alternate route. He'd been studying the map and didn't see many choices especially the closer they got to Saint Ignace, Michigan where there was only one way to get across the water and into the mainland of Michigan. If that gang were smart, they would keep watch on the bridge and ambush him there.

If forced, he could always go south, but that would take him around Chicago, which was the last place he wanted to go. Despite the radiation from the dirty bombs, there were still gangs roaming around the toxic city. He preferred to take the scenic route as it always meant fewer people on the road.

It was too much to think about right now because he needed to sleep. He entered the barn and knelt down next to Laney who had volunteered to take the next watch. She was sleeping on her back making her snore lightly. Collette faced the other way. He put a hand on her shoulder and shook it a couple of times while whispering her name. It took a few tries before she opened her eyes.

"Is it time?"

Winters nodded.

"Okay."

Winters rose up and extended his hand. She grabbed on and stumbled while standing.

"Careful there."

"Oh man, I'm tired," she said while arching her back.

"You gonna be alright."

Laney nodded and then yawned. "Yep. Just give me a minute."

Winters gave her a bottle of water and led her outside telling her about the two Caddies.

Laney gulped down some water and asked. "So, like, how are we gonna get out of here?"

"Not sure yet. I'm hoping they'll come back by, which is why I want you to keep an eye on the road."

"I can do that."

"At this point, we're going to have to drive at night and hope not to pass anyone."

"Okay. Go, get some sleep. I'll get Collette up in a few hours."

"Wake me if those cars drive back by."

"I got this, Cole. Go…go…get some sleep," said Laney as she shooed him away.

She sat down after Winters collapsed on the hay. It had been a long night, but especially for him because he had the extra baggage of worrying about them. He didn't like the idea of bringing them into a war zone. He never said anything about it, but then he never did ask them to come either. If he had to begin with, she would have said yes in a heartbeat. Collette would have done the same thing.

Laney took the cap off the bottle of water and took a large gulp. She owed him. Hell, the whole town owed him and rightly so. Had he not killed them, then right about now, she'd just be getting home after a long night of partying. She scoffed at the thought. Partying my butt. Fulfilling my duties was more like it.

She winced remembering when Fowler called her a prostitute and making demands. "I'm not a friggin prostitute." There wasn't a choice in the matter but then had to admit that there was a choice. It wasn't a great choice because her family needed to eat. "Damn it. I am a prostitute. Hell, I even worked double for more food." She slumped her shoulders in disgust. "They even took my virginity."

She stood up and shook her arms while twisting around in a dance. All the girls did this as a way to fight off the negative thoughts. It was something to help remind them that those bastards forced them to have sex and pay them with food that they stole. It was all of their food, and they took it. They raped us and kept raping us. We did not have a choice.

She stopped dancing and looked at the butterflies on her leg remembering getting them with Finley and Collette. It hurt at first, but then you got used to it. They agreed on butterflies because of the rebirthing metaphor.

She broke out a smile because she was finally transforming into something much stronger than before. She wouldn't let those bastards win and get depressed with something they did. It wasn't her fault. It wasn't Collette's fault, or Findley's fault or any of the other girls.

She took a deep breath to help calm down. She hated being alone, and this was why. Idle time produced idle thoughts. She sat back down and checked the M4 to keep busy. She relished the training Sergeant Hicks gave them. She thought her father and grandfather taught her everything there was to know about guns while hunting with them. Sergeant Hicks, however, showed the best way to line up a shot, how to squeeze the trigger, to breathe, to field strip a rifle and most important, how to think while in a firefight. He kept putting them through the Urban Warfare course until they each passed with a high score.

The training helped immensely while going after Butler who was trying to escape. She knew just what to do to stop him. Then there was that creep Fowler. There wasn't a moment of hesitation nor any regret either because he deserved it like all the others back home.

Laney looked at her watch. Ugh. What felt like an hour to her had only been thirty minutes. Still another two and-a-half hours before Collette's turn for guard duty. This was going to be a long wait, so she grabbed the backpack Sergeant Armstrong gave them and rummaged through it. She smiled pulling a bag of Hershey Kisses out. The man knew exactly what teen girls liked.

CHAPTER 67

JACKSON MICHIGAN

Scar was confident after firing a grenade at the cops that it would scare the hell out of the rest of them, at least for a while. He left Bassett and Burns to hold the fort down while Meeks drove him and Amber to the other side.

As they were coming up to Waldron Road, they spotted a couple more pickup trucks filled with citizens coming down the road. The trucks hit the brakes when they saw the cop car, but Meeks threw his hand out to wave at them.

"Hell, I'd think we were cops too," said Meeks.

The lead truck got the message and picked up his speed pulling out behind them as they passed by it.

They reached Taylor's position and pulled up to them. Rounds flew over their heads as they got out and shuffled up to them.

"They seem pretty optimistic," said Taylor.

"How many?" asked Scar.

"Not sure but from all the gunfire, probably six, maybe seven."

Scar hoped they'd be more of them but no matter, they'd fire a grenade at them and shut them down for awhile. He wanted to get back into town and get a SITREP. As it was, he was hearing reports relayed to him because they were out of range. What he did know was that most everyone was out of the hospital, but causalities were high. The remaining guys were regrouping with Eddie.

There was still no word from Nate, Elliott or Reese. He was holding out hope, but he had it in the back of his mind that they were dead. There was no time to mourn, and he wouldn't indulge in it until he knew for sure.

Scar pulled the launcher out and grabbed a grenade. He peeked over the hood of the car and calculated the distance. He pointed it up and squeezed the trigger.

The grenade landed right on the top of the cop car with another spectacular explosion. It took out all the cops, and suddenly there was an eerie silence as flames shot up in the air.

"Damn, that thing is something," said Taylor.

"Yeah, it is," Scar responded. "Badger, I need some of your guys over at Bassett's position."

"Whaddya got in mind?"

"I need to get back into town."

"Gonna leave me that grenade launcher?" asked Taylor.

"Ah…no. Besides, you've got the SAW."

"Never hurts to ask."

"Just keep this exit open."

"Not a problem."

Scar looked at Meeks and Amber. "Let's go."

Meeks raced up South Jackson Road and barely slowed down as he took a right on Kimmel Road, which paralleled the college where everyone was gathering. He was pleased to see Nordell's Block Captains had coordinated transportation up and down the road to pick up anyone on foot. They would deliver them to the college and then head back out to look for more stragglers.

Each time Meeks passed someone they would run and hide from them because of the squad car they were driving.

"Got to ditch this damn thing," said Meeks.

"Still might come in handy," said Scar.

"Where we headed?"

"Downtown. Last I heard, Nordell was still holding firm."

They were still six miles away and out of range of the small radios. The closer they got into town the more chatter they were able to hear.

Scar keyed the radio."

"Gunny, Gunny, this is Scar, over."

It took a couple of tries before Nordell replied.

"What's your status?" asked Scar.

"We've got ourselves a Charlie Foxtrot." Nordell was using a polite way of saying they were 'screwed.' Ali Baba has us surrounded. Anyone that escaped from the hospital headed to Eddie's position. He's leading a force down my way right now."

Scar nodded at Meeks.

"What's your fix?" asked Nordell

"Coming up Business 127 in about five."

"Roger that."

Scar lowered the radio. Nordell took a chance to give his fellow citizens as much time as he could. It was a risky gamble but worth it to the retired Marine. His only concern was the safety of his people. Now, he would need help if he were going to make it out of there.

He looked inside the bag at the remaining three grenades. He would need to pick his targets wisely.

Scar turned to Amber in the back seat. "Where's that map?"

Amber dug it out of her bag and handed it to him.

"Meeks take a left on High Street. I want to come up Francis, which goes right into downtown."

"Whaddya got in mind?"

"Won't know till I lay eyes on the situation."

Meeks flipped on the blue lights as he turned onto Francis Street. So far, they hadn't run into any Jijis. The quiet residential neighborhood was abandoned of all signs of life, which was a good thing because it meant the citizens were gone.

Meeks slowed down as they passed through the Morrell Street

intersection. They didn't see anyone, but Meeks proceeded with more caution as they were approaching the downtown area.

"Up there," said Scar as he pulled his binoculars out. "On Washington."

"I see 'em," said Meeks.

Two vehicles were blocking the intersection with four Jijis manning the blockade.

"Take a left here."

Meeks turned onto West Franklin Street and drove a block and a half before finding an ideal driveway to hide the squad car. He pulled it into a dirt driveway between two houses and parked it in the back.

"Let's go."

Black smoke climbed high in the sky as sporadic gunfire echoed throughout the area. Everyone grabbed their gear and scooted between houses to reach Wesley Street. They ran down the street before coming to a narrow stretch between two buildings, which was blocked off by a wooden door on a fence.

Scar came through it crouching low to the ground. He peeked around the corner and looked both ways on Washington Street. Jijis were at all the intersections as far as he could see.

There were so many different ways for the enemy to come in that it was going to be difficult at best to take them all out and stay alive. They needed to hit them fast and get the hell out of there.

Scar keyed his radio and called Nordell. "We're up on Washington on foot between Jackson and Mechanic."

"And Ali Baba?" asked Nordell.

"They've got all the intersections blocked on Washington. I've got an M three-twenty with three grenades left."

"Three huh? I still got one RPG."

"Get everyone together, and we'll take out the barricades on either side and slip your guys between them."

"Eddie here. We'll keep 'em busy on this end."

"Roger that and whenever you're ready. It's getting hot in here," finished Nordell.

CHAPTER 68

Ending the transmission, Nordell had a decision to make. He had one more RPG and needed to use it shrewdly. He had ordered his sharpshooters down from their perches, but it was leaving them exposed on all sides. However, Eddie's guys will keep the enemy busy on the north side while Bobby regroups and comes back to hit them on the east side.

The west side was his main dilemma because he had a lot of guys two blocks down and a whole lot of Jijis still coming in.

He turned to see Hollis running across the parking lot with his squad. That was the last of them on this end. Now they could move down the street to help those guys escape.

"Let's grab these vehicles and move 'em down the next block," ordered Nordell. "I want to clog up that intersection. Let's move!"

Nordell wanted to draw the enemy down Michigan and use the last RPG on them before escaping down a narrow alley, which ran straight across three blocks passing right by Scar's position.

Pickup trucks, vans, cars of all types peeled down Michigan and parked end to end blocking the street. Nordell then ordered the rest of the vehicles they would use to escape into an alley.

Satisfied with their exit Nordell led half his men west towards the approaching Jijis, while the other half kept an eye towards the east side.

A feeling of relief washed over Nordell as his sharpshooters began to exit the last two buildings. The last thing he wanted was to have the enemy surround the building cutting off all exits. Thankfully, none of them was wounded. Despite losing many of his men, none of them had serious injuries. This was because of the enemy's use of the RPG's. It didn't injure only killed. So far, their gunfire had been mostly ineffective but to scare his men away. However, Bobby did report several casualties on his team.

In the distance, he could hear the sound of M4's echoing. Eddie's guys were finally engaging.

Nordell grabbed his radio. "Bobby, Bobby, are you in position?"

"We are Nick."

"Then light 'em up," responded a frustrated Nordell. He had to take a second and remember that most of these guys were not former military. They did not have the innate decision-making abilities trained men had under pressure.

The crackling of gunfire erupted on the east side.

"Scar, Scar, come in," said Nordell.

"Gunny."

"Be ready to take those barricades out. We'll be coming down that alley next to the parking lot."

"I see it."

"If you don't hear from me, do it when you hear the boom-boom."

"Roger that."

Nordell then began to engage the enemy along with the others. He fired only a few rounds not seeing any clear shots. He just wanted to keep their heads down for a few more minutes. They still had four men coming down the City Hall building. It was a thirteen-story building and was a bear if you were out of shape.

"Nick," yelled Hollis. "They're coming in."

Nordell turned to the east and saw them gathering down Michigan Avenue. He lifted his binoculars and saw at least twenty take up positions on either side of the street.

"That didn't take long," Nordell grumbled to no one.

Hollis and his squad opened fire on them stopping their advances.

Nordell was running out of time. They needed to leave now before the enemy swept around them and cut off his new exit.

He jogged down half-way down the block and took another look through his binoculars. He could see one yelling out orders to the others.

"What would you do in this situation?" Nordell asked himself. "I'd call for an RPG and take out the barricade.

The revelation caused Nordell to scream his orders. "Fall back, fall back now."

Hollis got the message and ordered his squad to move back.

Just as they did, an RPG came racing down the street. It hit the middle car and blew up in an ear-piercing explosion.

Nordell dropped to the ground knowing what was coming. He looked up to see the concussion knocked some of the fleeing men to the ground. They were rolling around in pain but didn't appear seriously wounded.

Nordell ran toward them and saw Hollis moaning on the ground. His eyes were glassy, so Nordell folded him over his shoulder and took off with him in a fireman's carry as others carried the dazed. He plopped him in the back of his pickup truck and left him there. He didn't have a spare moment to see how he was doing.

He grabbed the last RPG and jogged back over to the smoldering barricade. He used the smoke as cover as he scanned his targets and picked one. The man holding the RPG launcher was reloading.

Nordell shouldered his and took aim all in one concise movement. He didn't have to be too accurate. He just needed to hit the side of the building. He pulled the trigger and watched the bluish white smoke stream behind it. He squatted down and covered his ears just as it impacted the brick building.

It blew out a hole in the building spraying rock chips in all directions. Bloodied Jijis lay dead on the pavement. It did its job.

Scar heard the first explosion and ordered Meeks and Amber to cover him.

The three walked with purposeful steps out in the street as Scar held the loaded M320. It was five hundred feet on one side and three hundred on the other target. He opted for the one further away first. Still an easy shot. He kept his heart rate and breathing under control and pulled the trigger. It thumped out and sailed through the air in a slight arc before landing dead center killing everyone around it.

Amber kept watch on the other target and saw them turn their way. She opened fire first, emptied the magazine as Meeks joined her. They continued to suppress their return fire as Scar reloaded.

He didn't want to rush it, but at the same time, he needed to hurry. They were exposed out in the middle of the street. He locked his big frame in place and tightened his grip before squeezing the trigger.

It took off in the same slight arc and exploded with the same deadly effect as the last one. Bloodied corpses lay haphazardly on the ground.

"Come on," ordered Scar as he began running toward them. He wanted to see if they had any spare grenades. He was the first one there and looked inside the burning car.

Nothing.

He then looked down at the next intersection. Three Jijis were coming their way.

He raised his rifle and picked the middle one. He fired a three-shot burst. The first bullet hit him the chest while the other two blew through his face.

The remaining two Jijis split off in opposite directions. Amber swung her rifle to the left and led him by a step. She squeezed the trigger on full auto and tripped him over. He tumbled to the ground covered in blood as she riddled him with bullets.

Meeks stayed on full auto as well but was behind his target as he ran towards a parking lot on the right. Unfortunately for the fleeing bad guy, there was a chain-linked fence. As started to climb over it, Meeks caught him in his side. The Jijis head fell forward, and the body dangled mid-stride over the fence. He fired again for good measure.

They heard vehicles roaring and watched as Nordell's guys came screaming down the alley zipping across Washington Street heading south.

The relief for Scar was brief because they still needed to get themselves back to their squad car. Amber led the way, and they ran back the same way they came. They crossed over Wesley Street and through a big parking lot exposing them again. Relief didn't hit them until they finally reached the small passageway between two houses and then across the street to their ride.

Just as they plopped down in their seats trying to catch their breaths, the radio came alive with Nordell calling Scar.

"We are away, but it looks like we got ourselves a tail."

CHAPTER 69

Nordell led his men south but was being followed by two vehicles.

"We've got two tangos on our six," he reported over the radio.

"What road are you on?" asked Scar reaching for the map sitting on the dashboard.

"We're coming down Francis."

Scar didn't like where they were headed. The college was just a couple miles away, and there might be people still trying to escape.

"Whatever you do, stay away from the college. Do not go that way."

There was silence.

This would leave Nordell with little choice but to go down 127, which would ultimately lead them to the cops. Their pursuers needed to be taken out before then; otherwise, they'll be surrounded…again.

"Roger that. We'll head down 127."

Nordell's convoy consisted of six vehicles, one of which was a cargo van, crammed with his men. They had two motivated SUV's following them. They were staying far enough away but were still firing at them. All they needed to do was to keep tailing them until they drove them to the cops. It was risky to pull over and engage them because Nordell wasn't sure if they had an RPG. Chances were high they did.

Scar turned to Meeks. "Let's go."

Meeks started the car and crept down the driveway. His heart sped up as he exposed the squad car by backing out onto the street. He hung a left on Jackson Street and stomped on the gas.

Scar picked up the radio. "We are away, I repeat we are away. Everyone get out while you can. I repeat, abandon the town."

The radio stayed alive with dispirited acknowledgments.

Scar turned to Amber. "You got any power bars?"

"Yep. Meeks?"

"Yeah, I could use one."

Amber handed them out.

They woofed down the much-needed food in silence and drank water to wash them down.

Meeks relaxed some the further away they got from downtown. This road went through an isolated part of Jackson with houses that sat in a stretch of woods. He knew the area as he'd been down here many times. He was surprised they hadn't run into any fleeing citizens although it had now been over three hours since the attack started. He figured they were either gone or hiding.

They came up to Francis Street, and Meeks took a right before speeding down the street.

"Find out how far up they are," said Meeks.

Scar keyed the radio. "Gunny, Gunny, what's your fix?"

"Getting ready to take the curve onto McDevitt."

"We just passed the cemetery," Scar answered back.

"You're about a mile back."

Meeks floored the gas pedal. The engine on the cruiser roared like a lion as he pushed the needle past a hundred miles per hour. He let off the gas when he saw the road curve up ahead as it turned into McDevitt. The tires squealed in protest as it swung around the bend. He over-steered the backend and had to wrestle the wheel to regain control before punching the accelerator once more.

No one said anything but all were thinking the same thing. That was a Reese move, and they still had no word on her or Nate and Elliott.

It was a mile and a half to 127. Meeks was closing in on Nordell's convoy as he had slowed down a little to allow them to catch up. It was a gamble, but his guys kept the Jijis back with a constant barrage of gunfire.

It took another minute before they caught up with them or so they thought. A van was up ahead not an SUV. There was a third tail.

"You got them cop lights on?" asked Scar.

"Yep."

"Pull up beside them like you want to pass 'em. Amber get your window down."

The air blew all around them as Scar and Amber lowered the windows. Meeks got in the other lane and had no problem powering up beside them.

The van didn't react as he would have had he known who was in the squad car. The Jiji put his hand out and waved Meeks by.

Scar nodded to Amber, and they both stuck their weapons out the window and started firing. Bullets ripped into the thin metal of the glassless van as brass shell casings bounced on the pavement. Both emptied their magazines in seconds forcing it down into the culvert. The front end of the van then lifted up off its wheels before crashing into a tree and landing on its side.

"There they are," shouted Meeks overcompensating for the loss of hearing from the gunfire.

The two SUV's were just ahead.

Meeks picked his speed back up. They needed to hurry because they were coming to US 12 where all the cops stood guard.

Scar keyed his radio again. "Gunny, we're coming in behind them."

"About damn time."

"We had a third one to take out first."

"Great. We're getting too close to 12. I'm gonna take a right on Harper."

"Roger that," said Scar familiar with the road. "Badger, Badger, you there?"

"We hear you. I see you're bringing the party down our way?"

"What's the status of Waldron Road."

"Refugees have been trickling through. Cops haven't been too interested in getting blown up, so they've been keeping their distance."

"Can you get up on Jackson Road and get over to Harper Road. Bring the big gun with you."

"I can do that."

Harper Road was a paved road but turned into a narrow dirt road that ran through the farm fields. There was nothing but barren fields and some wooded areas here and there.

Scar let go of the radio and threw in a fresh magazine.

Meeks continued to gain on the two SUV's and was about to get over into the other lane but noticed muzzle flashes just before a round smashed through the back window and straight through the windshield.

"What the hell?" yelled Scar.

"Get down," snapped Meeks. "There's one on our tail. Damn bastard snuck up on us."

More rounds hit the bumper as Meeks swept the car from one lane to the next.

Amber twisted around in the backseat and pointed her M4 at the back glass. She yanked the trigger sweeping the gun back and forth to knockout the glass. Hundreds of tiny glass bits flew away from the spider-webbed window. She used the butt of her rifle to finish tearing out a section of the glass.

She aimed at the front passenger as he leaned out the window of the Ford Expedition. He was just far enough out to become a big target, but she didn't have a good angle.

"Get over to the right," she yelled at Meeks.

He looked in the mirror and saw her dilemma. He pulled back into his lane.

She squeezed the trigger spraying the Expedition. One of the rounds found its mark as the Jiji dropped his AK-47, which hung on its sling bouncing against the door. The SUV slowed down, and the dead Jiji was pulled back inside. It then picked up its speed again but kept its distance as two Jijis continued firing at them.

Meeks cursed in frustration as the SUV in front of them started shooting as well. They were trapped between them.

"Screw this," yelled Meeks as he jammed on the brakes. The wheels screamed for a second and then bit the grass on the shoulder as Meeks swung into the empty ground to the right. The backend slid from side to side in the dirt before straightening.

Up ahead, Nordell's convoy took a right onto Harper Road while behind Meeks, the big Expedition jerked into the field.

"You two get ready," ordered Meeks. "I'll bring 'em 'round your side but brace yourselves, we're going into a full spin."

Meeks had done this many times in the past as a youth. He and his buddies used to get out into the fields after the harvest and tear them up. They call it drifting these days but back then, they didn't have a name for it other than just pure fun, especially after a few beers.

He waited for just the right moment and then floored the gas before turning the wheel. The tail end of big cruiser immediately started sliding in the dirt. Meeks had no problem keeping the slide under control.

Amber threw her foot against the other door to brace herself. She had to fight the G-force but managed to hold on while firing her M4.

Scar used the seatbelt strap to stay in place and had an easier time because of his big frame.

Both kept their weapons on full auto and sprayed the side of the Expedition as they whipped around it. The passengers on that side didn't stand a chance as rounds slammed through the windows.

Meeks kept pushing the cruiser and started coming around the other side of the SUV. The surprise move took the Jijis off guard, and they weren't able to return fire. Scar and Amber peppered the vehicle killing the driver.

The SUV came to a stop.

Scar and Amber jumped out and ran to the SUV with their weapons at the ready. It was a bloody mess inside. All four passengers were honeycombed with gaping holes.

"C'mon," said Scar.

They jumped back into the cruiser and Meeks was about to hit the gas when he pointed down the other end of the field. Four cop cars were turning onto Harper Road.

Scar grabbed the radio. "Gunny, you've got four cop cars coming in behind your tail."

"Well, it's officially a party then," replied Nordell. "Listen up, I know this area well. We're stopping to take cover in a wooded area. It's about a five hundred yard stretch of woods to Jackson Road…Badger, are you there?" asked Nordell.

"I'm here," said Taylor over the radio.

"I need you to go past Harper Road. As soon as you pass by the wooded area, get into that field and keep going until the woods ends. Then hang a right, they'll be a small line of trees that'll keep you hidden, and that's where I want you to open fire."

"Hell ya, that sounds like a plan," laughed Taylor.

"Scar, can you come in behind them?"

"You got it, Gunny."

Nordell stopped his truck on the narrow dirt road. On either side of him were so many trees, that it kept direct sun from lighting the area leaving it in constant shade. He had chosen the area with purpose because he knew the advantages of being covered on both sides while putting his enemy at a disadvantage. They would think they were protected, but they wouldn't know just how thin their cover was. A friend of his had owned the farms on either side of the road and used to come down here for target practice.

He grabbed the SAW from the back and ordered his guys to dismount. He had them line up in the woods. The enemy was approaching so Nordell fired a salvo at them in case they didn't see him. They immediately stopped.

He then ordered a man to get out through those trees to flag Badger in. He didn't want him to get lost.

His pursuers began to open fire on them, so he stood behind a tree like the rest of his guys did. He'd let Ali Baba get it out of their system for a few minutes while Badger flanked them.

His radio then came alive. It was Badger. "Keep your heads down boys."

Nordell let out a snicker and yelled out to his guys to get ready.

A moment later, the SAW opened fire and began to deforest the thin trees as branches snapped and dropped to the ground. Badger swung the big gun back and forth. Beside him were four others who started shooting their M4's.

Screams pierced the air as rounds ripped into the enemy from non-stop gunfire.

Nordell swung around from the safety of his tree. He started marching toward the Jijis' position while firing the other SAW. The rounds penetrated the front end of the first SUV and took out two Jijis who were using it as cover from Badger's gunfire.

Two engines came to life from squad cars trying to flee the battle.

Meeks saw the backup lights down the tree-covered road. "Got a couple of pansies coming our way," said Meeks.

"Pull in there," ordered Scar.

Meeks tore into a driveway of a farmhouse.

They got out of the car and hustled up the road each taking cover behind a tree.

Their hearts began to pound as they waited for their prey. Meeks wiped the sweat from his forehead and pushed his blonde hair back. The cars would pass him first and then Amber before going by Scar. Like the other day while in Port Huron, he would have to fight the urge to open fire on the first car.

He peeked around the corner of the tree and saw it coming. There were two cops inside, and they looked discombobulated and scared. Badger must have really put a hurting on them for them to be taking off like this.

The second car was now coming by him. He nodded at Amber, and all three came around at the same time with guns blazing. They were only a few feet from the cars, and it didn't take but a couple of three round burst to take them out. Blood splattered the interior as rounds went through them killing them instantly. It was messy but effective.

CHAPTER 70

Once they finished killing the two fleeing cops, Meeks drove up to Nordell's position. Scar got out of the cruiser keeping his weapon at the ready as he walked toward the perforated smoking vehicles.

Bloodied bodies lay everywhere, but still, he wanted to be careful. It didn't take too long to see he was overly cautious. The devastating effect of the two SAWs on these vehicles cannot be described other than to say it was complete. Everyone was dead including the vehicles. It was total destruction.

Scar looked up ahead and saw Nordell coming his way holding the SAW and then he heard Taylor stomping through the woods.

"Dumb bastards didn't stand a chance," said Taylor as he broke through the tree line with his guys.

"Hell no. Thanks for coming in," said Nordell.

"Oh, hey, thanks for the invite," smiled Taylor.

"How many have come through your exit so far?" asked Nordell.

Taylor scratched his head. "Hard to say, but probably three hundred maybe a bit more."

Nordell grimaced. It wasn't enough, but he wasn't sure how many were already dead or had taken off in a different direction. He wanted to keep the exit open as long as they could, but his wishes were dashed when Bassett came over on the radio.

Scar answered the call.

"Our position is collapsing. Hadley hauled ass up to us. The cops have broken through the barricade by using an armored bank truck. They are headed to our position, and there's going to be too many for us to handle."

Everyone scrambled back to the vehicles.

Scar was conflicted because he wanted to fight the cops, but at this point, he needed to make sure he could still get his men out of there. If the cops had the forethought to have an armored truck on hand, then they might now be flanking them. If that happened, they'd all be done.

They reached US 12 and took a left where Bassett had moved to in order to monitor their precious exit.

Scar got out and greeted him.

"I sent Burns to recon it, and he's coming back now," said Bassett pointing down the road.

"When did they come through the barricade?" asked Scar.

"Just before I called you."

Nordell parked his pickup and joined them as Burns came speeding in and screeched the tires.

"There's two of them," said Burns.

"Armored trucks?" asked Scar.

Burns nodded. "They're side-by-side with a bunch of pickups and cruisers right behind them."

"How many cops?" asked Nordell.

"Probably all of them. I couldn't really count 'em. There's a bunch of them on foot in between the vehicles, behind them. They're moving at a steady clip."

Scar hoped Nordell was thinking the same thing he was. They were done here. Their responsibility had shifted from protecting the fleeing population to getting their men out of there. The town was lost, and anyone who was still there was on their own.

While they could take on the cops, they would only be able to hold them off for a little while, but by doing so, they'd endanger their own exit. The cops would eventually flank them, and they'd be forced back into town where the rest of the Jijis would pick them off one by one.

He looked at Nordell who was staring through his binoculars at the bend in the road waiting for the cops to come around it.

"Gunny," said Scar.

Nordell turned to him with a dejected look on his face. Scar knew then that they were thinking the same thing. Fight another day.

Scar turned to Bassett. "Corporal, let's pack it up."

Bassett nodded and grabbed the radio to call Hadley who was now at the other barricade to get the men out of there.

Meeks and Amber stood with Scar as he waited for their last vehicle to turn south onto Waldron Road, which would take them to the Ohio border.

He looked down the road and saw the armored truck coming around the bend. He had an urge to use his last grenade but thought better of it. Better to escape without the cops knowing where they were than to engage them in a quick act of revenge.

He fell into the seat and leaned his head back. They had lost many good people today, but the frustrating part was not knowing who was dead or had been taken, prisoner.

His forces were now either scattered or lost, and his dwindling supplies were non-existent, as they had left them back in Jackson. He had to take solace that they helped a large number of citizens escape and did so while staying alive.

CHAPTER 71

IRON RIVER WISCONSIN

A fly landed on Winters's face waking him from a deep sleep. He shooed it away and looked down to see Laney's arm across his chest. He was confused for a few seconds because he'd fallen asleep next to Collette. He looked at his watch and was surprised to see it was three o'clock. He'd been sleeping for nearly six hours and hadn't woken up one time.

He slid her arm off him, got up and grabbed a bottle of water before heading outside to look for Collette. Clouds had moved in and turned the sunny morning into a dreary afternoon. He looked over to where he had kept watch and didn't see her. He then looked down the field and found her standing on the road. She didn't appear distressed, and it didn't concern him. She was probably just bored, so he headed down there to meet her.

She waved her hand as he approached. "Hey, Cole."

"Well, hey there, Cole…ette," said Winters.

"Ah, I love that our names are, like, the same," she replied as she gave him a hug.

"You know, I've never met a Collette before."

"And I've never met a Cole."

"So, anything happened out here?"

"Nope. Those Caddies never came back, and I've not seen anyone else either."

"How long have you been out here?"

"A couple of hours. Laney woke me up, and we hung out for, like, a little bit."

"If you want to get some more sleep, you can," said Winters.

"Nope. I'm good. I, like, slept really good and no spider bites."

"Well, that's good."

"I've been, like, walking around with the binoculars, and looking at stuff."

"Guard duty can get pretty boring."

"Tell me about it," said Collette as she moved back into the field. "But these binoculars are, really cool though. I saw a bunch of birds and a fox. I think it was a fox. It was kinda small and reddish a bushy tail."

"Sounds like a fox to me."

"It was really cool," she said with an obvious joy on her face.

Winters got a kick out her ever since her acting stunt the other night. She poured her heart out yelling for help so he could save Laney and Findley both of whom had been taken, hostage. She did this after being held hostage herself when her 'john' used her as a shield. The poor thing was so terrified when he put a bullet into his head that she couldn't even move. Now, she stood her ground and was a creative thinker.

"C'mon let's get something to eat," suggested Winters.

Collette nodded and began to head back when a chill ran down Winters's spine. He saw in his peripheral vision a car speeding towards them. Without hesitation, he wrapped his arm around Collette and dropped to the ground. The vehicle zipped by without slowing down, so Winters lifted his head to see it was a pickup truck with some gang-bangers in the back.

Winters pushed off her and rolled over to watch the truck. He then turned to the other direction to see if another one was coming and saw nothing but an empty road. Collette crawled on her stomach beside him with the binoculars pointed at the truck.

"Looks like the same guys."

"Yeah, that's what I'm thinking."

Collette lowered the glasses. "Guess they're pretty pissed off at us, huh?"

"Probably so. That and they want these trucks."

"How did they know? Didn't we kill them all?"

"One or two probably ran out the back."

"Well, that sucks."

"Yes, it does. But thankfully, we pulled over."

"You think?"

"Yeah, there's no way we could have outrun them."

"So, what are we gonna do then?"

Winters looked at her face. She wasn't anxious but more curious. "Not sure yet, but whatever it is I don't think we should be in any hurry."

"Well, we got more supplies than they do."

"Yes, we do."

"So, we can outlast them," she said in earnest.

She was correct; they could outlast whoever was searching for them. They had everything they needed and then some. The biggest problem was not knowing where the enemy was and waiting for them to make a move. You never knew how long it would take. These gang-bangers could be well motivated to wait days, maybe even weeks. They may have roadblocks up ahead or to the south.

"Whatcha thinking?" asked Collette.

Winters hesitated, as it was too much to explain.

Collette tilted her head. "Road rules, Cole,"

"Of course, how could I forget," said Winters, as he reached over and pulled some grass out of her hair.

Collette ran her hand through her black hair and shook her head. "All gone?"

"Yep."

"Good. Now, road rules."

Winters scoffed and then stated his concerns about their situation.

Collette nodded as she absorbed what he was saying. "Why don't we find a car to steal and look around in that?"

Winters raised an eyebrow impressed with what she said. "Now, you're thinking like a good soldier."

"So I'm not just a pretty face?" she asked jokingly.

"Or a pretty princess."

Collette laughed. "Oh, yeah, that shirt."

"So, what else should we do?" asked Winters wanting to find out just how creative she was.

"Well, for starters, we should, like, mix up these supplies and put an equal amount in each truck and, like, hide two of the trucks. Back when we had to turn in our supplies, we hid some in separate piles, that way if they, like, came looking and found one, we'd still have more."

Winters nodded. He had already thought about leaving two of the trucks behind and coming back for them later, though it would be better to get all three out of there. He needed more information before he decided which way to go.

For now, it was a waiting game, and he wouldn't make a move until he was confident the way was safe for them. While he wanted to get back to Jackson and deliver much-needed supplies, another day or two wouldn't be life or death.

CHAPTER 72

WASHINGTON D.C.

Green hopped in his car and pulled out of the parking garage to go meet with the former FBI man, Jacob Gibbs and his son Kyle. He called earlier and had something he wanted to show him that couldn't wait until their next meeting out in Manassas.

Green agreed on the condition that he brings some beers. He had already promised his friend Sam to go out for a beer. He needed one after learning what had happened today in Jackson.

The cops had assisted Mordulfah and his new army in storming the town and pushing the Shadow Patriots out. They took control of the small city and were in the process of rounding up any stragglers that weren't able to escape.

Causality numbers weren't in yet, but early estimates put the figure somewhere around forty. Green didn't know if that included some of the citizens. No telling how many of them had been taken, prisoner. There was probably enough young girls to satisfy Mordulfah's perverted thirst. Green cringed at the thought but had to remember whom they were dealing with and be honest about it. He was a pedophile plain and simple and needed to be killed.

The taking of the town had been devastating news and Green wouldn't be able to relax until he had all the details. He didn't know if Winters was one of the dead or if he had even made it back there yet. When he last talked with him, he said he was bringing in supplies but had to go to Iowa first. He had a couple of teenage girls to get back home before he went to Michigan.

Green did some quick math and didn't think with all the mileage he would have made it back there yet. If he wasn't there, then how would he be able to find his guys? Will they have to come back to Winnipeg to regroup? That would take too much time, especially if they had prisoners to be rescued.

Mordulfah was the kind of man who liked to extract payment for deeds against him. He'd make a big spectacle out of it by turning it into a celebration for his men. He'd already taken heads from his own men, so it wasn't a stretch to think he would execute prisoners.

The thought sent shivers down his spine as he turned onto 21st NW to pick up Sam at the State Department. He saw him up ahead and double-parked.

"Hey, thanks for picking me up," said Sam as he climbed in and gave Green a fist-bump. "Damn car is in the shop again."

"No problem," said Green as he pulled away.

"What's up? You look stressed."

"I do?"

"Yeah, man, you do, which is weird because you should be celebrating with all the talk around town about the street art."

Green was surprised it looked obvious. He gave Sam a brief summary of what happened in Jackson.

"Oh, damn. Man, that sucks, and you've no idea who was killed?"

"No, I don't, but I don't think Winters was there, and I'm pretty sure, if they had him, I would have heard about it."

"Yeah, probably so."

"But yeah, other than that, the street art is a major hit, even with Reed."

Sam's eyes grew wide. "You heard from him?"

"Yep. Said he was leaving the art alone for now, that it would be a good release of pent-up frustration."

Sam started laughing. "Damn good thing none of them were of him."

"Exactly."

"I'll tell ya what though, it was all everybody was talking about at work," said Sam.

"Yep, same here. Although it was more in quiet whispers."

"Well, ya, can't blame them, seeing how Perozzi visits your building…often."

Green chuckled. "Not anymore."

"So, what's Gibbs deal?"

"Not sure yet, but said it was important."

"Can't wait to hear," said Sam as he stared out the window.

Green headed over to where they had brought Perozzi's men after they kidnapped them. It was in an old garage with no chance of prying eyes spy on them.

Green tapped his horn and waited for the garage door to finish opening before driving inside.

Kyle stood off to the side holding a couple of beers from a cooler.

"Dad has some great news," said Kyle as he handed the cold beers to Green and Sam.

They walked into the office that had the same musky smell as the rest of the place did. An old metal desk sat against one wall and an old couch against the other. Wood paneling on the walls gave the room a 70's vibe, and it even had an old TV with rabbit ears sitting on a table.

"Major, thanks for coming by," said Gibbs extending his hand.

Green grabbed it followed by Sam.

"First off, the street art has really been a hit around town," smiled Gibbs holding his own beer up for a toast.

They raised their beers and clinked them before taking a sip.

"Amazing what a little thing like that can do."

Green nodded and told him about his phone call with Reed.

"Glad none of them were of him," said Gibbs.

Green didn't want to spoil the celebration but needed to give them an update on Winters and Mordulfah's attack in Jackson.

"That's very disappointing," said Gibbs. He held his beer up again. "To the Shadow Patriots."

"Here, here," came the responses before they took another sip.

"So, what's your news?" asked Sam.

"Glad we got the bad news out of the way first," said Gibbs. "I have two things to tell you."

Green looked at Sam before turning back to Gibbs.

"The first thing has to do with that laptop you retrieved from Pruitt's place. We've finally have been able to take full control of it."

Green raised an eyebrow at the news. He had taken the laptop along with all the cash before burning the house down with Pruitt's dead corpse sitting in his Porsche. They had been trying to break into the computer ever since. He didn't understand the process, only that if they could, it would take some time.

"We've got financial records of payments made to him and many others from Perozzi and Reed. It includes a list of people he's been using, and it can tie him to the murder of Senator Kelly."

Green let out a frustrated sigh. While it was good news, they still didn't have a way to make it public. They already had recordings of Perozzi and Reed talking about the bombings. What good was the information if nobody heard it?

Gibbs recognized the distraught faces on Green and Sam. "I know what you're thinking. So what? We have no way of getting it out to the public."

"That would be correct," said Sam.

"Well, there's other things, we've been able to retrieve from his computer like more blackmail pictures."

"Come on already," said Sam in an excited tone. "Get to it."

"I've got some salacious photos of Alexander Dauber with a whole bunch of girls, most of them in their early teens."

"Whose Alexander Dauber?" asked Green.

"He's in charge of all the broadcasting in the country. Everything you hear or see on the news or anything that's on TV, it all goes through his office."

"Everything?" said Green as he turned to Sam who had a grin from ear to ear.

Gibbs nodded. "Everything. He's the man, Reed and Perozzi have been using to get all the propaganda out to the masses and shutting down dissent. He's either been blackmailing or rewarding him with young girls this whole time."

Green took a gulp of beer and finished it off. "But will he play ball with us?"

"Oh, I'm sure he will. Besides his lovely wife, he has two teenage daughters that I don't think will be too happy to know he's having sex with girls their own age."

"No, I don't think they'd like that," said Green as he popped open another beer.

Gibbs finished his beer and reached for another. "Our only dilemma will be contacting him. He knows who I am and we can't expose you, Major."

"I could meet with him," offered Kyle.

"No, because if he finds out who you are, then he'll know it's me and Sam can't because he's a State Department employee. Any kind of a picture from any camera could be used to match up your ID."

Green thought about the situation. There was one person who could be trusted to do the job. "Then it has to be Stormy."

Gibbs considered this for a moment.

"They're already after her anyway," said Green.

They gave him a puzzled look, so he told them what happened earlier when a cop pulled her over.

Everyone then agreed she was the perfect person. She was someone you underestimated, and she could handle herself under pressure. Since Reed was already looking for her, it wouldn't expose anyone else in the group.

This next step was going to be their most dangerous move because they didn't know how Mister Dauber would react. Would he go along with them, relieved that Reed no longer had the pictures or would he call him for help? If this were the case, they would set Stormy up and grab her.

It was worth the risk because if they could get all the information they had out, then the country would scream for Perozzi and Reed's head and in turn the President. Exposing them would be a massive step in taking back the country. They'd lose all power and be exposed for what they really were, murdering traitors of America.

As always thanks so much for reading the Shadow Patriots series.
My goal is to end the series with Book Seven